GHOSTS AND SHADOWS
FELT, YET UNSEEN...

...nature's eternal conflict with ...isper Water" and ...rvest"

...truths of ancient ..."Return of the ... in the Thicket."

...into the world of ..."The Spanish ...ack Solitude."

...ortitude while ...antics of "The ...sistent Ghost."

Come join some of the best known horror writers of our time on an unprecedented excursion into the nightmares of childhood and the darkest corners of the human mind.

TABLE OF CONTENTS

HORROR GEMS

Volume 1
CARL JACOBI
and others

ARMCHAIR FICTION
PO Box 4369, Medford, Oregon 97504

For more information about Armchair Books and products, visit our website at...

www.armchairfiction.com

Or email us at...

armchairfiction@yahoo.com

RETURN OF THE SHOGGOTH

By
Gregory Luce

Copyright 1996 by Gregory J. Luce

"It's called *Return of the Shoggoth*."

"Return of the what?"

"Shaw-goth...at least that's how I pronounce it," Lucas replied. He lifted the film can and placed it on the workbench. "UPS just delivered it a couple of hours ago. I want you to run it as the final feature on the dusk to dawn show tomorrow night."

Timmons raised his eyebrows. "I've already got *Frankenstein's Daughter* built onto the platter. Besides, don't we have everything advertised in the paper already?"

Lucas shrugged his shoulders. "Who cares. I mean at 4:30 in the morning do you really think anybody's going to give a rat's ass whether they're watching *Return of the Shoggoth* instead of *Frankenstein's Daughter?* Anyway, we'll be lucky if we've got ten cars left by that time, and half of those people are gonna be asleep...the other half'll be drunk or stoned."

Timmons' eyes squinted with doubt. "I don't know, Gary, what if somebody com—"

"It's no big deal, Len," Lucas cut in, "besides, this is a *very* special film."

"Yeah?"

Lucas patted the top of the film can. "This puppy cost me three thousand bucks."

Timmons' mouth flew open. "What?"

"Money well spent," Lucas replied confidently. "Next to *London After Midnight* this is probably the rarest horror film of all time."

"You're kidding me."

"It was made in 1935 by a one-shot independent film company called Arkham International Pictures."

5

"Never heard of 'em."

"Ever heard of H. P. Lovecraft?"

Timmons shook his head. "Don't think so."

"He was probably the single greatest writer of horror fiction of the 20th century." Lucas pointed at the rusty film can. "He helped write and produce this baby."

"What's it about?"

"Nobody really seems to know for sure," Lucas explained. "You see, most film historians have never even heard of it, and most of the ones that have tend to doubt the film was ever actually made. The general consensus is that *Return of the Shoggoth* was just a big joke perpetuated by Lovecraft, himself."

Lucas began to fiddle with the rusty latch on the film can. For the next several minutes he expatiated on the film's history to his politely attentive projectionist.

The origins of *Return of the Shoggoth* were clouded in obscurity. The concept had supposedly come from an independent filmmaker named Bud Pollard in 1934. Pollard, who was also a student of occult sciences and a lover of weird fiction, had approached Lovecraft about writing and producing a motion picture based on some of the fantastic creatures contained in the author's supernatural stories. Lovecraft, himself financially indigent, had induced an unknown benefactress to put up part of the needed funding, with Pollard supplying the balance.

However, this unknown investor had withdrawn her support at Lovecraft's urging midway through the film's production. It appears Lovecraft and Pollard had developed irreconcilable differences about the direction the picture was taking. Lovecraft felt certain things being incorporated into the script were inherently *dangerous* and had therefore, backed out.

Most film historians believed the project had been abandoned at this point (Lovecraft certainly destroyed all documents pertaining to it and never mentioned it in his correspondences); but over the years a handful of historians had insisted the film was actually completed. According to their accounts, Pollard himself had raised the remaining funds to complete the production.

They further claimed that *Return of the Shoggoth* had only been shown once—a preview screening in a small Rhode Island theater attended by a handful of independent film distributors. This one screening had supposedly ended in disaster, but no specific details other than vague rumors had ever surfaced. Most of these rumors described some sort of mayhem erupting during the middle of the screening. One account had several lives being lost, another had Pollard turning hopelessly mad and being sent to an asylum; but no one had ever unearthed any conclusive evidence as to what had actually occurred.

Only one print of *Return of the Shoggoth* was thought to have ever been struck, and this—along with the negative—was long thought to be lost.

Timmons looked up at his employer and stroked his beard. "You mean to tell me this movie's never been seen by a paying audience before?"

Lucas smiled and put his hand on Timmons' shoulder. "Bound to make headline news in a town like Cave Junction...isn't it?"

"Where did you find this thing?"

"That's the incredible part, some film-broker found it in the crawlspace beneath the stage of an old, boarded-up walk-in theater in Providence, Rhode Island."

"And you paid three grand for it?"

Lucas shrugged indifferently. "I'll make ten times that once we get it out on video."

Gary Lucas was the quintessential '90s entrepreneurial type. He owned and operated a small mail order video company specializing in nostalgic horror and science fiction films. He also owned the Frontier Drive-in Theater, a one-screen wonder just outside the tiny village of Cave Junction, Oregon.

Lucas lifted the lid on the ancient film can; a slight, somewhat musty chemical smell eructed forth. He looked at Timmons and said, "By the way, there's something very important I forgot to mention."

"What's that?" Timmons asked.

"This is nitrate film."

Timmons shrugged his shoulders and said, "What the hell is nitrate film?"

"Let me put it to you this way, Len," Lucas responded, "if you smoke your usual pack-and-a-half while you're building this onto the platter, you're going to end up in somebody's ash tray."

"You mean this stuff is flammable?"

"It might as well be solidified kerosene...one spark and...*poof!*...this place'll look like a crematorium at rush hour."

"This makes me nervous, Gary...what about the heat from the lamphouse?"

"Don't worry about it," Lucas replied in a self-assured manner. "You won't have any problems unless the film jams in the aperture plate, and that hardly ever happens. If it does, just kill the lamp."

"Before it kills me...right?"

Lucas smiled reassuringly. "Everything'll be fine as long as it doesn't come into contact with direct, intense heat. Just keep your smokes downstairs."

"What if it catches on fire?"

Lucas' eyes widened. "Run like hell. Don't even try putting it out...you can't. This stuff acts as its own fuel...it'll even burn under water."

Timmons smiled sarcastically. "You're making me feel real confident."

"And the fumes?..." Lucas continued, a playfully sadistic expression on his face, "...deadly poisonous." He shuddered. "Brrr!...what a way to die." He broke into a burst of soft laughter that left Timmons with a perturbed expression on his face.

"I don't think it's funny, Gary."

"Of course it's *funny*, Len. Look, you've gotta put this in the proper perspective. I mean were talkin' about a world premiere here."

"Right...at 4:30 in the morning. Who the hell's gonna care...or even see it for that matter?"

"I will," Lucas answered. "I'll be out in my car watching every frame of it."

Lucas turned to leave. As he reached the top of the stairs he paused and turned to his projectionist before descending. "Cheer up, Len. Even if the projection booth erupts into a wall of flames, I'll make sure Susie and the kids get your ashes."

* * * *

It was the Frontier Drive-in's mid-summer dusk to dawn show— five big movies for a meager six dollars a carload, with Spielberg's *Jurassic Park* kicking off the festivities. The weather was perfect, too. The thermometer had topped the 100-degree mark earlier in the day, and people came pouring out of the hills and into the theater to seek relief from the stuffy hotness of their non-air-conditioned homes. A packed house was expected, and Lucas hoped the Frontier's 320-car field would soon be filled to capacity.

The Frontier was one of the last vestiges of the "old time" drive-in theater. Built in the mid-1950s, its crumbling snack bar and creaky wooden screen had survived the detrimental effects of Mother Nature, as well as the advent of home video and multiplex theaters.

By 8:45 p.m., two sputtering lines of automobiles had stacked up along the theater's tree-covered dual entryway. They extended all the way back to the Redwood Highway and at times threatened to impede the flow of traffic along the busy roadway.

Lucas and Timmons watched the flow of in-coming cars from an upper window of the projection booth.

"One hell of a crowd," Lucas said, tapping his index finger on the window.

Timmons nodded approvingly. "Cross your fingers…maybe we'll hit 300 cars."

In spite of his apprehension about handling nitrate film, Timmons' film-platter preparation of *Return of the Shoggoth* had come off without incident. All five movies were loaded onto the platters and ready to go.

At 9:05 p.m., *Jurassic Park* hit the screen.

The first intermission was a nightmare—from the snack bar employees point of view, anyway. Patrons were stacked five or six deep along the Frontier's outdoor concession windows. Candy, popcorn, soda—the money poured into the cash register in an unchecked torrent, brought on by a munchie-induced feeding frenzy.

Upstairs in the projection booth, Lucas looked out over the field and watched the hungry hordes descending upon his overwhelmed concessionaires. But Lucas loved intermission breaks for more than just the revenue, he felt very keenly that it was one of his missions in life to re-educate all Americans with the nostalgic values of classic snack bar ads. Gazing out across the field, he waxed nostalgic as food-mongering animated images danced across the screen:

Add sweet cream butter
to hot pop corn,
mix it up, wrap it up,
Buttercup is born…

The second feature ended shortly after 1:00 a.m. This was followed by the usual mass exodus from the theater. When the second intermission ended and the third feature started to roll, there were less than 50 vehicles left on the field; and most of these were huddled in the first few rows, although a few carloads of partying teenagers remained to the rear.

Plan 9 From Outer Space was the fourth feature of the program, and midway through the film Timmons put on his glasses and peered out over the shadowy field: only 12 cars left. He was even a little surprised at that number considering the abysmal quality of the movie being shown.

At 4:05 a.m., Timmons began eyeing the film platters with increasing apprehension. In another ten minutes they'd be into the fourth and final intermission reel of the night. After that—*Return of the Shoggoth*. With his nerves starting to get on edge, he instinctively reached into his shirt pocket for his pack of Camels. "Damn," he muttered under his breath, remembering he'd purposely left them in the glove compartment of his car.

But at this time of the morning Timmons felt more than just a little uneasy about running nitrate film through the projector. No, it was more than that…

He'd come down with a real case of the jitters.

The Frontier Drive-in had a genuine family atmosphere when business was hopping; but when the hour was late and the cars had thinned out, that ambience of homeyness sometimes transformed into an aura of solitude that could—to say the least—be a bit unnerving to even the most stalwart of local out-in-the-country types. Surrounded on three sides by lofty, swaying pine trees and dense undergrowth, one could sometimes feel a wave of lonely eeriness flowing onto the barren speaker field, especially on moonless nights.

Yet, there was something else that was also bothering him. Something Timmons couldn't get out of his mind.

It was the history of that damned movie.

What was it Lucas had said about it? Something horrible had happened during the preview screening? Lives lost? A man gone mad? Timmons rubbed his hands together—they were covered with cold sweat. He wished the night was over already.

Out in his car, Lucas was feeling just the opposite. An unknown, never-before-released horror movie from 1935—what a coup! And here he was, about to watch it on his own drive-in theater movie screen. It was a baby-boomer, horror film-fanatic dream come true.

The final intermission was one of the longest Timmons could ever remember, going on seemingly forever. Ancient metal speakers, hanging deserted all over the darkened field, blared out their message through the cool early morning air:

"The show starts in ten minutes."

Lucas, himself his only active customer at this time of the morning, made one last dash for the snack bar where his one remaining concessionaire, Dana, was sitting on a stool, head-down on the counter, asleep. Her dark hair spread out over the counter like a long, flowing black mop-head.

"You have six minutes 'til Showtime."

Not bothering to wake her, Lucas went in through the side door of the snack bar and served himself. He hurried back to his car a few minutes later, carrying a barbecue beef sandwich, a large soda, and a bucket of popcorn. He settled back in his seat and waited.

"There's just two minutes remaining before Showtime."

Upstairs, Timmons was a nervous wreck. He watched tremulously as the final feet of the intermission reel fed through the hot projector. It was almost time.

"And now…Showtime…on with the show!"

Neither Gary Lucas nor Len Timmons knew what to expect next. The shrunken nature of the ancient film caused it to rattle more than usual as it fed down into the projector. Both men watched the screen light up in glorious black and white:

Arkham International Pictures
presents

"RETURN OF THE SHOGGOTH"

Produced by
Bud Pollard
and
H. P. Lovecraft

Lucas scanned the opening title cards as they flashed by, hoping to see familiar names within the cast and tech crew credits, but the only recognizable names were those of Pollard and Lovecraft. Toward the end of the title cards, Lovecraft's name appeared again:

Screenplay by
H. P. Lovecraft

Inspired by writings from the "Necronomicon" by Abdul Alhazred

Inside the projection booth, Timmons was far too busy watching the aged nitrate film wind its way through the heated lamphouse to concern himself with the contents of the opening credits. He stood almost mesmerized—one hand gripping the handle on the manual douser—watching the film clatter its way through the projector. As it passed through the aperture plate, the intense xenon light filtered through the film's ever-changing images, propelling them out onto the distant screen.

The film's story line appeared to be typical Lovecraft. Set in Arkham, Massachusetts, it concerned the theft of the legendary *Necronomicon* from a locked chamber of the Miskatonic University Library by a mad student of the black arts. His crazed intention was to use the blasphemous volume to conjure forth a cyclopean creature known as a shoggoth, which—according to Lovecraft lore—was a type of slithering, protoplasmic monstrosity whose ancient race was once controlled by the Great Old Ones themselves. The Miskatonic's only metapsychologist, an aged professor named Armitage, along with his assistant, sought to stop the madman from carrying out this nefarious scheme.

Although the acting by the lead players was certainly competent, the rest of the cast was somewhat less than professional—a few of them were even embarrassingly bad; however, the moody cinematography, particularly the contrasting use of light and shadows, was outstanding, in spite of the obvious cheapness of the overall production. Slouched down in the seat of his car, Lucas was completely fascinated by what he was seeing.

Suddenly, while watching a scene in a library, Lucas jerked up in his seat and pointed a finger toward the screen.

"Lovecraft!"

There in the background, standing behind a library counter, was a tall, gaunt bit-player. His long face and squeamish looks were undeniable...

It was H. P. Lovecraft.

Lucas' jaw dropped. "Son of a bitch!"

No motion picture film of Lovecraft had previously been known to exist, yet this was unmistakably him. There he was, the master of horror himself, standing in the background as big as life. One of the main characters, Professor Armitage, turned and complimented him on the magnitude of the library's occult section.

In a thin, anemic voice Lovecraft replied, "Thank you."

A moment later the scene shifted; Lovecraft was gone.

Up in the booth, Timmons had calmed down a bit. In spite of its shrunken nature, the film was flowing through the projector fairly well; and although one hand still remained firmly clasped around the manual douser handle, Timmons actually found himself watching parts of the forgotten horror film with a mild sense of curiosity.

Shortly before 5:00 a.m. an eerie scene began to unfold.

Dana, who had woke up shortly after *Return of the Shoggoth* started, was just pulling out of the theater after closing the snack bar for the night. As she drove down the exit aisle she noticed a peculiar event happening on the screen. A strange looking fellow, dressed completely in black, was standing high atop a lonely hill, clutching an ancient book.

"I'm working for a wacko," she muttered sleepily to herself as she drove out of the theater grounds.

Inside his car, Lucas was completely engrossed by the same scene. The film's central antagonist, a wretchedly evil fellow named Abner Whately, was about to invoke one of the ancient, conjurative powers found within the text of the dreaded *Necronomicon*.

Whately stood atop the rounded hill, looking into the darkened heavens. The wind howled about him and thunder rumbled above the ambient sea of static crackling through the ancient soundtrack. He then looked down into the blasphemous volume and read aloud the following cryptic passage:

"Ph'nglui nglw'gath ee-ya-ya R'lyeh somalhau thagn-yi fhtagn Tekeli-li! Tekeli-li!"

A slight chill shot through Lucas' body.

The reading of the incantation had started with a medium shot of Whately, standing erect, shouting aloud into the heavens; but midway through the passage the camera had cut to a close-up of his mouth, pulling back slowly to reveal the crazed expression on the madman's face. It was apparent to Lucas that the reading of the incantation had not been filmed all at once, but in two separate shots that were then edited together and later incorporated into the final version of the film.

"This is awesome," he mumbled to himself, his eyes riveted to the screen.

Timmons had also been drawn in by the weirdness of the strange ceremony. As the final words of the incantation reverberated from the speaker above the workbench behind him, he experienced the same chill of latent fear that Lucas had felt. He then noticed something curious.

His glasses seemed to be fogging up.

Timmons whirled about. To his amazement he saw a flowing shroud of fog-like vapor pouring out of the speaker above the workbench. It was very cool and moist to the touch. He was even further amazed to see that the strange, swirling mist had practically filled the projection booth.

"What the hell's goin' on?" he blurted out in a startled tone.

He took a step toward the speaker but started to stagger. A dizziness shot through his entire body as he inhaled the strange mist. His hand slipped off the handle of the manual douser.

"That the hell...somebody help..."

Timmons staggered across the booth. Reaching the top of the stairs, he gripped the railing and took one step downward; but his legs were no longer able to control the descending weight of his staggering frame and he went crashing downward, his body collapsing into a heap at the bottom of the stairs. He lay there, completely unconscious.

Upstairs, the cold vapor began pouring out the back window next to the workbench. Timmons always left it open for ventilation. The cloud of mist poured downward and began swirling about the large, undeveloped field located to the rear of the snack bar. It seemed to gather into a huge ball, churning and swirling, the vaporous stream from the window feeding it all the while. Larger and larger it grew, gyrating rhythmically in a counterclockwise direction. After a minute or two a luminescent glow, barely detectable, began to pulsate from deep within the ball.

It was then that the first sounds could be heard.

Somewhere from deep within the churning ball of horrific fog came a series of low gurgling sounds. They grew steadily louder until they sounded more like the sloshing of a great cauldron—*as though something was forming inside it.* The sounds became more and more expansive, gradually developing into a dull, yet constant drone of liquescent vibrations. Eventually the sound of twigs and underbrush snapping could be heard under the soft, liquid-like whisperings.

After several minutes, the flow of mist from the upper window ceased. The pulsating luminosity, which had been evident only moments before, had also faded completely. What remained though, was a gigantic, flattening sphere of fog, the dimensions of which were truly frightening. It was easily 100 feet in diameter and 20-30 feet in height at its swirling center-point.

Then, a curious thing began to happen. Two rolling shafts of mist, about 10 feet in height and exuding from either side of the vaporous mass, began to slither around the perimeter of the drive-in. Like long, winding arms, they slowly encircled the speaker field, following along the theater's outer fence.

Lucas, who's eyes were still glued to the screen, failed to notice the two shafts of creeping fog that had quietly merged together immediately below and in front of him, just behind the screen. The entire field was now completely surrounded by an eerie wall of cold mist.

It was then that the vaporous mass to the rear began to move forward.

Only two vehicles remained in the back row of the theater, and they were both parked within a few spaces of each other on the south side. It was in this direction that the churning mass of fog moved, flattening out all the more as it progressed. It skirted the edge of the snack bar and projection booth as it rolled toward the autos and their unsuspecting occupants. From within the curtain of advancing mist came the sound of earth and gravel being assailed by a rolling agglomeration of protuberant matter.

Inside the nearest vehicle, a '76 Ford station wagon, two teenage lovers lay in a deep slumber brought on by the hot passions of several hours earlier, totally oblivious to the strange vapor now cascading over the top of their vehicle. Neither could feel the subtle, yet distinct vibrations of the tremendous physical mass that oozed toward them under cover of the cold, deadly mist. It was only the explosion of shattering glass and twisting metal that brought them partially to their senses. An instant later, slithering protoplasmic appendages had engulfed their half-naked bodies, tearing them asunder within seconds. They were gone before they could even scream; yet, for one flirting instant before death, their half-wakened senses had detected the piercing sound of an unearthly voice:

"Tekeli-li! Tekeli-li!"

The sound of speaker poles being pushed over echoed across the field as the great mass rolled on toward the next vehicle; but here it did not stop, it simply rolled over the auto at frightening rate of speed, crushing the sleeping occupants within. Then it paused—hesitating— as if trying to decide in which direction to move next.

Up in the sixth row, mill worker Louie Clowser—the only person awake in the theater except for Lucas—was finally beginning to nod off when his pet Doberman, Nellie, began to growl and fidget in the back seat.

"Nellie...what's up? Gotta take a whiz?" He cupped his hand over his mouth in a deep yawn, then reached down and opened his car door. "All right, girl...come on."

Before Clowser had put one foot to the ground, the dog had leaped over the back seat and charged across his lap, hitting the ground at a dead run.

"Nellie! Come back here!"

The streaking Doberman, growling viciously, was overcome by a rush of predatory instinct. With fangs bared, it charged directly toward the monstrosity hidden within the swirling mist.

"Gosh darn dog!" Clowser exclaimed as he rose up out of his vehicle. He then noticed the wall of fog that had surrounded the drive-in, in particular, the great mass of it that swirled near the back row.

"What in God's name... Nellie! Get back over—"

Before Clowser could finish his command, the charging Doberman had disappeared into the great clump of mist.

"Nellie!"

A moment later came the sound of savage barking followed by the yelping of an animal in terror. A squeal of pain came next, then all was silent—but only for a moment.

"Tekeli-li! Tekeli-li!"

Clowser was dumbfounded. "Holy crud. What the hell's happening here..."

Fearing for his dog's life, he began walking briskly, then trotting toward the great white mass. He then noticed something that made his feet slow and his eyes widen.

It was moving toward him.

Clowser stopped dead in his tracks.

He stood watching the creeping mound of fog as it rolled over the parking ramps. Like a vaporous wave of destruction, it crept closer and closer. At that instant Clowser realized his dog was dead, and whatever had killed it was hidden behind the wall of mist that was now moving in his direction. Then, for just a moment, the fog seemed to part; Clowser instinctively leaned forward to get a better look...

In spite of Timmons' predicament, *Return of the Shoggoth* was still winding its way through the projector. The reflected light of its moving images on the screen cast a pale illumination over the field. Within this dim light, Louie Clowser detected some type of motion behind the curtain of fog. Peering into the mist, his straining eyes caught only the briefest glimpse of something moving; yet, what he saw in that fraction of a second was so terrifying, so abominable, that it sent him stumbling in a blind panic toward the exit gate, screaming hysterically all the way.

Then again came that horrible vociferation:

"Tekeli-li! Tekeli-li!"

Lucas' eyes had been transfixed to the screen since the start of the picture. It was only the blood-curdling screams of Louie Clowser running past his car that broke his attention from the hokey-looking monster that was waddling across the screen.

He rolled down his window and called out to his fleeing patron, "Damn, mister…it ain't *that* scary."

It was then that Lucas himself noticed the shroud of fog that encircled his theater. Startled by this strange sight, he jumped out of his car. He could still see Clowser stumbling across the parking ramps, making his way toward the exit gate. A few seconds later the terrified mill worker disappeared into the mist. Lucas then heard what sounded like a body smacking into the wall next to the exit gate and collapsing.

"Son of a—" he cried out in startled concern. "Are you okay?"

There was no response.

Lucas' attention was then distracted by something that dropped his jaw and raised his eyebrows:

The shadow of a giant tentacle passed over the screen!

Lucas did a double take. For a moment he thought it might be some sort of weird visual effect contained within the film itself, then the sound of more speaker poles being knocked to the ground perked his ears. He turned around just in time to see the cumulous mass of deadly fog swallow up another vehicle. The sound of shattering glass and bloodcurdling screams reverberated over the grounds. The tentacle emerged again and slithered across the parking ramps, probing in his direction.

It's hard to imagine the kind of horror Gary Lucas felt at that exact moment. Horror for him had always been the rush of adrenaline he got from watching his favorite old black and white horror movies, or the shuddery chills he felt when reading a good Robert Bloch story late at night, or even the smile that would cross his face while looking at a Feldstein-drawn monstrosity in an old EC comic. Horror had—in a very real sense—been a good friend to him for many, many years.

But not now.

In an instant his heart began to pound like a jackhammer; his entire body quivered with sudden, unexpected fear. Then, like Clowser before him, Lucas turned and ran. But instead of running blindly into the ring of cold mist, he slowed his approach, then stopped momentarily in front of it. Stepping carefully, he moved a foot or two into the cool vapors only to find himself reeling with dizziness. Lucas threw himself backward and crawled back out onto the open field. He looked over his shoulder:

The thing in the mist was getting closer.

Rising to his knees, Lucas saw only one remaining possible escape: the towering screen that was still alive with the black and white images of *Return of the Shoggoth*. The screen was anchored by a number of tall wooden supports, and on one of them was a ladder that ran up the backside, all the way to the very top.

Lucas rose to his feet and staggered to the ladder. He paused for a moment to shake the cobwebs out of his head, then started to climb.

As he rose above the field, he could hear the sound of other vehicles being attacked by the slithering monstrosity below. From the backside of the screen though, Lucas could only see the exterior frontage of the theater and the highway that skirted it. But his ears couldn't shut out the terror-stricken death-screams that ripped through the cool morning air. Lucas heard one auto start its engine and move across the field in the direction of the exit gate. He thanked God as he saw it emerge safely from the surrounding wall of fog and go speeding down the highway.

When he reached the top of the ladder, he looked over the crest of the screen. The dim light of dawn was starting to creep up over the Siskiyou Mountains to the east. Lucas looked down on the speaker field and saw the twisted remains of several cars that had been ripped apart, including his own. What was even more horrifying though, mind numbing in fact, was that from this vantagepoint—easily 50 feet off the ground—he could see the general shape of the hideous creature that lurked below. He screamed in horror and almost plunged to his death as he briefly lost his grip.

On the screen immediately below him, *Return of the Shoggoth* had been fast approaching its hair-raising climax. The crazed Whately, through the abhorrent magic of the *Necronomicon*, had succeeded in conjuring forth a dreaded shoggoth; but Whately had paid the ultimate price for his evil treachery, being savagely destroyed by the very creature he had invoked. The monstrous entity—which actually looked more like a huge, woolly carpet with men carrying it from underneath—now ran wild through the hills near Arkham. Professor Armitage and his assistant stood on a small rise outside the city as the horrible creature approached.

The professor unrolled a small scroll and read a strange passage that echoed across the theater from the remaining handful of functioning speakers:

R'lyeh kjan'ef ske-sar ernlk'ja pag'n! pag'n!

At that moment, the creature on screen let out a horrifying bellow and disappeared into thin air. At the same time, the cosmic monstrosity on the field below began to thrash wildly about, writhing as though in immense pain. Its otherworldly screams of agony swept across the sleepy valley:

"Tekeli-li! Tekeli-li! Tekeli-li!"

The ring of fog that had encircled the grounds abruptly rushed in and swirled about the monstrous shoggoth, this time in a clockwise direction. Lucas could see a pulsating glow that was suddenly visible again from within the bulging mass of protoplasmic matter. The creature continued to thrash about in a frenzied manner, leveling everything in its path. Suddenly the pulsating glow became intensely bright, causing Lucas to look away and shield his eyes. Then, just as quickly, the great light faded into darkness. Within seconds the obscene monster seemed to collapse in upon itself, shrinking into a small, brownish glob, then disappearing altogether. Out of the southwest, an early morning breeze dissipated the wandering mist that remained.

Lucas made his way quickly down the ladder, jumping down the last few feet. He scurried around to the front of the screen. The last seconds of *Return of the Shoggoth* were playing out above him, fading away in the early light of dawn. He looked out across the field—the murdering creature had turned his lifetime dream into a charnel house. He fell to his knees and began to weep. Then he looked up at the screen and saw something that sent another wave of horror through him...

The end of the film had jammed in the aperture plate!

Lucas saw the screen go white as the film burned away. He whirled about and saw a great flash of light in the window of the projection booth as the nitrate film burst into flames.

"Len!" he screamed.

Lucas bolted to the snack bar. In the few seconds it took him to reach it, the upper floor had already turned into an inferno. He grabbed the side door and tried to open it, but there was something on the floor inside, obstructing his entrance. After pushing hard against the door, he realized what the problem was:

Timmons' body was blocking the way.

With a supreme effort, he pushed the door open just enough to squeeze through. The deadly nitrate fumes were already billowing down the stairwell. Lucas pulled Timmons' body back from the entryway and swung the door completely open. He dragged the unconscious body of his projectionist to a safe distance from the burning building. Then he stood up and looked back at the blazing structure.

The brilliance of the flames seemed to wane in the early morning sunlight and along with it, the nostalgic dreams of an overgrown babyboomer. *Return of the Shoggoth* was gone forever, and for Gary Lucas, movies under the stars would never be the same again.

A BLACK SOLITUDE

By

H. RUSSELL WAKEFIELD

"Only the dead can live in this room."

I HAVE no explanation of this story, in fact, one of my reasons for telling it lies in the hope that some reader of it may provide one. I rather dislike being left in such an elucidatory void. I got permission to tell it from Lady Foreland; she is sure the Chief would not have minded. I shall probably tell it very badly, for I am an organizer of writers by profession, not a writer myself. The "Chief" was Lord Foreland, the first and greatest of the newspaper peers; none of his many successors can hold a candle—or should it be a telephone?—to him. I was his personal, private secretary for six years. I got the job directly after the Kaiser War when I was twenty-two. I was a callow, carefree, confident youth in those days, still housing a number of small pieces of shrapnel, but otherwise healthy enough, and very proud of serving such a celebrity.

The events in this narrative occurred at Caston Place, the Chief's most renowned country house. This was a famous specimen of early Tudor manor house, in Surrey, charming rather than beautiful, perhaps; though never have I seen such exquisitely mellow brick. The grounds were unarguably lovely. The great lawn—finest turf in the world—lined by Lebanon cedars, the flower, rock, water and kitchen gardens, all show pieces and deservedly so, the best private golf course in the Islands, snipe in the water, meadows down by the strolling, serpentine Wear. Well, if I were a millionaire that's the sort of cottage I would choose. The interior, too, after the Chief's purse had mated with "Ladyship's" taste, had been most delicately modernized without a trace of "vulgarized." I was there about thirty weekends in the year and I grew to love it. It was a great old gentleman, an eternally young old gentleman and it died, like so many other gentlemen of my times, in the wars. And also, like many such gentlemen, it had a secret, which died with it.

My little bedroom was almost at the end of the east wing. It had once been, I fancy, the dressing room of the big bedroom next door

22

to it. To my surprise I found that this big bedroom was never used, even when the most lavish house parties came for the weekend. It was not kept locked, but no one ever slept there.

One day I went in and inspected it. By any standards I had known up till then it was a *vast* room, and somehow vaguely unprepossessing. It had very dark oak paneling and a great oak bed. Two full-length portraits flanked the fireplace.

The owners of Caston had fallen on sufficiently mediocre days not to be able to afford to live in it, though the rent the Chief paid for it must have gone far to reconcile them to such exile. Portraits of their forebears—the majority third-rate daubs to be accurate—liberally littered the walls. The Chief told me there'd always been a "sticky" streak in the family (though the latest generation were tame enough) with a notorious name for cruelty, improvidence and various and versatile depravities. These portraits certainly, for the most part, bore this indictment out. They were a baleful-looking crew, men, women and children, and their decorative value exceptionally meager. But the two in the room, as I will call it from henceforth, struck, it seemed to me, a new and noxious low. They were man and wife, I suppose, and fitting mates. They were both in the middle forties, I should say, period, early Stuart, judging from their garb. The husband had a very nasty pair of close-set beady eyes and his lower lip—a family stigma— was fleshy, puffy and pouting, the lip of an insatiable and un- scrupulous egoist and sensualist. He carried his head bunched forward and his chin down, as though staring hard at the artist and giving him the toughest piece of his mind. The lady was a blonde, and sufficient in herself to give blondes a bad name. She had the lightest blue eyes I ever saw in a face, almost toneless. They were big, too far apart and as hard staring as her spouse's. Her mouth was just one long, hard, thin line of scarlet. Her expression was ruthless and contemptuous, as though telling the painter he was an incompetent— which was true—and informing him it would be a case of "off with his head" if he didn't hurry up. I remember thinking that if he'd ever seen the color of his fee, he was lucky. When I looked at them I found them staring back at me and I felt I would *not* let them stare me down. I thought how lowering it might be to find those four evil eyes on one when one woke up in the morning, and that it might not be too jocund to turn the light out knowing they were there. (In some frail moods it is difficult to differentiate entirely man and his effigy.

And that goes, if you know what I mean, for *dead* men—and women—too.) These twain looked, if I may so put it, as though at any moment they might step down from their frames and beat me up.

WELL, here was a small mystery and I made up my mind to solve it. It wasn't as if Caston was over-supplied with bedrooms. Those old houses are smaller than they look, in this sense, that many of their rooms are, to our ideas, ludicrously large, and there are too few of them. I knew Ladyship could have put the room to very good purpose if she'd so chosen. Why didn't she so choose? It was puzzling. I was new to the job, and it was not part of it to ask possibly awkward domestic questions. So I waited my chance and presently it came.

One day, when I was on my own down at Caston making arrangements for a big staff party the Chief was throwing, I took a stroll round the grounds with Chumley, the butler and a great character. The very first time I stayed at Caston, the Chief sent for Chumley and in his presence said to me, "This is my butler, the best butler in England, and a very great rogue. Owing to his defalcations and the house property he has purchased therefrom, he is also a very rich man. No doubt eventually he will go to America, the devil, the spiritual home of the best British butlers. Never, my boy, let me catch you giving him a tip."

"Well, sir," I said, "*may he* give *me* one sometimes?" The Chief was in a good humor, luckily, and passed this rather saucy remark. In fact, he said it showed I had a promising eye to the main commercial chance. (After the Chief died he *did* go to America, and some years later he sent me his photograph seated at the wheel of a Rolls Royce, a cigar in his mouth and an Alsatian sitting beside him. An eagle amongst doves!) Well, on this occasion we were strolling about on the lawn and I asked him, glancing up at its windows, why the room was never occupied. "His Lordship's brother, Sir Alfred, had an unpleasant experience there," he replied, "but please do not say I told you."

"What sort of experience?"

"I don't quite know, but he started screaming out one night and went straight back to London first thing in the morning. He never came here again and died very soon after."

"And it has never been used since?"

"Only on one occasion, sir; the editor of the *Evening Sentinel* slept there later on and he looked very *green* at breakfast the next morning. I think he must have said something to his Lordship, for he gave me orders the room wasn't to be used again."

"Was that Mr. Spenland, the present editor?"

"No, sir, Mr. Cocks, the former editor.

"He also died soon—within a week, as I remember it."

"Odd, Chumley!"

"Possibly, sir, but keep what I've told you under your hat, if I may use that expression. I made some inquiries in the village and they weren't surprised at all. Until his Lordship took the house the end of that wing was blocked up and never used."

"Why?"

"Hard to say, sir. Not considered lucky, I gathered."

"That's nice for me, sleeping there!"

"Have you been bothered, sir?"

"I don't think so. I get some funny dreams, but that's the food and drink, I expect. Not what I'm used to. But how d'you mean, not lucky?"

"They kept a tight mouth about that, but Morton, the game-keeper, told me there's supposed to be somebody or something still living on in that room."

"*What* a yarn!"

"Yes, sir," agreed Chumley doubtfully. "None of the maids will go in there alone after dark."

"Just because they've heard tales about it!"

"I suppose so, though one of them got a fright some years back. Anyway, don't tell his Lordship I said anything. He's a bit touchy about it; he likes all his possessions to be *perfect*." A very shrewd remark!

"No, all right," I promised, and we resumed discussing the business of the hour.

THAT night, just before going to bed, I paid a visit to the room. I had been busy with mundane and concrete matters. I had dined well, so it was with a very disdainful and nonchalant air that I climbed the stairs. At once, it is no use denying it, my psychic outlook changed. I suddenly realized that Caston when empty, was a very quiet, brooding place, and that I had never quite liked being alone in it, it was a bit "much" overpowering for a "singleton."

The weather had soured during the evening, clouding over with a falling glass and a fitful rising summer wind. My little enclave at the end of the passage seemed peculiarly aloof and dispiriting. Chumley's enigmatic remarks recurred to me with some force at that moment and with a heightened significance. I thought of those two dead men, the one who'd screamed and the other who'd looked "green"—what a word!—at breakfast. However, you know the feeling. I didn't want to open that door, and yet I knew if I didn't I should have kicked myself for a craven and never—or at least not for a long time—got it out of my system. My year at the War had taught me that each time one funks one finds it harder not to do it next time. All of which may sound much ado about precious little, but you weren't standing facing that door at midnight on July 20th, 1923! Well, with a small whistle of defiance I turned the handle of that door and flipped on the lights. Anti-climax, of course! Just a huge old room like any other of its kind. And yet was it quite normal? Well, there was that commonplace feeling everyone has experienced that someone had been in there a moment before, that the air was still warm from that someone's presence; perhaps rather more than that; perhaps, quite absurd, of course, that one was being observed by someone unseen. My eyes ran round the room swiftly and then settled on those criminal types athwart the fireplace. They had their eyes on me pretty starkly. "Avaunt!" they seemed to be saying, or whatever was the contemporary phrase for "Beat it!" I stared back at them. "Not till I'm ready!" I replied out loud in a would-be jocular way. There was an odd echo in that room. It seemed to swing round the walls and come back to hit me in the face. Then I heard a scraping noise from the chimney, Jack-daws nesting in it, no doubt second-brood; my voice had disturbed their slumbers. I moved further into the room. The rustling in the chimney grew louder. "Well, good night, all!" I said facetiously, but there was no echo. I tried again; no echo at all. That was a puzzle. I shifted my position and said good night to them once more. This time the echo nearly blew my head off and something tapped three times on one of the windows. I suddenly felt that uncontrollable atavistic dread of ambush and glanced sharply round behind my back. "I'm not afraid of you," I said loudly. "Do your worst!" But somehow I knew it was time to go. I paced back slowly and deliberately, turned out the light, banged the door and went to bed.

What a history that room must have had, I thought, to have been blocked off from the world like that for years. And now the ban was up once more. Strong medicine there of some sort! What sort? And there was only some thin paneling and plaster between it and me. I kept my ears pricked, for I was a bit on edge, my subconscious was alert and receptive.

I went to bed and presently to sleep. Sometime in the night I awoke hearing something, which, my subconscious told me, I had heard several times before, but now, *consciously* for the first time; it was a kind of *crack* like the flipping of giant fingers, twice repeated. A displeasing, staccato, urgent and peremptory sound, the source of which I quite failed to trace.

Now the Chief, like most self-made men, especially in his profession, had some queer "old friends," many of who had been associated with him in his days of struggle, but had, for the most part, been left far behind in the success marathon. The Chief had not a trace of snobbery about these; so long as he liked them and they amused him they remained his friends, rich or poor, successes or duds and, in several cases, reputable or not. Perhaps the queerest of all these was one, Apuleius Charlton. This person was generally deemed a very dubious type and a complete back-number, the last belated survivor of the Mauve decade, with a withered green carnation in his frayed buttonhole and trailing thin clouds of obsolete diabolism. Incidentally, he belonged to a cadet branch of a very "old family." As a sinister monster of depravity I found him sheer Disney and so did the Chief, but he had unarguably superior brains, a kind of charm, and an ebullient personality. In fact, *personality* is quite too flaccid a word; he was *Sui generis*, the sole member of his species. There was a strong tinge of Casanova about him; he shared his brazen candor, occasional brilliant insight, his refusal to accept the silly laws of God and man as binding upon himself, his essential spiritual loneliness. He was a big hefty creature, an athlete by right of birth, with a huge domed head, large watery eyes and jet-black hair, the fringe of which he tortured into twin spiral locks. Between them was a small, red magical mark, a three-pronged "moon" swastika. He had been everywhere in the world, I think, and his travel tales were legion and sensational and owing something, no doubt, to an ebullient imagination. He was then barred from a number of countries, rather unhumorously, for while his bark was Cerberian, his bite was vastly over-rated. He had, no doubt, acquired certain monies by various modes of false pretenses, but never a sizable hoard; and those he diddled were, I am sure, consummate mugs who just asked to be "taken." He said so himself and I believed him.

HE HAD written copiously on many subjects with an air of complete confidence and authority, and in his youth had been a goodish minor poet of the erotic, adjectival Swinburne school, but somehow he never had any real money. That was his incurable malady. There are a number of, such vagrant oddities in the world, lone wolves, or rather, I think, they remind me of great ostracized, solitary birds, forever winging their way fearlessly and hopefully from one barren place to another, wiry, wary, and shunned by the timorous and "respectable" flock. He had written stuff for the Chief's publications before his name became so odoriferous, climbed with him in several parts of the world, for he was a brilliant and scientific mountaineer, and gone with him on esoteric drinking bouts in the wine countries, for he knew his epicurean tipples and taught the Chief to judge a vintage. Lastly, and immensely most important to himself, he was a magician with a cult or mystery of his very own invention and a small band of very odd initiates indeed. Hence the swastika and much ponderous and eleusinian jewelry on convenient parts of his person, including a perfectly superb jade ring. I know jade and this piece was incomparably fine. (You will hear of it again.) For this aspect of his ego the Chief, not necessarily rightly, expressed the most caustic contempt, telling him the only reason why he and his rival Merlins and Fingals shrouded their doings in veils of secrecy—and this went for Masons, Buffaloes, Elks, and all other mumbo-jumbo practitioners—was that they had nothing to conceal except the most puerile and humiliating drivel worthy of their Woolworth regalia, and they were ashamed to disclose such infantile lucubrations and primitive piffle. All the same some people were definitely scared of old Apuleius, and no doubt he had a formidable and impressive side. He was sixty odd at this time and very well preserved in spite of his hard boozing, addiction to drugs and sexual fervor, for it was alleged that joy-maidens or Hierodoules were well represented in his mystic entourage. (If I were a Merlin, they would be in mine!)

Of course he never figured in house parties, but the Chief had him down to Caston now and again and, I know, sent him a most welcome cheque at regular intervals.

In November of this same year, the Chief and his Lady went away for a month's holiday to the Riviera, and just before he met old Apuleius in the street looking a bit down at heel and told him he could doss down at Caston while he was away, that I would look after him, and that the cellar was at his disposal, but that this invitation did *not* extend to his coterie, particularly the Hierodoules! Poor Apuleius leaped at this timely and handsome offer, and the day after the Chief's departure he appeared at the house bearing his invariable baggage, one small, dejected cardboard suitcase—at least, it looked like cardboard. I was on holiday, too, or rather half-holiday, for I got six to a dozen telegrams a day from the Chief and had made a rash promise to begin the cataloguing of his library. (I may say he had two other secretaries to do the donkey-work.) But I had plenty of spare time to shoot golf and catch some of the nice little trout in the stream. So there were old Apuleius and I almost alone for a month and all the best at our disposal. He treated me always with some pleasing but quite unnecessary deference, for I was the Czar's little shadow and a lad worth cultivating. Besides he liked me a Little and he didn't like anyone very much. I resolved to examine this psychological freak, because I never could decide how much of a charlatan he was and how much he believed in his own bunkum. Such characters are very dark little forests and it's a job to blaze any sort of trail through them.

He arrived, very sensibly, just in time for lunch and did himself extremely well. He was in great spirits and splendid form talking with vast verve and rather above my jejune head. I quite forget what it was all about. He slept for a while after lunch and then began a prolonged prowl around the establishment, which he had never properly inspected before. I went with him, for the unworthy reason that the house was full of small, highly saleable articles and he had a reputation for sometimes confusing meum with tuum when confronted with such. At length we reached my little enclave and there facing him was the room. "What's that?" he asked, staring hard at the door. "Oh, just a bedroom," I replied. Suddenly he moved forward quickly, opened the door, and drew a quick, dramatic breath. At once he seemed transformed. You have seen the life come to a drowsy cat's eyes when it hears the rustle of a mouse. You may have noted the changed demeanor of some oafish and lugubrious athlete when he spies a football or a bag of golf clubs. Just such a metamorphosis occurred in Apuleius when he opened that door. He became intent, absorbed, *professional*, I felt compensatingly insignificant and meager.

"Nobody sleeps here?" he said.

"No," I replied.

"Not twice, anyway," he said sharply.

"Why?" I asked.

HE WENT up to the criminal types and scrutinized them carefully. And then he pointed out to me some things I had not noticed before, a tiny figure of a hare with a human and very repulsive face at the right-hand side of the gentleman, a crescent moon with something enigmatic peering out between its horns on the same side of the lady. "As I expected," he observed in his most impressive manner, and left it at that.

"Well, what about it?" I asked impatiently.

"That would take rather a long time to explain, my dear Pelham," he replied, "and with all respect, I doubt if you would ever quite understand. Let me just say this. Such places as these are as rare as they are perilous. In a sense this is a *timeless* place. What once happened here didn't change, didn't pass on, it was *crystallized*. What happened herein eternally repeats itself. Here time, as it were, was trapped and can't move on. Man is life and life is change so such places are deadly to man. If man cannot change, he dies. Death is the end of a stage in a certain process of change. Only the dead can live in this room."

"And do they?" I asked, bemused by this rigmarole.

"In a sense, yes."

This effusion didn't commend itself to me. (Besides it was still daylight.) I countered with vivacity. "Well," I said, "you may be right, but the moment anyone begins philosophizing about time I get a bellyache. It is one of the prevailing infirmities of third-rate minds. Personally I believe it to be no more a genuine mystery than say, money, with which it is vulgarly identified. All this pother about both is due to a confusion of thought based on a confusion of terms. The word 'time' is habitually used in about sixteen different senses. If I were asked to define metaphysics, I should describe it as an acrimonious and sterile controversy about the connotation of certain abstract terms. But I'll give you this, the room has a bad name." (There was no getting round that, and he'd instantly spotted it. How?)

"It should not even be *entered* after dark," he said, "save by those who—well—understand it and enter it fore-armed."

"You say something happened here and eternally reacts itself. What?"

"Those two," he replied, pointing to the types, "made an experiment which in a sense succeeded."

"And that was?"

"Once again I am in a difficulty. These dark territories are such new ground to you. You must understand there are no such entities as good and evil, there are merely forces, some beneficent, some injurious, indeed, fatal, to man. He exists precariously poised between these forces. Those two, as it were, allied themselves with the forces noxious to man; what used to be called selling oneself to the devil. These things are beyond you, my dear Pelham, and I should not pursue them. It is one of the oldest mysteries of the world, the idea that if one can become all evil, drink the soma of the fiend, one immortalizes oneself; one becomes impervious to change and so to death. Actually, it is not so. It cannot be done. One cannot defeat death, but one can become what is loosely called an evil spirit, a focus for a concentration of destructive energy, and, in that limited sense, undying."

"Of course, you're right, that's all cuneiform to me," I replied staring up at the ambitious pair. "But what's the result? What happens then?"

"Well, those two made that attempt. I can tell that for certain reasons, and achieved that limited success. They practiced every conceivable wicked and unspeakable thing. This room was their laboratory, their torture-chamber; it reeks of it. When they died, they became chained to this room. It is their *Hell*, if you like so to put it."

"In what state are they?" I asked not knowing whether to laugh or cry. "I mean are they conscious? Do they know, for example, you are discussing them?"

"To begin with 'they' is a misnomer. 'They' are *one*; male and female principles have been fused and the feminine predominates, for it is the more primitive, potent and dangerous. The resultant 'It' is not conscious in our sense of the word, it has no illusion of *will*. It is a state we cannot understand and so cannot describe. It has been absorbed into the very soul of that power which is inimicable to man and is endowed with its venom. But it cannot roam; it is anchored to this room. To destroy man is It's delight. In that It finds It's *orgasm*. What occurs in this room is the eternal generation, condensation and release of murderous energy. After dark, for it cannot be released in daylight, this whole room will be soaked in and embued with that energy."

"How does It destroy?"

"It can do so simply by fear and fear can kill. Once in India I passed through a cholera-infected area. The very road was thick with bodies, but more of them had died from sheer fear than the disease. It would kill *you* by fear, but It could not so kill me. It would have to— well—*overpower* me to destroy me. I am coming here tonight."

"I shouldn't!" I said hastily. "I'm not sure the Chief would— permit it. If anything happened to you, he'd be furious."

"It will not. I know the only safeguards against and antidotes to these forces. So leave me now. I will start to prepare my defenses. I will see you at dinner."

So I went off to do some work, completely baffled and somewhat uneasy in mind.

AT DINNER Apuleius was preoccupied and portentous, and actually drank nothing but water, a sure sign he was taking life seriously. I was preoccupied too. I knew perfectly well that the Chief would have shoved down a formidable foot on the whole thing, but I wasn't the Chief. Apuleius had been given the run of the house and I had no authority to control his movements within it. All the same, looking back on it, I think I acted feebly and that I should have exercised a veto however arbitrary, and kept him out of that room that night. All I did was to employ persuasion, and quite ineffectually. "My dear Pelham," he propounded, "this is a challenge I must accept. I have devoted much of my life to this crusade of safeguarding man from those black forces which, unknown to the blind and unpercipient, are forever striving and with ever increasing success to break down his resistance and shatter him. If I fully succeed tonight I shall cleanse that room and make it harmless, white and habitable again. I shall be very thankful if I can do the Chief this service."

"But supposing they are too strong for you?" I protested. "That energy may be more virulent and vicious than you reckon on."

"That is a risk I must take. So far I have always conquered them, and I can rally mighty forces to my aid. In this sign,"—and he touched the swastika on his forehead—"I shall conquer once again. Have no fears."

I must say he looked impressive, exalted, when he said this.

After dinner he again disappeared for a while and I tried to do some more work, but of all jobs cataloguing a library is the most soporific. I dozed off and presently woke to find him standing before me. He had repainted the swastika, which gleamed somberly.

"I am ready," he declared, "and now I will rest for a while. I will enter that room at five minutes to midnight."

"What kind of ordeal do you think awaits you?" I asked. "Or do you mind telling me?"

"The moment I enter that room I shall pronounce certain formulae, what you would loosely call incantations, I shall then, to use a military metaphor, entrench myself within a defensive and concentrate my whole spirit on rallying to my side the powers of white, the forces of salvation. They will come to me. Already the black forces will be concentrating upon me; the tension will increase every moment. Sometime the black will strike and the white will lash back, the grapple will be joined. When those dark forces have done their worst and been repelled, white will have been reestablished in that room, the sting of evil, of destruction and of black will have been drawn. I shall be exhausted and soon pass into a coma from which I shall awake refreshed, hale and with added powers. And then we will enjoy our holiday together, my dear Pelham, and drink deep, having cleansed this lovely house of its ancient doom.

"I wish I could be with you in that struggle," I said doubtfully.

"It is unthinkable," he replied forcibly. "It has taken me forty years to learn how to conduct this fearful quarrel. I could not extend that which protects me to you. You would be inevitably destroyed."

"Just killed?" I asked repressing a blasphemous itch to laugh.

"More than that, though that for certain. You might never be seen again."

Now, I will be frank, it did seem to me that already there was a tension, a sense of malaise in that great room where we were sitting. The wind had risen to half-a-gale and the rain had come with it. The old house seemed like a ship heaving at its, moorings. The windows shook, the curtains stirred, the wind went roaring by. And really for the first time I knew old Apuleius to be a strange and formidable fellow and no figure of fun, and that that shining emblem on his brow

33

might have more than a derisory significance. I grew very restless; the current stirring my nerves seemed to have had its voltage raised. I should have liked to have gone out into that storm and walked the tension down. Odd, distorting little pictures formed and vanished in my mind's eye; masks of evil, a flaming body hurtling through the sky, a ring of sultry fire, a dark stream of birds, a bloody sword. I shook myself and fetched a drink. Apuleius was sitting now, motionless, his chin on his breast, his hands gripping the arms of his chair. And presently the clock chimed three times, it was a quarter to midnight.

"No drink, Apuleius?" I asked, to break the silence.

"No," he replied. "Alcohol relaxes, and I require the utmost stiffening of my spirit. If I had known what was before me I would not have drunk at lunch."

"Then put it off till you've prepared yourself properly!"

"No," he replied, "it must be tonight."

"Look," I urged, "you realize there will only be a thin wall between us. If you're in any trouble bang on that wall and I'll come fighting."

"Have no fear," he said, "all will be well."

"Yes, but if it isn't will you bang on that wall?"

"In the last extremity I will, but it will not be necessary. And now the time has come."

WE GOT up together. I took the tantalus of whiskey with me and a syphon. I had no intention of sleeping and I felt like some Scotch courage. The gale was now at its height, screaming wickedly round the house; a fit night for black and white, I thought, as we mounted the lightly creaking stairs. We parted without a word at the door of my room and Apuleius went on. Just before he opened that door he raised himself to his full height, touched the mark on his forehead, turned the handle and strode in. To this day I can see him there in my mind's eye as clearly as I did twenty-three long years ago. Then he disappeared, and I went in and closed my door. I sat down in an armchair, knocked back a big drink and tried to read. But I was half-listening all the time and couldn't concentrate. What was happening on the other side of that thin wall? I cursed the wind, which waxed and waxed in venom drowning all small sounds. I could hear their straining timber roar as the great cedars fought the gale. The room seemed charged with a heightening tension. I had felt something like it before in the dynamo room of a great power station, when those

34

smooth spinning cylinders seemed to charge and shake the air with the power they so nonchalantly and quietly engendered, a power that in its essence remains a mighty mystery to this day.

I tried to visualize what Apuleius was doing. Sitting inside his magic circle, I supposed, murmuring his protective runes, straining to keep back that which strove to pass the barrier. I concentrated all my will upon it and presently I had the strangest illusion of my life. It was as though I was seeing into that room, as though the wall had become almost transparent and I was gazing through its thinning veil. Apuleius was sitting there in the middle of the room surrounded by a faintly illuminated ring. His eyes were staring, his face contorted into an odious rixus, his mouth moving convulsively. On the carpet just outside the ring huge shadows were crouching, other shadows of dubious and daunting shape were leaning down the walls. All seemed to have their heads pointing at him. All the time the lighted ring grew slowly dimmer. Suddenly there came, repeated over and over again, that horrid cracking of giant fingers, the lights in my room flickered, reddened and sparked. And then there was a dazzling flash of lightning and a blast of thunder, which went roaring down the gale. I could stand no more and leapt to my feet.

SUDDENLY I heard Apuleius scream, once quickly, the second a piercing, drawn-out cry of agony. And then came a frenzied beating on the wall. I dashed out into the passage and flung open the door of the room. It was dimly lit, it was quiet, it was empty, the only movement, the slight stirring of the long, dark window curtains. I ran along to his room. Save for the little cardboard suitcase it was empty too. I shouted for him until Chumley came to investigate whether I had really gone crazy, or was merely very tight. He was wearing, I noted, a mink-collared dressing gown over a pair of the Chief's most scintillating monogrammed silk pajamas.

And on that mildly farcical note I will end the story of that night. For Apuleius was never seen again. Of course, most of the few people who cared in the least whether he was alive or dead believed he'd done a bunk for reasons not unconnected with the constabulary. He was soon forgotten for he had long ceased to hit even the tiniest headlines. He had disappeared before and now he'd done it again. Good riddance! When the Chief heard my story he flew into a considerable fury though not with me, for he was a fair man and agreed it was not my function to control his guest and a man more than twice my own age. He wanted to believe the done-a-bunk theory naturally enough, but he realized it was dead against the weight of evidence. He had the room locked up and gave orders no one was to enter it without his or Ladyship's permission in the future.

The years passed and so presently did the Chief, no doubt to put some ginger into celestial or infernal journalism. I got a very nice job in his organization for life, I hoped, but then came the war and I transferred my talents temporarily to the M. O. I. In 1941 I was for a time bomb-jolly through being flung out of bed and hard up against a wall when my Kensington house was next door to a direct hit.

I had still kept in touch with Ladyship, then living very sensibly in a safe area, and one morning in June, 1944, she rang me up to say she had just heard Caston had been damaged by a fly-bomb and would I go down and see what had happened.

Poor sweet old place! The doodle had dived clap in the middle of the courtyard, which had, of course, enclosed the blast—and that was that. Those Tudor houses were lightly built of delicate brick and lots of glass, so Caston was no more. Center block pulverized, right wing still collapsing by stages when I arrived. My old left wing just a great mountain of debris, bricks, beds, furniture, pictures, clothes—an incredible chaos spangled everywhere with that lovely old glass. The rescue squads were digging in the center wing for the bodies of the caretaker and his wife. A bulldozer and cranes rolled up while I was there. I climbed up the monstrous and pathetic pile feeling sad and full of memories. On the summit I picked up a piece of canvas and, turning it over, found I was being regarded by the palest eyes which ever stared from a woman's face above a long, thin streak of scarlet. I threw it down again, *that* was not the sort of souvenir I relished. As I did so, I saw something glitter from between two broken bricks. I pulled it out and there was a sea-green jade ring on the splintered bone of a fleshless finger. I got the rescue men to dig around there, but we found nothing more.

That ring is on the desk beside me as I write these words. It is lovely beyond all telling. How it happened to be where I found it is, as I have told you, a matter for you to decide.

STRANGE HARVEST

By

DONALD WANDREI

Trees, plants, vegetables had mysteriously developed will power of their own had cast off the dominance of man.

THE sun had scarcely risen when Al Meiers shoved himself away from the breakfast table and lumbered to his feet. A big, powerful man even for the Shawtuck County region of husky farmers, he had a face like tanned leather and arms whose hair lay swart over muscles like cables. He was all bone and solid flesh. Though past fifty, he strode with the ease of youth.

"That was a good breakfast, maw," he drawled to his almost spherical wife. She smiled out of eyes that had smiled through drought, storm, plague of locusts, and depression.

"Get along with you. Them apples'll never get picked with you aloafin' around here all day."

"Them apples'll be down by night. Hank!" he roared. The harvest hand, dripping of suds and rainwater on the doorstep, hastily smeared his face with a towel.

"There ought to be over two hundred bushel," said Al.

"Maybe more." Hank, a wiry drifter, slouched beside Al as they passed the chicken-coops. Roosters crowed, hens squawked out of their way, and the spring chickens beeped in alarm. Al made a splendid figure even in his dirty overalls, a bronzed giant of the soil.

They passed the pigsty where sows and porkers squealed over a sour-smelling trough. The sun stood just above the horizon, and the warm air held that peculiar scent of late summer—smell of cattle and manure, of clover, hay, and wheat, of baked earth and ripening vegetation.

A wagon loaded with empty bushel baskets stood by the barn. Al hitched the horses and took the reins. The team of Belgian Grays ambled down a dirt road.

"It's been a good year for crops," said Al. He jammed tobacco in an old corncob pipe and lighted it without loosening the reins.

"Yeah. Only there's something funny about 'em this year."

"Yeah. They're bigger. Biggest ever."

Hank spat out a hunk of plug. "That ain't all. They kind of shake even if there ain't no wind. As I was sayin' yesterday, I got to feelin' pretty queer when the tomato patch kind of shook when I was hoein' it."

"Giddyap!" Al bellowed. The team clattered faster. He inhaled and blew out a cloud of fragrant smoke. "Uh-huh, I don't know what's got into things. Best weather and best crops we ever had but something's wrong. Last fall the crops started growin' again about harvest-time. The damnedest thing. It wasn't till October we got all the spuds in and the corn-crib full."

Hank looked uneasy. "I don't like it. There been times when I, well, I just didn't feel right."

"Yeah?"

Hank lapsed into moody silence.

"Yeah?" Al prodded.

"There wasn't any wind yesterday but I swear the north clover patch flattened out when I started to mow."

"Yeah? You been seein' things." Al was noncommittal. Hank kept silent.

"I never saw corn grow like this year," said Al after awhile. The horses clopped along. "Ten foot high if it's an inch. Fred Altmiller was sayin' the other day that he figured on gettin' a hundred fifty bushel to the acre. Nary an ear less'n a foot long."

Hank moped. "Last time I went through your corn was the damnedest racket you ever heard. You'd of thought a storm come up. There wasn't a cloud nowhere. Wasn't any wind."

"Layoff the corn likker," Al jibed.

"Wasn't corn likker," Hank protested. "It's the crops are queer. I'd of bet there was somebody around when I weeded the melons last week. Sounded like voices."

"What did?"

"Why, just everything. Whispers, like the corn was talkin'."

Al snorted. "You're headed for the bughouse. I been here for thirty years an' I never hear tell of such a story."

"It's so! It's been goin' on all summer!"

The wagon bumped through fields of ripe wheat and oats, lurched around an immense boulder, and rattled up a hill where cows munched at grass strewn between stones and scrubby trees.

Al agreed with Hank but he wouldn't admit it. The first principle of stolid people is to deny the existence of what cannot be explained and does not harmonize with the run of experience. Ever since the phenomenal post-season growth of vegetables and fruit last fall, he had been wondering. The spring planting, the perfect weather, bumper crops, truly miraculous yields—these blessings were offset by certain evidence that had made him increasingly uneasy. There was the matter of waving grass on still days. He hadn't yet gotten over the way the trees hummed one hot afternoon when he was spraying the apple and cherry orchards.

"Anyway, it's been a good year," he repeated. "Them apples are prize winners. The trees are bustin' with 'em."

The wagon bumped across the hilltop and the horses plodded down. "Just look at 'em, just look—well—uh," his voice petered out.

Yesterday an orchard of Jonathan's had occupied this acre between two small hills.

Yesterday.

Today there was only torn soil and furrows stretching toward the opposite hill.

Al gaped and his face turned a mottled red. Hank's eyes popped. He opened his mouth and closed it. He stared as if at a ghost. He ran a finger around his neck. The sun slanted higher. The field lay bright and newly ploughed. But there were no apple trees.

Al blasted the morning air with a howl. "Some dirty thief has swiped my apples!" he yelled.

Hank looked dazed. "There ain't any trees, ain't any apples, ain't nothing."

Al sobered. "Not even roots."

"No stumps," said Hank.

They stared at the bare ground and at each other.

"The orchard walked off," Hank suggested.

The horses whinnied. The red in Al's weathered face died out. It became a study in anger and bewilderment.

"Come on!" he choked and flicked the horses' flanks with a whip. They plunged downhill, slewed onto the field, and followed the furrows over the looted soil, across undulating mounds, and straight through a field of wheat. There was a swathe like the march of an army.

"It can't be. I'm dreamin', we're both crazy," muttered Al.

Hank fidgeted. "Let's go back."

"Shut up! If someone's swiped my apples I'll break him in half! The best crop in thirty years!"

Hank pleaded, "Listen, Al, it ain't only the apples. The whole trees're gone, root an' all. Nobody can do that in a night!"

AL DROVE grimly. The horses galloped over a hill to the road and followed it as it wound down toward a small lake between terminal moraines. There they jerked to an abrupt halt under Al's powerful drag.

Al glared. Hank's eyes roved aimlessly around. He fumbled for a chew, which he bit off and absently, spit out. He tried to loosen an open shirt. He didn't want to see what he saw. "So help me God," he muttered, "so help me God," over and over, like a stuck phonograph record.

Here stood the orchard of Jonathan apples grouped around the pond; a half-mile from its accustomed place, but otherwise intact.

Al leaped out, a peculiar blank expression on his face. He walked with the attitude of a cat stalking prey.

The orchard of Jonathan's wavered.

There was no wind.

The orchard looked for all the world like a group debating. Whispers and murmurs ascended, and the branches shook.

Hank leaned against the dashboard. Tobacco juice dribbled from his gaping mouth and watered his new crop of whiskers.

"Come on!" snarled Al. "Get them poles and nets. We're gonna pick apples!"

But he did not need to pick apples. He reached for a luscious red Jonathan hanging low on the nearest tree. The branch went back, then forward, like a catapult. Al ducked. The apple smacked the wagon. Both horses whinnied and raced off. As if that were a signal, the orchard launched into violent motion. A noise like a rushing wind rose. The treetops bent and lashed as in a gale. Apples showered the farmers, darkened the air, bounced and squashed painfully from faces and shins and bodies.

The ungodliest yell ever heard in Shawtuck County burst from the throat of a hired hand whose terrific speed carried him after the careening wagon out of the picture, and the county.

LARS ANDERSEN was walking along a path with a scythe on his shoulder to mow some odd plots of hay, early that morning. His Scotch collie bounced beside him.

The path went around a vegetable garden and then paralleled a windbreak of elms. Now it is a well-known fact that any intelligent dog will have nothing to do with grass or mere vegetables.

The collie, being a dog of rigidly conventional habits, made a beeline for one of the trees. Whatever he intended to do was postponed. The lowest branch of the tree curved down and not only whipped his rear smartly but lifted him a good dozen feet away. He yelped and tore home like mad.

Lars had a thoughtful expression on his face as he turned around and headed back. He guessed he didn't feel much like mowing today.

Old Emily Tawber fussed with her darning until mid-morning before laying it aside. "Jed can wait for his socks," she muttered crossly. "I can't cook and sew and tend to the crops all at once, and them watermelons ripe for market."

She put her mending back in the big wicker basket, pulled a vast-brimmed straw hat over her head, and went out in an old rag dress that she used for chores.

She stomped across the yard and through her flower garden to the melon patch. There were about fifty big melons ready for picking. She would pile them up alongside the path for Jed to load and take to market in the morning.

"Land's sakes, I never see such melons in all my born days." Old Emily stuck her arms on her hips and surveyed the green ovals. These were giant watermelons, three and four feet long, weighing a hundred pounds or more. She had been surprised throughout the summer by their growth.

"Well, the bigger they be, the more they'll fetch," she decided and went after the first one.

It must have been on a slope for it rolled away as she approached.

"Well, I swan!" said old Emily. "Things is gettin' to a pretty pass when you can't get at your own seedin's."

She walked after the watermelon. It rolled farther. Old Emily became flustered. She increased her stride. The melon bumped unevenly in a wide circle around the vineroot. Old Emily panted after it and it wobbled crazily always just ahead of her.

Old Emily began to feel dizzy. She guessed the sun was too much for her. She wasn't as spry as she used to be. The world reeled around. The melon kept going, while she paused for breath, then it rolled all the way around, came toward her, and crashed into her ankles. The blow sent her sprawling. This was when peril first entered her thoughts. She staggered to her feet and from the patch.

"Watermelon won't get me," she crooned. "Watermelon run along but he won't get me. Don't let old watermelon get me." This was all that anyone heard her say during the rest of her earthly existence.

THE harvester thundered as Gus Vogel gave it the gas and it clattered toward his wheat acreage.

Gus hollered, "With this weather we'll be done come night!"

"If the machines don't break down," bawled brother Ed above his machine's racket.

"Wheat is two dollar 'n a quarter a bushel," Gus chortled. "I bet we get a hundred bushel to the acre this year."

The two machines rattled along a dirt road that was little more than weed-grown ruts until a tawny sea appeared beyond the brook and cow pastures.

A full half-section in extent, the field of ripe grain rolled away in a yellow-brown flood shoulder high, the tallest wheat within memory, headed by two-inch spears with dozens of fat grains.

Gus and Ed jockeyed the harvesters into the near corner of the field. Those long rows erect as soldiers would soon go down in a wide swathe. The three hundred twenty acres of wheat were worth over seventy thousand dollars.

Gus roared lustily as his machine lurched ahead and the blades whirred to reap, "Let 'er go!"

As if struck by a mighty wind, the wheat flattened against the ground in a great area that widened as the harvester advanced.

Not a breath of wind stirred. The air hung warm and fragrant, the sunlight lay mellow on ripe grain, meadowlarks caroled morning-songs, and the black crows cawed harshly high overhead. But the wheat lay flat, mysteriously, in a large strip. Beyond this strip, the golden ranks rose tall again, but a myriad murmuring issued from them like voices of invisible hosts. The hair prickled on Gus's scalp. He looked behind him. Not a stem had been cut by the reaper, and the full ears were intact. In a sudden vicious, unreasoning rage, he drove the combine ahead at full speed, and the blades sang a song of shirring steel, and the wheat went down in a racing band farther ahead at a faster pace than he could achieve, and the slicing blades whirred idly over the prone grain.

Then Gus and Ed stopped the machines and climbed out. Gus knelt over and bent his face low to study this extraordinary field. A patch sprang upright like wires, lashing his face. Gus gaped, popeyed. The veins stood out on his temples in purple. Somewhere within him something happened and he pitched to the ground, his face livid, as Ed ran to his aid.

NOT least among the remarkable events in Shawtuck County that morning was the saga of the fugitive potatoes.

The potatoes were only a small planting of an acre or so that Pieter Van Schluys had raised. They should have matured in early August but they didn't. They kept on growing and their tops got bigger and greener and lustier. Pieter was a stolid Dutchman who knew his potatoes as well as his schnapps.

"Dere iss something wrong," he solemnly told his American frau. "Dey haff no business to grow furder. Already yet dey haft gone two veeks too late."

"Dig 'em up, then," said the bony Gertrude. "If they're ripe, they're ripe. If they aren't, you can tell quick enough by diggin' a couple out."

"Ja," Pieter agreed. "But it iss not right. Potatoes, dey should be in two weeks already."

"Maybe if you weren't so lazy you'd of dug 'em two weeks ago."

"Dat iss not so," Pieter began, but Gertrude tartly gathered dishes and pans with a great noise.

Pieter blinked and rose. It was hard to have such a shrewish frau. In this *verdammte* America, *frauen* were too independent. You could neither boss them, nor beat them.

He rolled to the door and waddled past a silo to the barn where he took a potato-digger from a mass of tools. He leisurely filled a well-stained meerschaum pipe, which had a broken stem, and lighted it. A couple of geese honked sadly as he passed in a cloud of burley smoke.

Pieter paused by the potatoes to wipe his sweating face with a kerchief bigger than a napkin. "Gertrude," he muttered, "she iss no better as a potato."

Having expressed his rebellion, he dug and heaved. The tubers did not come up. Pieter strained, struggled, perspired. The heap of earth grew larger, but no potato appeared.

"Dat iss some potato," Pieter muttered. "Himmel, vat a potato it must be."

Pieter looked at his planting. "Diss iss not right for a potato," he spoke in reproof, and shoveled more soil away.

Had his eyes deceived him? Or had the plant actually sunk? He looked at the vegetable tops with thoughtful disgust. It seemed beyond question that the leafy tops were considerably nearer ground level than when he arrived.

"So?" Pieter exclaimed. "Iss dat how it iss? So!"

He scooped again. He watched with a kind of bland interest at first, then a naive wonder, and finally anxiety. It did seem that the potato was getting away from him. No, that could not be. He must have taken too many schnapps last night. Or it was too hot. He wiped perspiration off his face with a sleeve of his blue denim shirt. The potato was as far below his digger as ever, and surely his eyes did not befool him when they registered that the potato's topmost leaf was now at ground level. Quite a heap of soil lay beside it. The rest of the potato patch stood as high as before. Only this one pesky tuber had sunk, unaccountably.

Pieter dug deeper.

The mound of dirt increased. The hole grew larger. The elusive potato continued to slide below his digger. It was maddening. There must be a cave as big as the Zuyder Zee under this vegetable. He might fall into it with the plant!

His slow brain, obtaining this thought, brought him to a momentary halt. But no. Ten years he had farmed here, ten years he had harvested. It was very strange. Pieter did not feel quite so chipper as after breakfast, and he certainly had not been jovial then. Pieter became stubborn. The devil himself was in this potato. The devil was leading him to hell. Or nature had gone crazy. Or he had.

Pieter shoveled and scooped, but the tuber dug down like a thing possessed, a mole, a creature hunted. The pile of dirt had spread far by now, and Pieter stood in a deep pit with the potato still below him. He had reached sandy, thin, base soil. He was angry and stubborn. He dug till his arms ached. He panted in Dutch and cursed in English.

He muttered, he swore.

"Something iss crazy or I am," he decided and made a half-hearted plunge at the vanishing vegetable.

"You seem to be having some difficulty. Can I be of help?" inquired a polite voice.

A stranger stood on the rim of the hole. The stranger wore old corduroy trousers, a stained work-shirt, and a slouch hat. He had amused gray eyes. A briar pipe stuck out of his mouth. He twirled a golden key idly so that the chain wrapped round and round his forefinger. His face was full of angles, and a peculiar mark, not a scar, possibly a burn, made a patch on his left temple. By that mark, Pieter recognized him from hearsay as a comparative newcomer. He had bought the Hoffman farm a mile out of Shawtuck Center on County Road C somewhat over a year ago. He paid cash, and claimed the odd name Green Jones.

Pieter scowled. "Danks, but I vill manage. De potatoes iss hard to dig diss year."

The stranger's jaw fell open. "You don't mean to tell me you're digging potatoes! Way down there?"

Pieter felt acutely unhappy. "Ja."

"You sure plant 'em deep! Why don't you try for those nearer the surface?"

Pieter stared glumly at Green Jones, then back at the potato plant, now a good five feet below ground level, and still going down in the crater he had dug. Damn the potato! Damn the stranger! Damn all this business!

"Ja," said Pieter. "Be so kindly as to help me out."

Green Jones lent a willing hand, heaved while the rosy Dutchman puffed, and helped him scramble up. "Dat vas very good of you," Pieter thanked him.

"Don't mention it."

Pieter marched to the next cluster of potato tops, spat on his hands, and made a ferocious jab at the ground. His digger sank a foot. The tuber sank a foot and a half. Pieter glowered.

"Haw!" exploded the onlooker. Pieter glared murder. Green Jones chuckled to himself and blew out a cloud of pungent smoke.

"How you did it beats me, but I never saw anything like it!" Green Jones walked off in great good humor, a lank figure striding down the road, leaving behind him the aroma of fine tobacco, the echo of his chuckles, and a wrathful Dutchman.

"Potatoes!" Pieter muttered. "Himmel, everything iss crazy mit de heat."

Like the first, this second group of fugitive potatoes seemed to be burrowing into the earth. The magical submersion was too much for him. He reeled toward his farmhouse to drown his troubles in a sea of schnapps.

THE incident at Loring's farm was notable for its spectacular brevity. Mrs. Loring wanted to can corn. Lou Loring said he'd haul her in enough for the winter. Between other chores, he went to his sweet-corn field about ten o'clock with his daughter Marion.

Marion held a bushel basket and would have followed him down the rows if there had been any stripping.

Lou reached for an ear.

The ear moved around to the other side of the stalk. A weird caterwauling went up from the whole field and the stalks, standing ten feet high and more, seemed to shake.

Lou hesitantly pursued the ear. The cob returned to its original position. Lou batted his eyes. Marion gave a peculiar squawk and raced pell-mell for home.

Lou swore and reached for another ear. Did the whole stalk revolve? Or did the ear slide away? Was he out of his head? The furious sounds of the cornfield alone were enough to make his flesh creep.

Between the rows of corn, pumpkins had been planted. A few weeds grew, and a sprinkling of wild groundcherries. Lou reached for a lower ear and in so doing almost stepped on one of the groundcherries. The plant leaped straight up and fell a foot away. The roots moved feebly, began to sink in the soil, and the groundcherry rose gradually erect.

What with revolving ears of corn and leaping groundcherries, Lou felt that he needed a day off, to have his eyes examined. And off he went.

THE main hangout in Shawtuck Center was Andy's general store. On Saturday night, Andy usually did a whale of an illicit business in Minnesota Thirteen, a strain of corn that eager moonshiners quickly and happily discovered made superior whiskey. Weekdays were dead, especially the early days. But the way farmers began drifting in on this Tuesday was a caution. A dozen had collected before noon. Andy did not know what it was all about, but the corn liquor was flowing. There were rickety chairs, empty barrels up-ended, and nail-kegs a-plenty to hold all comers.

The universal glumness was a puzzle to Andy. "How's tricks?" he asked when Al Meiers came in.

"So-so." Al twiddled a cracked tumbler, drained it, clanked it on the counter.

"Something wrong?"

"We-ell, no."

"Here, take a snifter of this."

"Don't mind if I do." Al gulped the drink.

"You ain't lookin' so well, Al."

Pieter Van Schluys waddled up.

"Hi, Pieter, why aren't you hauling in?"

Pieter glowered at the speaker. "Dose potatoes," he muttered, "dey iss full mit de devil!"

"So?" Andy perked his ears. An amazing interest developed among the rest of the group.

"Ja, I dig fer vun potato and so fast as I dig, de potato dig deeper. Ja. I tink dere iss a hole so big as China under dose potatoes or de potatoes iss, how you say it, haunted, ja, else I am crazy mit de heat."

"I'll be damned," Al broke in, "and I thought I was seein' things. Listen!" He told of the orchard that walked away. Hesitantly at first, this big farmer almost pleaded for belief, and when he saw that the jeers he expected did not come, he warmed to his tale like a child reciting a fairy-story.

"That must of been your hired hand went by here like a blue streak in that old jalopy a couple hours back," Andy guessed.

"Yeah. Hank lit out. I don't blame him much. I don't s'pose he ever will come back."

Ed Vogel had a grim face. "I just saw Doc Parker. He says Gus had a stroke when we was mowin' this mornin', but he'll pull through. Only there wasn't no mowin'. The wheat don't cut. It just lies down an' then springs up again. You'd of thought it was alive and knew just what I was gonna do."

"My apples ain't worth a dime a bushel now," said Al. "After they got through throwin' themselves around, they was so banged up they ain't even good for cider."

Ed wore a reflective air that turned to a scowl of apprehension. "Say, if things go on like this, we won't have no crops this year. We're ruined."

UNTIL he spoke, not one of the farmers had fully realized the extent of the disaster that faced them. Each had been preoccupied with his own worry. The fantastic rebellion of nature was a mystery. Now Ed's remark drove home understanding of what they were up against. If this was not all a collective hallucination; if they were as sane as ever and had witnessed what they thought they saw; if they had no more success in harvesting than they had had so far—then they were bankrupt, ruined. They could pay off neither mortgages nor debts. They would be unable to buy necessities. They would not even have food for themselves, or seed for next year's sowing.

"I wouldn't eat one of my leapin' apples for a million dollars," Al Meiers declared, and meant it.

"What are we gonna do?" Ed asked helplessly. "We can't all be batty. Somethin's wrong, but what? No crops, no food, no cash. Crops are bringin' high prices this year, but we're done for."

Andy peered over his shell-rimmed glasses. "Why don't you go see Dan Crowley? Maybe he could help you out."

"Good idea," Al agreed, lumbering to his feet. "How about it, boys?"

"Sure, let's see the county agent."

Gloom hung thick on the anxious group that faced Crowley.

"Take it easy, boys," Crowley advised genially. He was county agent for the Department of Agriculture. He was fat and bald. His nose stood out like the prow of a ship and stubble covered his jowls. H smoked black, twisted, foul stogies that smelled to heaven. His feet were on the desk of his office when the farmers came and there his feet remained while he puffed poisonous clouds and listened. His muddy blue eyes were guileless. Dan Crowley looked harmless, hopeless, and dumb. They were deceptive traits. Dan had a good head. He just didn't believe in extending himself needlessly.

"So that's how it is," Al Meiers finished. "I'm ready to move out of the county now and burn the damn wheat to the ground."

"Now, now, Al, don't be that way. You know I work for you all."

Pieter Van Schluys moped. "Ja. Vat good iss dat?"

"Plenty. Just leave it to me." Dan hooked his thumbs in his armpits and leaned farther back.

"You haff an idea?" Pieter asked hopefully.

"Sure thing. Now run along while I'm thinkin' about this. I'll get it straightened out." Dan was vaguely definite. The farmers filed away.

SHAWTUCK CENTER grew more and more restless as the afternoon waned and farmers arrived with newer and wilder accounts of the pranks that nature was playing. Andy's general store buzzed with anxious and angry voices. The population of Shawtuck County was made up almost exclusively of hardheaded Dutchmen, Scandinavians, and Germans who had settled through the mid-West during the great immigration waves of the late nineteenth century. They were a conservative, strong working, sturdy lot. They clung to past customs and some of the superstitions learned in the Old Country. The town simmered with tales of witchcraft and hauntings, of the Little People, of goblins and evil spirits.

What caused this strange revolt of the plant kingdom at Shawtuck Center? Nothing of the sort seemed to be afflicting the outside world. And what possible action could he take? He could at least make a field inspection for a special crop report.

Dan went out, climbed into his official car, and headed out of town on County Road A.

The land, under the warm, mellow light of the sun, gave testimony of abandonment, without the voice of any farmer. Harvesting ought to be in full swing, but not a figure tramped the fields, not a reaper moved. Here and there stood threshers, harvesters, wagons, farm implements, and combines.

Yet the fields, though deserted, were not wholly silent. This was a day of quiet, such a day of stillness and ripe maturity as often comes at harvest time; but ever and again, as Dan drove along, he saw strange ripplings cross wheat and hay fields, watched clover sway, heard a sound like innumerable murmurous faint voices sweep up from grains and grasses and vegetables; and one patch of woods was all an eerie wail, and infinite restless disturbances of flower and leaf and blade set the forest in motion; while the wild chokecherry and sumac nodded in no wind and shook for no visible reason alongside the dirt road.

Dan felt uneasy. All summer there had been little signs, increasing evidence, that a change had come over nature; and now the rapid and sinister character of that change became intensified with its completion. The trees, the plants, the vegetables had mysteriously developed a life and will-power of their own. And they had cast off the dominance of man.

Dan drove on through back roads, and twisted over cart paths, weaving in and out around Shawtuck Center during the afternoon. Everywhere he went, he found the same uncanny solitude, the constant whispers whose speakers remained invisible, alfalfa and barley and corn that quaked though no presence was near and rarely a breath of air stirred. The sun was sinking when Dan headed homeward, and it seemed to him that new and deeper murmurs issued from the bewitched fields and the enchanted woods. But he had learned one fact, and it puzzled him.

The phenomena were limited to the valley where Shawtuck Center lay in a bowl of low hills.

Returning to his office, Dan passed a group to whom Pieter Van Schluys was relating again the saga of the fugitive potatoes. "So dere I vass, fife feet down already, ja, and der man, de Jones person, he stand dere and laugh. Himmel, maype it vass funny as a funeral, nein?"

Dan wondered why anyone should be amused by such a strange occurrence. He went thoughtfully into his office and looked at the routine blanks and forms on his desk.

He could well imagine the results if he reported the facts to Washington. "Meiers's apple orchard walked away last night and the trees planted themselves around a pond on the Hagstrom farm because they liked it better there." And, "The Vogels' wheat refuses to be harvested. Kindly advise proper action to take." Or, "Emily Tawber's melons object to being picked. Does she lose her guarantees under the federal Watermelon Pickle Price Support Program?"

No, Dan decided, if he sent in these official messages, he would only be fired and replaced. His only course was to make a further investigation in search of a cause for the bizarre happenings.

He went to the wall and studied the large map of Shawtuck County. It showed the size and location of every farm, the variety and acreage of every crop. He drew a rough circle around the area of the phenomena. At the center of the circle lay the farm of Green Jones. Dan decided to pay Jones a visit.

As Dan turned in at the private road by the mailbox lettered G.

Jones, he noticed immediately in the twilight that the land had not been tilled at all. Jones was no farmer. Only lank weeds grew in his fields.

Dan stopped at a gray old frame house guarded by elms and maples. Lights burned in the ground floor windows.

Dan heaved his bulk out with a sigh and lit the inevitable stogy. He rang the bell, and presently a tall, thin man with an angular face appeared at the screen door.

Dan said, "I'm the county agriculture-agent. Mind if I drop in for a few minutes?"

Jones replied firmly, "Why, yes, I do mind. I've a lot of work to do and I'm pressed for time."

"So'm I." Dan blew a cloud of reeking smoke at Green Jones. "I have to get off a special crop report to Washington tonight."

"What have I got to do with that? I don't grow any crops," said Jones, frowning.

"Maybe not. Maybe you just help to make other people's crops grow."

A wary look came into Jones' eyes. "What do you mean by that?"

Dan said slowly, "It's like this. There's been queer things going on around here all summer. All year, in fact, ever since you moved in. Walkin' trees an' gallopin' potatoes and God knows what all."

Jones spoke with a tone of bored indifference; "I heard some of those wild rumors."

"They ain't rumors. I went out for a look-see this afternoon. Crops an' everything else that grows have gone crazy all around Shawtuck Center. There's a borderline maybe 3 quarter-mile wide where things are kind of uncertain, an' after that the trees an' such haven't anything wrong with 'em. So I looked at my map and saw that the center of that circle is right here."

Green Jones straightened up coldly. "Are you implying that I have some connection with these phenomena?"

"Implying? Hell, no, I'm tellin' you."

Jones regarded the county agent with peculiar, shrewd appraisal. Finally, after appearing to weigh many matters, he shrugged and said, "You win. Nice crop detective work. I suppose I might as well take you into my confidence. I don't want a lifetime's work wrecked in a day." He stepped aside. "Come in."

The parlor was severely furnished. Besides a sofa, several chairs, and a desk, Dan noticed two prints on the walls: one of Burbank, and another of Darwin.

"Have a chair," his host suggested.

Dan sank into a wing-backed piece that promptly collapsed under his weight.

"Dear, dear," Jones protested. "That was a good chair."

Dan eased himself into the more substantial sofa and blew his nose violently to indicate that he was sorry but unembarrassed. Unfortunately, he dropped his stogy, which left a scorch on the thick blue carpet amid a fine powder of ashes.

"My beautiful rug," mourned Jones.

"Sorry," mumbled Dan.

"Never mind. It's done."

"An' everybody hereabouts is done for the way things are goin' now." Dan steered back to his original topic. "Jones, I don't know who you are or how you done it but you sure raised hell with the crops."

Jones slouched against a mantelpiece. From far away came an insidious drone that Dan could not quite identify. His host idly twirled a golden key on a chain. He looked cool, slightly detached, and yet there was a deep passion behind his features. "Right. My real name doesn't matter. I'm a botanist. Some years ago I got the idea that vegetation seemed to show a sort of rudimentary awareness. It couldn't be called intelligence. I noticed how tree roots turned off and travelled considerable distances straight to underground water pipes. Then there is the fly orchid that acts with almost human ingenuity. It attracts, traps, and devours insects.

"I became convinced that there was a kind of dormant awareness in the plant world. It would be a great achievement for science and a possible blessing to man if plants possessed instinct and science could develop it to reason or at least the power of free motion. Then food materials, like animals could seek a water supply and largely do away with the harmful effects of drought. I worked on that line. I didn't get far until other scientists discovered that ultraviolet rays, even the ordinary illumination of electric lights, could be turned on plants all night long and they grew almost twice as fast as other plants. Physicists found that various cosmic radiations produced definite effects on vegetation and could cause radical changes.

"Two or three years ago, I found that a universal radiation isolated first by Diemann greatly accelerated all activity of plants. I built an apparatus to capture and to concentrate that radiation. I turned the intensified radiation loose on some hothouse plants and they grew like mad. I decided to experiment on a larger scale, and bought this farm because it was in a secluded district. For the past year I've been bombarding vegetation around Shawtuck Center with Diemann's radiations. You know the results—abnormal growth, mobile powers, and apparently rational, rudimentary impulses. That's the whole story. Now I've laid my cards on the table."

DAN knitted his brows. "You say the ray makes plants *think?*"

"No, I don't know that it does. All I know is that Diemann's radiations have always been essential for the growth of plants. I proved that by trying to raise flowers in an insulated hothouse. Nothing I experimented with would grow at all without Diemann's radiations. I reasoned that a concentration of the rays, if strong enough, might cause abnormal developments and hasten the evolution of species. I'm only experimenting and recording data as I go along. There seems to be something more than instinct developing, but it's too early to call it reason."

Dan said, "Hmm. Why did everything happen today? That's kind of suddenlike if you've been usin' this ray for a year, ain't it?"

The stranger shrugged. "Yes, but remember, I too am almost as much in the dark as you are. I know the cause of the change but I don't know the how or why or what. I must observe for years to determine these factors. Possibly there was a dividing-line. On one side stood inanimate vegetation, constantly but feebly irradiated. Then my concentration of Diemann's ray built up the change until its influences reached their climax last night and inanimate plants crossed the line to animation."

Dan suggested, "You might be smart if you quit now."

Jones looked aghast. "But my experiment has hardly begun! Think of what mankind may learn as a result of my researches! The whole course of civilization may be affected!"

"Yeah," Dan answered grimly. "That's what I'm afraid of. If this goes far enough, there won't be anybody left. Animals won't get no food except each other an' we won't have much except animals an' they won't last long. If the crops lie down or walk off an' can't be harvested, how're we gonna live?"

Green Jones looked thunderstruck. Dan could not help having a half-liking for him. He was obviously sincere, and evidently had meant well when he began his experiment. It was not wholly his fault that it had worked out differently from the way he expected.

"I didn't realize the change had gone as far as that." The botanist twirled his key, but his mind was elsewhere.

Dan stood up. "Jones, you're in a tough spot."

"Yes?"

"Van Schluys is pretty dumb an' so are a lot of the boys but sooner or later they're gonna start thinkin' like I did about why you were so tickled when he was tryin' to dig spuds. Or they'll pin you down on the map. God help you when the boys come tearin' out here hell-bent for your hide. You ruined their crops an' they'll tear you limb from limb."

For the first time, the botanist came all the way down to earth from his remote dreams, speculations, and theories. His face paled a bit. "That was a bad mistake on my part, I'll admit." The ghost of a smile hovered in his expression. "Just the same, it was a sight for the gods to watch that Dutchman pursue his fleeing potatoes."

"Take my advice and move out while you can," Dan said gruffly.

The botanist seemed unnerved. "As bad as all that? But I can't leave my experiment unfinished!" he cried shakily. "Besides, how'll I get away? My car's broken down."

"If your experiment's worth more'n your hide to you don't blame me for what happens. But I guess this is official business, so I could use my official car to drive you to the next town if you wanted to leave tonight."

MR. JONES carefully, moodily, replaced the gold key in his pocket. He seemed to be undergoing an inner struggle to make up his mind.

"Where is the machine?" Dan asked out of idle curiosity.

"Next room." The scientist's indecision and worry fell away. He snapped erect. "I've got myself into a jam all right but it's too late for regrets. I'll take your kind offer if you'll give me an hour or two, say til ten o'clock, to collect my data and a few belongings, I'll be ready to go."

"An' you'll turn off the rays?"

"Yes, I promise." His voice was eager, sincere. Dan knew men and knew that Jones would keep his word.

"I'll be back at ten sharp. Better not let anyone else in."

Dan left, jubilant over the success of his visit. He had discovered and he had eliminated the menace to Shawtuck County agriculture.

It was eerie driving through the woods. There was neither moon nor wind. The stirless air lay like a cool and weary sleep over the aging world; but the autumnal quiet that should have prevailed was missing. There were great rustlings abroad and dark movements among the blacker masse of trees and crops, a continuous ghostly murmur issuing from the shapes of things possessed. The entire landscape seemed restlessly alive. There were voices without speakers, and slow creeping without breeze or visible agency; and Dan felt the impact of dimly remembered legends from childhood, about haunted woods and forest where witches resided, the Druids of the trees, the gnomes, and the Little People who lived under blades of grass and toadstools. It would be strange indeed if somewhere in the long ago, Diemann's radiations had been stronger when the world was younger and all manner of growing things had then owned powers of life and motion that declined through the ages, leaving only ancestral memories for record until Jones brought back to nature its ancient gift. They were mysterious and disturbing activities that obsessed Dan as he drove toward town; and he was glad to leave behind him the soft and wailing wide whisper of inarticulate things, as the lights of the town drew near.

BACK in his office, having firmly shut the door, Dan cocked his feet on the desk and smoked interminably. A small shaded lamp on the desk kept the room in semi-darkness. The air became stale and bluish with smoke. Through the half-curtained windows, he watched figures drift by; arguing farmers; worried old crones; harassed and hopeless and blank faces, strong ones and weak ones, some dull and others furious, all showing the paralysis, the demoralization that the revolt of nature had produced. Beset by events alien to their lives, they were unable to cope with them, much less understand them. The only refuge lay in herding together and trying the forced gayety of town, with plenty of potent drink, as an antidote; as if the courage of the individual might return through combined strength and association with his neighbors. It was a night of rights, altercations, and bitter argument, and rowdy choruses from Andy's store.

Dan folded his hands on his lap. He had no desire to mingle with them until his task was finished. Tonight would see the end of the strange harvest, and tomorrow he could worry about the crop reports to Washington. The day's work had been strenuous, for him. He dozed, being one of those fortunate mortals who can snatch a catnap under almost any circumstances.

He could not have slept long. It was only just past nine when he blinked awake. He had a vague impression of some distant and receding roar, echoing through slumber to wakefulness; but all he now heard were the sounds of a few racing feet. The street outside his window was deserted.

Dan regarded the window and the empty sidewalk for perhaps a minute before a thought struck him with such force that he sent the chair spinning away as he crashed to his feet and pounded out.

The street was almost deserted. The tumult of less than an hour ago had subsided. A few broken windows, a picket-door hanging askew, some smashed bottles, and a couple of overturned kegs in front of Andy's store were the only remaining evidence of the crowd. The one person in sight was an old woman with infinitely wrinkled face and slow steps passing the Church.

Dan called, "Where's everybody?"

Old Mrs. Tompkins peered out of ancient eyes. "Eh? They all went out to the Jones place."

"What!"

"Lordamercy, you don't need to yell so. I ain't stone-daft yet. They're gone and much good may it do. Pieter was telling his story and I don't know who it was decided Jones could say a-plenty about these goings-on. I'm a religious woman, Dan, but I tell you, if it's this Jones who's the cause of all this grief I'd—"

Whatever she thought was lost on Dan who jumped into his car and sped off toward the Jones farm.

Dan hoped to overtake the angry farmers. He didn't know exactly what he could say or do, but he thought they would at least listen to him. Dan sympathized with their feelings. They had been baffled, scared, and ruined by the perverse results of Jones's experiment. There was a certain justice to any punishment they might inflict on him. But Dan could see the scientist's side too; his passion for discovery in unknown fields; his willingness to experiment, whatever the cause; his primary purpose of aiding humanity and increasing the general good. The experiment had got beyond control. Vegetation given a new power had responded in a far more willful and independent manner than Jones anticipated. He could scarcely be blamed for the curious developments, which had occurred. He might have hoped to benefit mankind, but the character of Diemann's radiations had ruled otherwise and given the plant kingdom a new vitality that fought human control.

There were differences and changes in the farmlands through which Dan sped. He remembered well the Hanson grapevines, but they had somehow vanished, leaving only torn earth. And the Ritter chestnut grove—of which no trace remained, save deep furrows.

As DAN approached the Jones place, he felt a sudden tightness in his chest. A crowd of farmers surrounded the house, milling around.

Beam of flashlights and glow of lanterns cast flickering lights and shadows on alarmed faces. The surging mob seemed checked. Then, to Dan's amazement, they all suddenly broke and fled to their autos. They raced away, leaving Dan alone in the moonlight.

An ominous chill came over Dan as he stopped his car. A vast, dark mass, a writhing mound, engulfed the house. Dan got out and stood paralyzed for an instant. Forest trees and cultivated fruit trees, flowers and climbing vines, vegetables of countless variety, bushes and brambles and berries, representatives of all the plant life of Shawtuck County had converged here and overflowed Jones's place. And Dan heard an indescribable sound, a strange, eerie, inarticulate murmur of vegetation.

Now he heard other sounds, the sharp crack and tinkle of broken glass, the splintering of wood, and he knew that the windows and the very frame of the house were giving way. Suddenly there came a cry, a scream for help from within, and he barely recognized the voice of Green Jones. A great shudder convulsed the tangle surrounding the house. There was nothing familiar in the now loud, incessant, and threshing roar of vegetation; a weird tumult such as the wildest gale had never produced.

With unaccustomed agility, Dan leaped to the rear of his car. He habitually carried a variety of new farming aids that he demonstrated as part of his duties, products such as weed-killers, insecticides, fertilizers, and implements. Among these was a portable flame-thrower designed for burning out infected fields and blighted trees that he had been showing off in recent weeks. He grabbed it and aimed the nozzle at the heaving mass. A burst of intense flame struck and clung to the tangled foliage of shrubbery and vines and trees. Briefly, then, a sad sound flared up, like a many-bodied, subhuman, voiceless thing crying for life.

Now a great rent appeared in the mass and even the front of the house began to burn. Dan shut off the stream of fire but carried the thrower with him as he ran inside the burning structure.

His bulk was unused to such exertion, but he gave a convulsive leap when he saw the dark branches and vines beating at the side windows of the parlor, and watched a pane smash. He hurled himself against the door to the next room with a force that burst it from its binges. He looked at a dynamo that hummed a faint drone on the floor near the doorway, its brushes occasionally sparking, and connected with an object that occupied the whole center of the room. It looked like a huge metal box. Its plates glowed with a pulsing and ghostly radiance that shifted between soft silver and the crimson of fire. Near the ceiling above it and completing the circuit by thick cables that pierced the metallic concentration box to whatever mechanism lay within, hung a globe between anode and cathode. The globe swam with blinding mist, a purple, impalpable force that streamed out constantly and almost visibly in all directions. The giant globe had a sound all its own, a peculiar, intense whine, at the upper range of audibility.

The rear window to the room had been burst, and a flowing tide of plant growths had already enveloped part of the machine. Jones lay on the floor, evidently knocked unconscious when the mass burst in. For an instant Dan used the thrower again. The vegetation burned into ashes, and suddenly the huge globe melted with a violent flame of purple and red and silver streaked with blue.

Dan dragged Jones from the burning house. The night air became filled with one loud, prolonged, and mournful wail that faded into an inchoate murmur, an inarticulate whisper, then silence. Gone now were the eerie voices and the purposive movements.

Only the crackle of flames and pungent smoke came from the dying house and the dead mass.

Harvesting of crops proceeded normally around Shawtuck Center the following day. The destruction of the machine had also destroyed the newly acquired powers of the plants and fruits and vegetables.

Dan often wondered about that last night. Had the growing

things, impelled by some dawning intelligence, converged to destroy their creator, or to encompass and protect him and his machine? He never knew. While Dan watched the burning house, Green Jones must have regained consciousness. He had walked away down the lonely roads of night.

FLING THE DUST ASIDE

By
SEABURY QUINN

And their bodies would die if they didn't go back to them by morning...

WADE BARLOE looked disgustedly at the fog-swathed beach and drummed a devil's tattoo on the rail of the hotel veranda. Next to a nightclub at 10:30 in the morning there was no place quite so forlorn as a beach resort in foul weather, he reflected. Why the cock-eyed devil hadn't he gone up to New York with Muriel when that telegram came from Aunt Matilda?

If anyone enjoyed poor health it was his wife's old aunt who could always be depended on to stage a relapse of one of her many undefined maladies whenever her favorite niece went for a holiday. That time they'd gone to Yellowstone...the old lady had been dying, judging by her telegram. Muriel had flown back to New York, and when he followed her reluctantly a week later he found the old girl chipper as a cricket on a warm hearth and vowing Muriel had hardly spent an hour with her. Now—he reached for a cigar, bit off its tip with more than necessary violence, and snapped his lighter.

Damn! Out of fluid again. He searched his pockets for a match and struck one. A little puff of sea breeze came from nowhere and extinguished the small flame as neatly as a snuffer puts a candle out. Somehow profanity seemed woefully inadequate just then, so with a sign of vexation he stepped into a dark angle of the hotel porch, hunched his shoulders to form a windshield and struck a second light.

"*Oh!*" The little cry, half-sob, half-terrified exclamation startled him as an unexpected pinprick might have done. As the blue of the first flame of the match changed to a clear yellow he saw two terrified eyes staring into his.

They were wide, startled and questioning, greenish-violet in shade, fringed with heavy lashes. Above them slim brows lifted like twin circumflexes in a mixture of surprise and fright. He supposed there was a nose beneath them and a mouth under that, but neither of these features was visible, for the owner of the eyes held a hand before her face as against a blow.

"What happened—what is it?" she gasped as the flame gathered strength. "Who—"

"Sorry!" Wade apologized as he backed away. "I didn't see you in the shadow."

The girl lowered her hand and her lips quivered as if she tried to smile. "I'm sorry, too," she told him. "I must have fallen asleep on the settee, and I was just having a bad dream—about a house afire, I think, and I was in it and couldn't get out..." She left the sentence hanging in midair.

HERE was an awkward situation. If he left her abruptly it would seem churlish; it would sound fatuous to repeat he was sorry he had startled her; just standing there and saying nothing would seem inane, too. "Are you all right now?" he asked, not that he had any misgivings, but merely for the sake of filling in an awkward pause.

"Oh, yes!" she spoke with what seemed more than necessary emphasis. "You see, I'd been trying to get up courage to go and hear the Guru's lecture, but somehow I lacked the nerve, so I came out here..." she left another sentence uncompleted.

"Oh, you mean the Mahatma?" Barloe smiled tolerantly. "The Little Bad Man from India?"

"*Is* he a Mahatma?"

"I wouldn't know. Probably he's just a faker playing hookey from a Coney Island sideshow. Why were you afraid to go in and listen to him?"

"I'm not quite sure. Somehow, this Oriental mysticism frightens me. It seems so utterly..."

Wade smiled in the darkness. He was getting used to her truncated sentences and had already found she could make her meaning clear without the need for rounding out her periods. At first he had not recognized her, now he placed her; the little mousy girl whose room was three doors down the corridor from his. Not exactly pretty, but not quite homely. She might have been quite attractive if she'd been willing to let herself go cosmetically. Somebody's rather frumpish secretary, or a salesgirl in a quite unstylish shop, he thought, spending a whole year's hoarded savings on a two-week stay at the shore. To get a man? Her chances could not have been less if she'd attempted to go whale fishing.

"Well," deliberately he blew the smoke away from her, "if it'll bolster your morale I'll go in with you." Just in time he kept himself from adding, "I've nothing else to do."

THE main parlor of the hotel was bright with women's evening dresses, orchid, salmon, blue and ice-green, to which the men's sports coats of Harris Tweed and hound's-tooth checks were an incongruous contrast. The Pandit Vikrim Adjeet Singh was finishing his discourse as they tiptoed in and found seats by the door:

"Your Christian Gospel speaks more truly than you know when it declares there is an earthly and a spiritual body. We of the East have known it for thousands of years. We know man has a physical body composed of solids, liquids and gases, and an etheric or astral body, which is composed of the four subdivisions of the ether, a body formed of our desires, which at the will of the Adept can leave the fleshly form and take the free, unfettered spirit to far places—a body which may live long after the decay of the gross flesh."

"Guru," a lady with a great many diamonds and wrinkles to match spoke from the rear of the hall, "how does one go about the process of—er—astralization, if that's the proper word?"

The smile the Guru bent on her was wise and secretly amused. "Dear lady, that is not for everyone to know. A little learning is a dangerous thing, as your poet has so aptly put it. Especially such learning as that. When the astral form is separated from the flesh the flesh lies dormant, to all appearances lifeless, and unless the astral form returns within a period of twenty-four hours what you call death ensues. Then the spirit wanders bodiless and homeless through the ether till the end of time."

"But, Guru," the dowager persisted, "what is the process—or is it formula?—by which the astral body is released?"

The Pandit's pointed eyebrows went up in acute angles, and his smiling mouth described a capital W. The sharp ends of his little black mustache curved upward like a pair of horns, the sharp black beard on his chin jutted forward. He looked like an amiable but nonetheless mischievous Mephistopheles. "The formula, dear lady, is a simple one. First of all, the Adept has to clear his mind of all thought. That is not so easy as it sounds. Few Easterners and practically no Westerners can do it. However, it is possible, as every Adept knows. When all worldly thoughts have been erased from the mind, so that it is a clear, unmarked page, the Adept slowly recites, *'Oom, oom, oom!'*

which is the word for the Ineffable. Time after time he repeats the mystic greeting to the Infinite, breathing slowly, so that the word comes from him with all the vital principle of breath. At last the word ceases to have meaning, and gradually the world and all things mundane fade from his consciousness, then—" the small, dark man's small, dark hands spread in an all embracing gesture— "then the spirit takes its flight and scales the Akashic heights, free from the dross of flesh, free from all the binding ties of base, material existence."

"But is there any value—any practical value—in this power?" the old lady persisted.

The Pandit gave her a hurt look. "What is practicality?" he asked, much as Pilate once asked, "What is truth? Suppose you have a loved one. Between you and your beloved there stretch a thousand earthly miles. You wish to know where he is, what he does, how greatly he yearns for you. If you have learned the art of astralizing you can fix your thoughts on him and in a second—in the twinkling of an eye— be with him, though all the waters of the seas and all the mountains of the earth are set between you. You can, yourself invisible, behold him in the flesh, see what he does—"

"Good God, I wouldn't want my wife to have that power!" whispered a stout, gray-haired man to a slim redhead seated cuddlesomely beside him. "If she could see me now—"

"Boy, would you ever have the process servers on your trail!" the little redhead supplied with a giggle.

"Let's get out o' this," Wade whispered to his companion. "The man's a driveling fake if ever I saw one."

The girl was gazing straight before her, eyes fixed in an almost hypnotic stare, lips parted, as if she contemplated some vision of beauty and eternal life.

He rose quietly and left her.

"Of all the balderdash I ever heard—" Barloe bent to untie his shoes—"of all the silly twaddle"—he slipped into the trousers of his pajamas—"telling a lot of silly women—" His muttering grew silent, and a grin formed at the corners of his mouth. "You wish to know how your beloved is," he seemed to hear the Pandit's silky voice. "You wish to know what she does, how much she yearns for you..." H'mm.

He lay down on the bed and crossed his ankles, crossed his hands upon his chest as he had seen the hands of deceased friends disposed by the embalmer. For a long moment he lay there relaxed, mentally repeating, "Nothing—nothing—nothing!" till his brain seemed clear of thought as a freshly vacuumed rug is clear of dust. Then slowly, breathing out the syllable so softly that it sounded like a sigh, he pronounced "*Oom—oom—oom!*"

If you repeat a word often enough it loses its associative meaning and becomes just senseless sound. *Oom* hadn't meant much when he first pronounced it, after fifteen minutes' steady repetition it had no more meaning than a bird's chirp.

What kind of double-distilled assininity was this? This nonsense had gone far enough, he'd been the world's prize chump to pay attention to that faker—

HE OPENED his eyes, looked about him. How the devil had he gotten this far from the bed? He had no recollection of rising—good Lord! As peacefully as any corpse laid in its casket his body lay upon the bed, hands crossed upon its chest, eyes closed, lips parted. Of all outlandish things! He took a startled backward step and next instant found himself in the corridor. Although he had felt nothing he had passed through the locked door of his room as if it had not been there. How—what? Glancing downward he received another shock. Beneath him was the carpet of the hotel corridor, a rather worn broadloom figured in big off-pink roses on a mauve background. Right through his legs the roses of the carpets pattern showed, not clearly, but as plainly as if viewed through a light drift of vapor. He held a foot up for inspection. The form was there, but not quite as he recalled it. Instead of being suntanned it was pale, not tallow-white, but lightly shaded, as if delicately technicolored, and somehow it seemed younger. The hardened, slightly bunching sinews of his calves were smooth and supple, like the pliant muscles of a lad.

A full-length mirror hung upon the wall some fifty feet away and he stepped toward it briskly, then brought up with a sharp exclamation. He had no more than thought, "I must get to that looking-glass" —and he was there. A dome light in the ceiling shed a diffused glow, and in the mirror he could see the pattern of the carpet and the wallpaper reflected. But no reflection of himself. Though he stood squarely before the looking-glass it gave back no more image than if he had not been there.

"...and I told him, 'Well, if *that's* all you want with me you can just go—"' Sharp as tinkling silver came a girl's voice raised in acid narration as two young women stepped from the elevator and made toward him. Stark panic seized him by the throat. Although he had not made a complete inspection he knew that he was unclothed, for the momentary glance he'd cast on his legs showed that the pajama trousers which had been his sole garment had not astralized when he did.

For an instant he considered flight, but before he could propel himself to the safety of his room the girls had reached him. "Yeah, an' what'd he say then?" one of them asked as she stopped before the mirror to fluff out her short blond hair, then passed on unconcernedly. She had looked right at—right through—him as she primped before the looking-glass, and had taken no more notice of him in his complete nudity than she did of the circumambient atmosphere.

So? So-o-o-o...

Long windows looked out from the fifth floor corridor toward the landward side of the hotel. He walked to one of them and put a foot upon the sill. "I'd like to be in New York now," he muttered. The wish was hardly a wish, scarcely more than the shadow of a thought, but in an instant he was out the window, passing through the fog-bound air so swiftly that when he glanced across his shoulder the lights of the hotel were just a blur in the mist.

Far below him, like a luminously-glowing worm, a B. & O. express train hurried toward Jersey City, but it was just a small trail of light glimpsed in the dark a moment before vanishing. The buzzing of propellers sounded like the droning of a monster hornet several hundred feet beneath, and a plane that sped toward Idlewild Airport showed for a moment. Then it too was left behind.

The fog was lifting now, and as he rushed northward the setting moon left the night dim beneath the high stars. Ahead of him, so far it seemed incalculably distant, glowed a net of scintillating points of light, the window-spangled bowl that was New York.

ORIENT HOUSE, the thirty-storied apartment house that stood fortress-like beside the East River, showed half a hundred dimly lighted windows in the darkness overlooking the black, oily tide, and he dropped toward a casement which he knew looked from Aunt Mattie's bedroom. He was not conscious of an attempt to lose altitude or speed, but naturally and unthinkingly as he would have slackened pace in walking, he slowed from his rushing, wind-swept flight to a slow, easy descent, soft as the downward wafting of a feather shed by a soaring bird. A moment he poised on the stone sill, leant against the heavy plate glass of the steel-framed casement—and was inside the house.

He stood in a big, ugly room with heavy Victorian furniture, hideous with oleographic copies of such *chefs-d'oeuvre* as Landseer's Stag at Bay, Rosa Bonheur's Horse Fair and Millet's Angelus. A blue-globed night lamp cast sufficient light for him to see the low mound formed by Aunt Mattie's desiccated old body under the bedclothes, the linen nightcap tied under her chin with two strings, and "transformation" which rested on the dressing table. Aunt Mattie slept with her mouth open, a circumstance which revealed the serviceable teeth she used at meals were masterpieces of dental technology, and at the foot of her bed slumbered Hans, the overfed and shamelessly spoiled pug-dog which was the chief companion of her latter years.

Barloe advanced a step and Hans raised heavy eyelids, sniffed fretfully, then rose as agilely as anything so obese could and turned to face him, the short hairs on his neck and shoulders rising in a hackle, and his rheumy old eyes glazed with fear. The growl he gave was more like a whine, and as he retreated a step the tremors of his back and flank muscles were visible.

"Hans!" Aunt Mattie roused and raised a high-veined old hand to pat the terrified dog. "What's the matter with my baby boy?"

"Gr-r-r!" muttered Hans, slinking toward his mistress. *"Gr-r-r-rf!"* In an instant he had burrowed underneath the covers, but the smothered sounds of his growls came through the blankets.

Aunt Mattie pressed a switch and twilight fled from the room as the chandelier blazed suddenly into life. She looked around, looked squarely at Barloe, then patted the small agitated mound where Hans lay shivering. "Silly boy! He's had another bad dream. No more chicken livers for him at bedtime!"

"Aunt Mattie!" Barloe whispered, but the old lady, whose hearing was abnormally keen for her age, continued looking through him, patting her whimpering pet comfortingly. "Aunt Mattie!" He spoke sharply, almost desperately, now. "Where's Muriel, Aunt Mattie?" The old lady showed no sign of having heard him.

He turned away. It didn't seem quite decent to look at the old girl in her dishabille. Muriel must be in her own room, the big room with the twin beds that Aunt Mattie kept for visiting relatives and friends. He faded through the locked door of the old lady's bedchamber, wafted down the hall to the guestroom.

The beds were primly made, percale sheets turned down above chenille coverlets, pillows covered with embroidered slips. No one slept in either of them. Plainly no one had slept in them for at least twelve hours. He crossed the room to the big wardrobe, seized its knob and pulled. Nothing happened. He was powerless to move the door. Then he remembered. Leaning forward, he went through the heavy oak of the panels as if they had neither solidity nor substance. The inside of the clothespress was as virginally empty as the beds. H'mm. Aunt Mattie must have made a quicker recovery than usual. Muriel was probably on her way back to the shore, and— How could she be? The last train for Stratfordshire left Jersey City at five-thirty, and should have arrived not later than eight. It had been after that when he had listened to the Pandit's lecture; now it was well after midnight.

He stepped back into the big empty guestroom, stood at gaze a moment, then, "I want to be where she is," he murmured.

THE bell-like tinkle of ice cubes against glass sounded, and a woman's delicate, light laugh came to him. He stood upon the threshold of a small, luxurious room. Before him on the polished floor there spread a lustrous Shiraz carpet, the quiet textures of damask and needlepoint complemented the patina of old, rubbed mahogany. The glow from parchment-shaded lamps illuminated the deep sofa with its brocade upholstery, the long coffee table littered with the miscellany of small, frivolous objects—old silver cigarette boxes, cloisonné ashtrays, a bronze lighter fashioned like a Grecian lamp, ultra-modern magazines and a lacquered tray set with bottles, siphons and a crystal bowl of ice cubes.

Behind the coffee table on the lounge a woman sat, a small, slight wisp of womanhood in oyster-white lounging pajamas trimmed with white fur. In one hand she held a glass of amber liquid, and the nails of her slim fingers had been lacquered copper-red from quick to tip, without half-moons. She had kicked her cross-strapped satin sandals off, and as she curled her graceful legs up under her he saw the nails of her small, pink-soled feet were varnished to match those of her hands. She was, perhaps, in her late thirties, perhaps a year or so older, and certainly she was far more charming than she had ever been at any time before, for her features were as delicately cut as those of an intaglio, with a throat-line perfect in its purity. Her short, intensely black hair was shot through with gray, which she seemed to display triumphantly because it called the more attention to her small, unlined, and classically beautiful face.

She swirled the fluid in her glass and the ice in it tinkled musically. "To us, my dear," she raised the glass and took a sip.

The man who stood before her shot a stream of seltzer into his tall glass and raised it toward her. "And to you, Muriel —and Wade."

"Poor Wade," she gave a small contemptuous laugh. "He's such a stuffed shirt. Such a beastly bore. If it were not for these brief intervals I think I couldn't stand him. Why, d'ye know, I don't believe he ever was a boy—he must have cut his teeth on Blackstone and learned the Statute of Frauds instead of nursery rhymes. I positively can't think why I ever married him!"

"Perhaps his income had something to do with it," the man commented dryly.

"Oh—money! Yes, he can make money, and when he's made it can't think what to do with it. When I come into my inheritance from Aunt Mattie—"

"Don't wish the old gal in her grave too fast, kitten. She's been quite useful to us."

The woman gave a throaty little giggle. "I'll say she has. She'd be surprised to know how often she's been gravely ill and needed her dear niece for company and comfort. Last year when Wade dragged me to Yellowstone I thought I'd just die of *ennui* while I waited for your wire. You do the *nicest* jobs of forging, Maitland. I don't know what we'd do without the telegraph—no signatures to verify, no handwriting to compare, just, '*Have had a relapse and need you. Come at once. Aunt Mattie.*' It's as simple as that, isn't it?"

"H'mm, yes; unless your ever-loving husband finds out."

"Oh, he'd never even suspect. He lives on such a high moral plane that he'd never think his little wife would two-time him. The poor innocent! Come and kiss me, honey-bug. I have to go back to my duty tomorrow or the day after. I daren't let Aunt Mattie be ill *too* long, you know."

Barloe felt a sudden giddiness, as if the world were spinning crazily on a loose axis. Muriel—and Maitland Hodges!

HE'D met Muriel seven years before when she had come to him for advice. She had been barely thirty then and he five years her senior. How it was with her he did not know, but with him it had been love at first sight. As she had said so flippantly, he had scarcely had a boyhood. Orphaned at eleven, he had been left to shift for himself, living unloved and unwelcomed with first one relative, then another. He worked his way through evening high school acting as a busboy in a lunchroom for his meals and a minuscule salary. At college he had waited on the students' table, been agent for a laundry, turned his hand to anything that came along. He lectured on sightseeing buses while he studied law and graduated near the head of his class. Then came a clerkship in Moran & Morgan's office, a junior partnership, finally full membership in the firm. He'd had small chance for amusement while he grew up, no time—or money—for the amusements his classmates indulged in. It had been all work and little play till he was nearly thirty-five—then Muriel.

He had always stood a little in awe of her, for she was a gentlewoman born and reared. Her broad *a* was as natural and as unaffected as her breathing, French was a second mother tongue to her, for she had lived in Paris till her thirteenth year. Everything she said or did was said or done with the assurance of one to the manner born, she looked like something right out of the pages of *Harper's Bazaar or Town & Country*.

Such social graces as he had Wade had acquired by observing others; his *savoir faire* was the result of a long trial-and-error process; even yet he felt embarrassed before the place setting of a fashionable dinner table.

She had not been slow to exploit her advantage, and though she married him and took his name and spent his money her attitude toward him had been more that of a mistress toward a faithful but slightly uncouth servant than of a wife toward her husband.

Barloe had known Maitland Hodges since school days. Hodges was a rich man's son who lived on the gold coast of Fraternity Row, wore good clothes, knew the right people, did the right things. Tall, blond, always immaculately groomed, his love affairs had been as numerous as they were deplorably thorough. Twice he had been named as correspondent in divorce suits. There had been "talk" of his and Muriel's friendship—or perhaps something more before she married Barloe. But Wade had shut his ears and mind against the scandal. "She never would have married me if she had cared for him," he told himself.

Blind anger, poisonous and suppurating, flooded through him as he looked at them. A "lady," was she, a gentlewoman *sans reproche?* She wasn't even faithful to her plighted troth, or to the obligation of her food and clothes and shelter. A cur-dog taken in and fed would have shown more loyalty!

He sprang at her furiously, struck the tall whiskey-soda in her hand. The liquid bubbling in the tumbler did not even tremble. His blow had been as powerless, as ineffectual, as an exhaled breath. "Muriel!" he choked, his voice gritty with rage. He heard himself cry her name, but neither she nor Hodges took the slightest notice.

"Damn you, you can't do this to me!" he dashed at Hodges, striking with both fists. He might have been a shadow beating at the solid substance of the man he hated. For something like a minute he continued his assault, then, knowing it was useless, gave up the effort. An astral body, it seemed, was powerless against material things.

The lights of the hotel were dim against the thinning fog as he descended from the upper sky and came to rest upon the window sill outside the fifth floor corridor. He passed through the plate glass pane, dropped to the carpet of the corridor and made his way toward his room. As he paused momentarily before his door, forgetting that he needed no key for admission, he saw, or thought he saw, the fleeting flicker of a pale, slim shape before the door three rooms away from his, one of those half-perceived but not quite seen images we sometimes have the impression of discerning just before we turn our heads to find that there is really nothing there.

He had some trouble getting into his body; it seemed cold, stiff, rigid with the rigor of the newly dead, and when at last he felt he had achieved re-entry he was numbed and chilled to the marrow. There was a feeling of profound lassitude, too, as if he had been exercising to the point of exhaustion, and despite the heart-sickness that possessed him he fell into a deep, dreamless sleep.

A NAMELESS, formless sense of loss crowded his mind when he awakened. His life was broken into bits and he could not reach down to pick up the pieces.

Somehow he went through the conventions of the morning, shaved, showered, dressed himself and went down to the dining room. The thought of food disgusted him, but he managed to get down a glass of orange juice and several cups of strong black coffee. Then he went into the library. Something incredible, something wholly out of his experience and beyond the bounds of possibility had happened to him last night. He didn't understand it, but he had to find out what he could about it.

He had no notion where to begin searching, but in the first volume of an encyclopedia he read:

ASTRAL BODY—A term used by Theosophists and Eastern mystics. According to their belief the soul has two bodies, one of solid matter, one of attenuated, perhaps gaseous substance, which is sometimes able to carry the spirit away from the physical body during sleep or trance and which may survive the death of the material body.

Under ADEPT he found:

An Adept, or Mahatma, who has acquired the power of astralization or separating his astral from his material body can sense the subtle material of the universe and can, by responding to the vibrations of Askashic records, see vividly the particular occurrence in the past to which he is attuned and also hear and to a degree feel, just as did the actors of the event which may be under consideration for review.

He shook his head bewilderedly. Dimly be sensed the import of the information he read, but just what did it really mean? Somewhere he had read that all events were photographed indelibly upon the ether, and remain a record *in perpetuum*, traveling ever outward in the limitless space of the universe, so that if a man possessed a telescope of great enough power he might look through the illimitable darkness of interstellar distance to see Henry V fight at Agincourt or Charles Martel defeat the Turks at Tours. That was all a lot of fantastic nonsense, of course, and yet.

HE WENT back to his room and lay down on the bed. *"Oom!"* he

71

pronounced softly while he strove to make his mind a blank. *"Oom— oom—oom!"*

This time it did not take so long, and as he looked back at his body lying on the bed he searched his mind for some scene in the past he might view. Rome? Persia? Babylon?

Babylon... The air seemed suddenly warmer, almost torrid, and his eyes were dazzled by a deluge of bright sunshine. The golden light shone on an immense granite staircase flanked right and left by terra cotta figures of winged sphinxes. Down the stairs there marched a troop of men in scarlet knee-length tunics and high pointed caps, and each one blew a ram's-horn trumpet set with intricate gold inlay. The braying thunder of their music shook the atmosphere. Behind the trumpeters came a throng of women clad in fluttering veil-like draperies attached to them by gold rings in their ears and on their wrists and ankles, and after them a double rank of tall black men with jewels flashing in their purple turbans and ivory staves in their hands. Then came a company of stately, tall women with unloosed black hair falling to their feet and serving them in lieu of garments, then copper-colored girls who played on harps and little drums and dulcimers, and then a regiment of soldiers dressed in silver armor with gleaming silver shields on their left arms and long spears in their right hands.

The pageant was breath taking in its splendor, erotic as a hashish-smoker's dream, sense stealing as the vision of an opium addict. Babylon the Mighty, Babylon the Glorious and Glamorous. A thousand scholars had described it from hearsay, but he had seen it; he was watching it as he might watch a parade down Fifth Avenue.

A little dancing woman flitted by, nude save for bracelets, anklets and armlets, black hair crowned with roses and floating in the breeze of her own movements, the metal bands upon her wrists and arms and ankles chiming sweetly. She cast a wanton, provocative glance at him, her red lips smiled an invitation, laughing black eyes signaled a summons...where had he seen such eyes, such bidding, luring lips?

He turned his back on the small, sweetly made strumpet. Muriel...Muriel and Maitland Hodges. There was unfinished business to be attended to.

All day he wandered restlessly, like a caged beast counting its bars. A dozen schemes for vengeance he considered and discarded. His legally trained mind rejected commonplace homicide as a means of re-quital. He had seen too many wronged husbands go to imprisonment or the chair to think he could plead the "unwritten law" successfully. But there *must* be some way…some way…

The answer came to him like an inspiration. His astral body was invisible, inaudible, to people in the flesh, but—Aunt Mattie's dog had flinched and cringed from him when he had astralized, had been in terror of him. And Muriel loved the old carriages in Central Park. He chuckled grimly. It was a trial.

THE Park was lovely in the twilight. The sky was gray as pewter and the sleepy birds made small noises in the branches. Here and there new stars peeped out and signaled one another as though messaging in code. Southward the light-jeweled towers of Manhattan thrust against the gathering dusk. The cab horse ambled lazily, head hanging down, heavy hooves almost shuffling on the smooth asphalt. Perched on the high seat of the hansom the driver dozed in somnolent content. The gent and lady down there would be his last fares today. They seemed to be that way about each other, ought to be good for a generous tip. Then he'd go down to MacSweeney's for a mug o' Guinness, maybe two, before he put old Gus in the stable and went home.

"Dear, I can't stand it," Muriel burrowed her sleek head into Maitland's tweed shoulder. "When I think of going back to that *gauche*, poker-faced Puritan I feel like banging my head and screaming. If he wouldn't always be so humble, so considerate, so—so dam' *good* to me…"

"Take it easy, kitten," Maitland drew her closer in the bend of his left elbow. "Your Aunt Matilda can't live much longer, and when you get your money— 'Reno, here I come!'"

"But I can't stand him, I tell you. He sickens, nauseates me. If— *oh!*"

Something like a man's form, something palely tinted like a dim reflection of a watercolor in a steamy mirror had come down to the asphalt of the Park Drive. The cabman didn't see it, nor did Muriel or Maitland, but the cab horse did. He checked his drowsy amble as if the reins had been jerked, reared on his hind legs and gave a high, frightened whinny—reared and plunged and beat the air with iron-shod hooves.

"Gus! What t'ell?" the cabman shouted, dragging at the reins with all his strength. "Gus, you crazy fool—" He plummeted from his high seat as the cab careened crazily, fell head-first to the soft grass at the roadside, and looked wonderingly after the racing horse and wildly swaying vehicle. "Wot in bloody hell?" he asked the unresponsive atmosphere.

The woman clung to the man in an oestrus of terror. The pounding hooves, the madly swaying vehicle, the flapping, unheld reins that beat the frightened horse to fresh exertion...the helpless, hopeless feeling of confinement behind the latched doors of the hansom...! "Maitland—Maitland, *do* something!"

Almost miraculously the cab escaped annihilation. Bicyclists dodged to left and right, motorists blew horns and swore and swerved aside, a policeman set spurs to his horse and galloped after it. At last, exhausted by his sudden spurt—for he was an old horse and hadn't run a hundred feet in fifteen years—Gus slackened speed, slowed from a frenzied run to a gallop, then to a sedate trot, and finally to a walk. Two minutes later he was standing by the edge of the drive, head down, sides heaving, lather drooling from his mouth.

Disappointment that was almost rage possessed Barloe. He'd counted on the frightened horse's flight to bring disaster, possibly disfigurement or death, to Muriel and Maitland. Here was anticlimax. He could frighten the cab horse again—all animals seemed terrified by astral shapes—but could he make it run away? It seemed far too exhausted...

"Don't Wade, please don't!" the eager, soft voice sounded just behind him.

He whirled about. "What—?"

She stood there, nude as Praxiteles' statue of Phryne, unclothed and unashamed as Eve before she tasted of the fruit of knowledge. He looked at her, lovely in her nudity. Even her hands and feet were right, narrow, sweetly shaped, with long, tapering fingers and high, arched insteps and slim toes, the kind of hands and feet that Alessandro Botticelli loved to paint. "Wh—why," he stammered, "you're—"

"Sarah Lee, the girl you took to hear the Guru lecture."

"But you're pretty—lovely—"

"Of course," she smiled almost tolerantly. "Don't you know your thoughts can shape your astral body? I've always been so colorless, so mousy, and I've always wanted to be pretty, so..."

Despite himself, he smiled. An uncompleted sentence again, and one that needed no completing to be clear. "What was it you asked me?"

"Don't persecute them any more. They're not worth it. If you *really* want revenge, why don't you leave them to each other?"

"You know about my—trouble?"

She nodded. "Yes, Wade. The other night when we came from the Guru's lecture I lay down on my bed and tried to astralize. At first I couldn't do it, but finally I succeeded, just in time to see you stepping from the window."

"You followed me!"

She nodded again, diffidently, almost guiltily. "Of course. Haven't you been my ideal since the first moment I saw you? You were so occupied with your thoughts you never looked behind you, and I kept almost at your elbow all the way. I saw you go into the old lady's room and frighten her fat dog out of its silly wits. I saw you go to Maitland Hodges' place and find your wife with him, and saw you try to strike them."

"But why…?"

Her luminously greenish-violet eyes were steadfast in the lovely pallor of her face. "Because I love you, Wade Barloe." Before he realized what she did she leant toward him and put her lips to his.

Their touch was lighter than the weight of a poised butterfly, but he felt it, and as naturally, as instinctively as a bird goes to its nest, he gathered her into his arms.

He could barely feel the pressure of her form on his, there was no warmth in it, and very little substance, hardly more than the light pressure of a breath, and yet…she seemed to melt into him, to become an integral part of him, blending her light, etheric substance with his, coalescing, commingling as one cloud does with another.

He had no words to describe the ecstatic sensation he felt. A man born blind who suddenly received his sight would have no words with which to describe his sensations at his first view of a sunrise, nor did Wade Barloe have words for the rapturous ecstasy that flooded him. He knew only that this was what he'd wanted, longed for since the hour of his birth, yet could no more envision than an earthworm could conceive the glory of the midday sun.

GENTLY, reluctantly, he put her from him, and it seemed that he was tearing out his heart as he did so. "Sarah Lee," he gasped brokenly. "Oh, little Sarah Lee, if only I had met you sooner!"

"You have met me, my dear."

"But I'm old enough to be your father—'

"Look at yourself."

"Look at myself? How can I? No mirror will reflect—"

"Look in my eyes, dear heart; and tell me what you see reflected there."

He looked into the greenish-violet irises, and saw the image they gave back; himself as he had been twenty years earlier, a young man, vigorous with youth, with muscles that moved easily and smoothly underneath smooth, pliant skin, eyes not yet dulled from reading legal texts, or cynical from watching fellowmen's frailties.

"You see?" she asked. "Your thoughts have shaped your astral form. You'll never change unless, of course, you wish to."

Her fingertips touched his face lightly as the breeze from a moth's wings. They crept up his cheeks like the searching fingers of a blind girl. "If we don't go back to our bodies within twenty-four hours they'll die. Shall we leave them where they are—never go back?"

He laughed. The first time he had laughed naturally in years, it seemed to him.

> " *Why, if the soul can fling the dust aside,*
> *And naked on the air of heaven ride,*
> *Were't not a shame, were't not a shame for him*
> *In this clay carcase crippled to abide?*"

he quoted.

"Who said that?" she asked.

"A man named Omar Khayyám."

"Omar Khayyám?" she repeated. Plainly, the name meant nothing to her.

"Yes, my dear, one of the greatest astronomers, poets and philosophers the world has ever seen. One of the greatest drunkards, too."

Her wide eyes dwelt on him in violet-green abstraction a moment. "I think that he had more sense drunk than most men do when sober," she pronounced.

"You're not the first one to say that."

She nodded thoughtfully. "No, I suppose not." Then, "Shall we leave our bodies—our 'clay carcasses'—where they are? They'll die if we don't go back to them before morning, you know."

The suggestion shocked him. It was almost like an invitation to suicide, yet— She was speaking again:

"We can leave Muriel and Maitland to each other. That's about the worst thing we can do to them...and we'll have each other till the end of time..."

He felt a sudden glow of enthusiasm. "And we'll have the whole of history to explore together," he broke in joyously. "We'll see Athens under Pericles and Rome under Augustus—the Glory that was Greece, the Grandeur that was Rome—"

She was laughing at him now. "'The Glory that was Greece, the Grandeur that was Rome!'" she mimicked. "Who cares about them when we have this?"

Once more she laid her mouth to his, and he felt tenderness and love and rapture such as he had never known flow from her body into his.

SONG IN THE THICKET

By
MANLY BANISTER

Is it true that an Undine can obtain a soul by marrying a human being?

JOHN DRAKE drove off the highway upon the dusty approach of Beauregard Avenue. All the streets are "avenues" in Burton County, although with the latest development style they deserved to be called ruts. Beauregard "Ruts," Drake thought with a high degree of dissatisfaction. Whyever he and Bev had chosen to settle in Burton County was something that presently evaded his more cognizant faculties.

Twelve thousand bucks...twenty years to pay it in...be dead by then. Drake tooled the sedan through a choking cloud of dust. Twelve thousand bucks down the drain—if you could call a cesspool a proper drain. There were no sewers in Burton County yet...they'd come later. Sewers would bite an extra twenty-five dollars a month out of his already inadequate income. He kicked himself for not having foreseen the sewer problem. Add that expense to house payments, car payments, insurance, lights, water, gas, food, clothing, and the sizable sum he had invested in a perverted lawn that refused to become grass...

He braked to a crawl and steered carefully around a big mud puddle in the middle of the road. A dollar and a quarter he'd spent this very day for a wash job, and damned if he was going to throw *that* away with a wild dive through that obscene patch of liquidity.

No wonder there was a puddle in the road, Drake mused viciously. The whole benighted country was clay from the surface to the center of the earth...and probably a few thousand miles beyond. No drainage through clay...clay! No wonder his lawn wouldn't grow! Gezwich told him that yesterday...no, it was this morning. You got to haul in topsoil, Gezwich had said, or put in sod. Need topsoil in any case...the builders buried the original topsoil under the junk they dug out to make the basement.

Drake had always thought dirt was dirt, and dirt was what grass grew in. Thirty bucks worth of seed and fertilizer—hours of backbreaking effort—and the yard was still a semi-sea of yellowish mud whenever it rained. When it didn't rain, the soil baked so hard you couldn't sink a pick in it. Oh, of course, he had a *few* sprigs of grass here and there…crabgrass grows anywhere.

Drake steered carefully around another puddle. There were not many finished houses on Beauregard Avenue. Drake had the last one, at the end of the street. There were several more about midway down, but all the other lots were still a-building. Lean skeleton houses lined the dusty road.

ANOTHER puddle. Drake peered at it with a frown of disfavor. Something about those puddles had set his subconscious mind to working. He could almost hear the whirring and clicking of mental cogs. The puddle was as ordinary as any, damp around the edges and wet in the middle. Otherwise, the roadway was covered with a thick, soft layer of dust. There wasn't much traffic on the back streets of Burton County, and Drake was sure those puddles had not been there when he left for work this morning. If it had rained in Burton County today, the roadway would at least be damp, wouldn't it…?

Drake coped no further with the problem of the puddles. He carefully negotiated the perimeters of several more and drove onto his own drive.

A flurry of pink and white in a yellow starched housedress of economical cotton fluttered at the kitchen door, hurtled out to the car. Drake opened the door.

"H'lo, hon. How's m'baby?"

Beverly Drake planted a luscious, soul-satisfying kiss on her homecoming husband's lean chops. They still had a couple of million kisses to go—and a couple of babies, too—before Bev would content herself with a mere look out the window as John came driving in. For the present, they were very much married, and very much in love.

"I'm *so* glad you're home, lover boy!"

Beverly was blonde, sparkling blue-eyed, warm and cuddlesome. Drake grabbed her to him and returned the luscious, soul-satisfying kiss she had so generously given him.

" 'Smatter? Trouble?"

He knew there was no trouble. Bev said it every night. She was just glad he was home and wanted him to know it. He knew it and was glad of it, too. Bev was all he wanted out of life—the rest of it could go hang.

He expressed the depth of his feelings with, "What's for supper, baby?"

She ignored his outburst of connubial passion.

"John there's something I want you to do for me before it gets dark…"

"Eh? Sure...anything at all, baby!"

He kissed her again, even more satisfying than before.

"Well!" she balked, pulling free. "Nothing like killing a dragon or anything! I just want you to drain a puddle out of the front yard."

He went up the kitchen steps into the house.

"Let it dry up, baby."

"But John...!"

He turned, chucked her under the chin, grinning.

"Anything for you, baby...after supper!"

He progressed into the living room, dumped his hat on a chair. He sprawled on the davenport. "Where's m'paper?"

"Pork chops for supper...to answer your questions in the order of their appearance," Beverly said, running one hand through his hair. She balanced herself delicately on the arm of the davenport.

"As for your paper—it's out in the middle of that nasty puddle I was telling you about!"

"The hell it is!" Drake swung himself to a sitting posture. "What kind of an idiot have we got for a paper boy? Get on the phone and have another sent over."

Beverly went dutifully to the phone, called the local distributor.

"He'll be by with it in about a half hour," she said, hanging up. "John, I want to discuss that puddle with you..."

Drake lay back on the davenport and reached for a magazine.

"Hmmm. Hope you told that guy what I think of his delivery..."

"John, the puddle..."

"Lots of puddles," John observed, whetting his glance on a four-color representation of pulchritude in the magazine ad. "There are puddles all over the road," he said. "What do you expect when it rains?"

"Did it rain downtown today?"

"Don't think it did...just out here."

"Not out here, it didn't. I've been home all day, so I know."

"Maybe a street cleaning wagon went by."

"Be sensible!"

"Okay. Maybe there's a water main bust."

"John—this puddle in front of our door..."

Drake's face went a trifle gray.

"Good God! Do you suppose *our* water main could be broken? And on *our* side of the meter? ...Oy! At the rate we're paying for water!"

He got up quickly and opened the front door.

"It isn't a broken water main," Beverly said matter-of-factly, "because the water doesn't flow. It just puddles. There seems to be a sag in the walk there, right at the foot of the steps."

Indeed, it did appear that the water filled a sag in the concrete walkway. It lapped out several feet on either side into the gruesome mockery of a lawn. John knew there couldn't be a sag there. The grade sloped from the house to the street…the walk itself was slightly crowned.

The evening paper lay, as Beverly had said, in the middle of the puddle, just beyond reach of a questing broom handle.

"Could you drain it?" Beverly suggested, referring to the puddle. "Dig a little ditch or something?"

"It'll dry up by morning," Drake protested dubiously.

"Are we to ask the Harrians to wade through it tonight? Remember…we're having them over for canasta. Or do you?"

Drake hadn't remembered, but he did now.

"Get me a broom," he said tersely, "and go on with supper. I'll sweep it away."

"Huh-uh."

"Huh-uh what? Must I get my own broom?"

"Nuh. No sweep."

"Nonsense. Get me a broom."

"It won't work, I say."

"Why won't it work? Get me that broom!"

"Okay, Canute. Have it your way."

She flounced into the house and a moment later the broom came bouncing out. Drake caught it and began to sweep industriously, sending the offensive puddle in foaming waves down the walk. Observing the damp spot that remained, he shook the moisture from the broom with complete satisfaction and went into the house.

Drake was in process of mangling his third pork chop when Mr. Barnes, the neighborhood newspaper distributor, knocked on the door. He passed the paper and a mumbled apology through the door to John.

"That's certainly a man-size puddle you've got there," he allowed. "You got a bad sag in your walk. What I always say about these houses they build nowadays, scamp the work, that's what they do! Never try to see a thing is done right. If you was me, I'd get hot after the contractor that left that sag in the walk. You get a puddle like that from watering your yard, you'll see it's a fright when it rains!"

With that, he politely touched the brim of his fedora, stepped off the porch and sloshed off through the puddle. Drake stared after him, nonplussed. It was almost dark, and the puddle gleamed silvery with sky light.

Beverly said over his shoulder, "I see it's back."

There was a tone of smug satisfaction in her words that stung Drake.

"I suppose you knew it would be?" he hurled at her.

"Yup. I swept it away three times myself today!"

"Get me that broom again!" Drake snapped. "I'll do some more sweeping—see if it's a water line bust or a spring in our front yard!"

"John, dear...your supper..."

"Hang supper! I've finished anyway."

He swept the water away again. During the last half of the operation, he had to have the porch light on to see by. Finally, there was only a damply gleaming streak reflecting the shine of the early evening stars.

Drake examined the ground on both sides of the walk and along the foundation, but there were no telltale streams of moisture bubbling from the earth or anywhere else. For the last time, Drake shook out the broom, stamped moisture from his soggy footgear, and went grumpily back into the house. He left the porch light on for the expected arrival of the Harrians.

Neither John nor Bev heard Ben and Zuelda Harrian drive up. A bedroom intervened between the living room and the driveway, and the TV set was making an exorbitant amount of noise. A loud hallooing and banging at the back door announced the arrival of the expected couple.

"The front door's for coming in," Drake greeted them pleasantly, switching on the drive light.

Zuelda, tiny, buoyant, vivacious and brunette, assumed a mien of mock indignation.

"Wade through that puddle? Or do you furnish a boat?"

Tall, handsome Ben Harrian, as dark and sombre as his wife was dark and sparkling, nudged her through the door.

"Go in, Zuelda!"

The expression was just like him, Drake thought...so grammatically proper. He could not imagine Ben saying, "go on in" like a native would have said it.

"Don't keep the man waiting with the door open," Ben concluded, and grinned at Drake as they passed through the kitchen. "That *is* a big sink you have in your front yard, Jack. Been watering the lawn?"

"That's the second time tonight somebody has blamed lawn watering for that puddle," Drake retorted. "I haven't got enough of a lawn to waste our high-priced water on. If there's a puddle there now, it's grown in the last hour. I've swept it away twice this evening. I don't know where it comes from...nor where it goes to!"

Ben lifted heavy, perfectly arched brows.

"Tut, tut...not so touchy, Jack! Sorry to tramp on your feelings, but it *is* a big puddle…"

"All right," Drake said. "All right! Let's go into the living room."

The living room emitted a blast of variegated squeals and giggles as Bev and Zuelda came face to face. The Harrians were really Beverly's friends, Drake thought, as he put their things away in the bedroom while Bev and Zuelda hugged each other.

The Harrians had arrived in the city, friendless, a few months ago, and Ben had landed a job in the shipping department of Drake's company. A background of extensive Old World travel and an uncanny familiarity with every backwoods hamlet in America made Ben a natural for the shipping department post.

Drake, of course, had been responsible for Beverly's meeting Zuelda. He'd invited the couple the first time, out of a desire to be friendly to the new man. Ben had accepted the invitation with a surprising warmth, and from then on; well, it had been like a rolling stone picking up momentum.

Not that he disliked Ben Harrian. Drake just was not a gregarious type, and the thoughtless remarks of others frequently irritated him. Ben was quite good at being irritating, and apparently without meaning to be.

Zuelda, now…she was cute and convivial and…well, hell!…it's natural for a man to take less umbrage with a good-looking woman than with another fellow, isn't it? Zuelda had a mouth like a fresh, red rosebud, deep, dark eyes that swam in a sea of gaiety, and a figure…Drake's neighbors *never* irritated him with things like that!

The group settled down to a comfortable game of canasta. The conversation was bright and sparkling. Ben was witty, Drake had to say that for him. He was extremely cultured, betraying in speech and manners an unusual education coupled with a wide knowledge of little known subjects.

Ordinarily, Drake enjoyed the Harrian's company well enough, but tonight a worry oppressed him. He didn't like things that went unexplained. Finally, he put words to his aggravation.

"The thought of that puddle is getting me down!"

"Tell your contractor about it," Ben observed judiciously, quietly studying his cards and playing with great care.

"You mean I should make him replace the walk. The walk doesn't need replacing. There's no sink in it. But where is that water coming from?"

"I wouldn't worry about it," Ben observed lazily.

"I *should* worry," Drake said stiffly. "It's my walk."

The game continued with something less of its former sparkle. Bev mixed and served cocktails, and spirits picked up again.

"It's either a busted water main or a spring in the front yard," Drake gloomed.

"How terrible!" Zuelda put in. "Your nice new house!"

Drake looked at her gratefully. Ben tapped his cards against a gleaming thumbnail.

"A spring? That's a possibility, Jack."

Drake tossed his hand on the table.

"Come on; Ben. Let's look it over. Maybe you can see something I couldn't the last time I looked."

ARMED with a flashlight, Drake flipped on the porch light and went out. The puddle was a black and shining smear at the foot of the steps, extending out a considerable distance along the walk and into the yard on either side. Drake flashed the torch over the far perimeter of the glistening slick.

"It's bigger than it was last time, and for the life of me, I can't figure what keeps it from flowing down the walk. Might as well be tar." He dipped the toe of his shoe into the pool. "But it isn't. It's water, all right."

Ben made a humming noise in his throat but offered no other comment. Suddenly he snapped his fingers.

"Might be a spring at that, Jack! I know a fellow who might be able to tell you something. Old Tom Ellers...he lives over near us, on a back street. Sort of a neighborhood handyman. He..." Ben stopped, at a loss for words.

"Go on," Drake prompted. "He what?"

"He...he's what they call a water witch..."

"One of those guys who twiddles a stick and finds water?"

"You might put it that way..."

"Ha!" Drake glared gloomily at the puddle. "I can find water without a stick. Here it is...see?"

"I mean," Ben put in, "that Tom could find out where it is coming from...if it is a spring."

Drake glanced sourly up at the taller man.

"You don't...*believe* that rot, do you?"

"Well..." Ben temporized. "I can't do it myself, but Tom..."

"Let's go in the house," Drake grumped. Ben's talk of the water witch irritated him more completely than anything else that had passed between them this night. "If I got a spring pouring up there, I can find it myself tomorrow!"

DRAKE could not find the spring the following morning, though he swept the puddle away once more before going to work. Far from being happy at not finding the evidence he sought, Drake was so put out he failed to notice that yesterday's puddles were gone from the road, though new pools of water gleamed among the row of houses under construction.

Having had the day in which to think over his predicament, he dropped into Ben's office shortly before quitting time.

"What'd you call that fellow, Ben?"

Ben looked up from a desk full of papers. "What fellow?"

"You know...last night...was it water witch?"

"Oh you mean Tom Ellers. Sure. Decided to have a try at it? Now, I don't guarantee Tom can actually tell you where that water is coming from, Jack..."

Drake waved a hand.

"I looked all over hell for a spring this morning. Didn't find any."

"Was the water still there?"

"I swept it away."

"It's gone now?"

"I...well...it's always come back before. Let me call Bev."

He scooped up Ben's phone, dialed outside, then rapidly dialed his home phone number. Beverly answered promptly.

"How's that puddle, hon? The one in front, I mean."

There was a brief pause. "It's back again, John."

Drake swore. "Sorry, honey," he apologized.

"That isn't all."

"Isn't all?"

"No. There's another one across the drive from the kitchen door, and a third one in the back yard!"

"Have you been..." Drake began suspiciously.

"Whatever it is you're thinking, I haven't. And it hasn't rained today, either."

"Uh...thanks. See you." Drake hung up, looked gloomily at Ben.

"Bev says it's back...and there's another in the side yard and one in back."

Ben whistled softly.

"You just *could* have a spring breaking out in several places. You'd better let me bring Tom Ellers over this evening."

"Sure, but...what could he do?"

Ben shrugged. "He might be able to give you a hint whether it's permanent or not...or show you some way to divert it."

Drake shook his head. "I can't believe in that kind of stuff."

Ben hoisted his shoulders again.

"Nobody does, really…except the water witches. Nobody believes in their ability…but they hire them every day to find water."

"Is that true? I thought water witching was some kind of fable…"

"Many water sources have been discovered by the so-called water witches. Fable or not, they frequently do locate water underground with nothing but a stick."

Drake gave in with a sigh.

"Okay. How about bringing this…Ellers around, hey? I don't know what good he can do, but maybe…just maybe…he can tell me for sure if I've got a damned spring running loose or not!"

ELLERS turned out to be a wizened little man of about sixty, gaunt as a pitchfork, sparsely topped with gray. His cheeks like old bacon rind were covered with a gray stubble. He was dressed in sordid blue overalls, and his wretched once-white shirt bore witness to at least a score of bachelor meals. He grinned all over, shaking hands with Drake.

"Pleased t'meet yew, Mist' Drake!"

Drake smiled affably as the little dowser ambled out of Ben's coupe.

"Ben…uh…tells me you're a…water witch, Mr. Ellers."

Tom Ellers' blue eyes turned frosty. He frowned.

"They ain't no sech thing as a witch, Mist' Drake. I'm a plain, natural dowser, that's all. I dowses for water…ain't no witchin' to it!"

Drake acknowledged his error with a look of pained embarrassment, hiding an inward smile.

"Do you think I've got a spring on the property, Mr. Ellers?"

The oldster stamped on the concrete drive, surveyed the lay of the land with a critical eye.

"T'tell 'e truth, Mist' Drake, if I was one of these geology fellers, I'd say there wasn't a chance in the world. This county is solid clay more than two hundred foot down, to bedrock. But that ain't the case." He fell musingly silent, scanning the slope behind the house and its thickets of scrub elm and willow. "No, sir, it ain't the case. There's lots of water here—I can feel it. I am one of them as can," he observed with a proud grin, "though I like the feel o' the stick for pinning it down. Let me cut a stick, now, and I'll be right with you."

Ellers stamped off briskly in the direction of the thicket behind the garage. Drake glanced inquiringly at Ben. The tall, dark man smiled easily.

"He's gone to cut a divining rod—the forked stick he uses."

Ellers returned in an instant, paring leaves and stems from a forked branch of elm.

"We c'n start aroun' in front," he hailed cheerfully, "by that big puddle, and come on aroun' thisaway…"

He led off quickly, with a spryness that belied his years, shucking the last of the leaves in the drive. He skirted the edge of the puddle on the sad description of lawn, raising the "rod" until it pointed upward like a V, in a peculiar, back-handed kind of grip.

Drake was not prepared for what happened next. He jumped as the rod whipped violently downward, swung back up another half arc between Ellers' arms and beat the air in front of his chin. The dowser's brown face mirrored his physical strain. His arms twisted, seeming to fight the vicious pull of the rod, and he found it difficult to keep his footing. Suddenly the old man stumbled and fell, losing his grip on the writhing rod.

Ellers got up with a shamefaced grin.

"You've sure got a lot of water under there, Mist' Drake. See how that blamed rod th'owed me? One nev' th'ow me befo', though I did hear tell of it happenin'."

He grinned, braced himself, and swung the rod upward. It flapped violently again, seeming to twist itself from the old man's grip.

"Plenty there, all right," Ellers grunted. "Naow, le's aroun' to side."

He led off again, and Drake hurled an accusing glance at Ben.

"Is that guy nuts or something?"

The half-grin of understanding he had expected from Ben did not materialize. The tall man's lean face suffused with a saturnine frown.

"You modern Americans don't believe in anything; that's your trouble!" he spoke harshly.

Drake shrugged, privately thinking that Ben Harrian must be nuts, too, if he took any stock in this sort of thing.

Ellers was in the side yard, his rod doing a witch's dance over the second puddle. "I'd say, Mist' Drake, they's a great big spring feedin' that pool, but you doan' see it runnin' out anywheh!"

Drake regarded the pool. The sun was below the horizon by now. It had been sunset when Ben drove in with the old fellow. Lingering twilight reflected from the surface of the pool, which seemed to ruffle, swirling, as if caressed by a brisk wind.

But there was no wind…not a breath. Drake peered more closely at the puddle. The surface was definitely agitated in brisk motion.

Ellers cupped the rod in his armpit and moved into the back yard where the performance was repeated. He held his rod up again, turning this way and that, seeming to read significance into the waving and waggling of the forked stick.

"I think, Mist' Drake, I can find fa' you where that stream is comin' from…"

The oldster took off at a high lope toward the thicketed slope. Drake took a step to follow, heard Ben call out to Ellers, then Ben's hand on his arm arrested him.

"He'll be back in a minute. The big spring, or source, is probably up there on the slope some place. No use our crashing around the brush after him…he'll go in a straight line through anything in the way!"

It was, Drake saw, almost dark. The sky still glared against the horizon, silhouetting the thickety ridge, which was now like a pool of ink.

DRAKE didn't know how long they waited. Ben passed the time with a few comments on dowsing, which he seemed to have gleaned from some place. It may have been ten minutes, or fifteen. Shadows gathered thickly on the drive until Drake could scarcely see the tall man's face. Before they knew it, darkness closed in. Stars sprang into being in the velvety overhead. Drake fumbled his way to the kitchen door, found the light switch just inside, and turned on the drive light.

"Your friend ought to be coming back pretty soon, hadn't he, Ben?"

Ben shrugged. "He may have gone farther than we think. No use shouting. If he's still dowsing, he wouldn't hear us."

Drake peered across the drive toward the puddle that had puzzled him with its seeming agitation. He clutched Ben's arm.

"Ben! The puddle…!"

The tall man swung around.

"What…?"

"It isn't there!"

"Sure enough!" Ben bit his lip. He looked sidelong at Drake. "How about…?"

Drake bounded through the house, nearly scaring Beverly out of her wits. A long minute rater, he returned slowly.

"It's gone."

"I checked the one in the back yard," Ben said.

Drake looked at him. Ben nodded.

"What the hell…!" Drake exploded.

"What can it be?" murmured Ben Harrian. "Jack, you don't believe in superstition, of course, but I've made a study of such things. Frankly, this business worries me."

"Your friend Ellers is what's worrying me!" Drake barked at him.

"We'd better look for him."

Drake went inside for a flashlight. It took an hour, casting about in widening circles, to find the little dowser on the thickety slope. A three-quarter moon rising in the east cast oblique light into a small clearing about two hundred yards from the house. They found Tom Ellers there...quite dead.

"Poor little devil!" Drake mourned as they picked their way back to the house. "I feel guilty as hell, having you bring him over here...

Ben's voice was a mumble in the darkness. "Forget it, Jack."

"We couldn't know he had a bad heart, could we, Ben?"

"Forget it, Jack!"

Drake nearly wept with remorse. "Ben, I..."

Ben's firm, slim hand came out of the darkness, shook Drake forcibly. "Forget it!"

Drake's teeth rattled. Momentary rage swarmed through him. But the shaking cleared his head. He felt his guts settle slowly back into place.

"Sorry, Ben...here, take it easy...here's the yard..."

They rounded the garage and went into the house. Drake did not see the shadow lurking there out of the moonglow. As the kitchen door closed, the shadow detached itself from the garage, drifted down the drive and into the night.

"Guess we better call the sheriff, Ben?"

"That is the usual procedure," Ben said gruffly.

Drake moved toward the phone. Ben put a hand on his arm. He made a motion signifying a drink in Beverly's direction. Beverly understood, sped worriedly into the kitchen where they kept a fifth under the sink.

"Better let me phone," Ben said.

He made the call quickly, curtly, and turned to Drake.

"Bev is bringing you a drink, Jack. Pull yourself together. The sheriff and his men will be here in a few minutes. Don't mention the puddles to them."

"The puddles?" Drake had forgotten the puddles. "Why?"

Ben grinned tightly. He tapped his forehead with a stiffened finger.

"*That's* why. They'll think you're crazy enough, having a dowser over. Let me do the talking. You just answer what questions are asked of you."

"But, Ben, how about those puddles...?"

"Forget the puddles, Jack!"

Drake felt anger flare in him again. Ben Harrian was master of this situation. He, Drake, in his own house, was a nincompoop. He blamed Ben for accentuating his distress. Beverly appeared suddenly and jammed something cold and firm into his grasp. He tilted the glass, drank. His feelings subsided.

It was a long night. They had to go back to the body, of course, with the sheriff and two of his deputies. Flashlights bobbed in the thicket, pale swords of luminance in the stark glare of the moon. When they came upon the body, Sheriff Hamilton sent a deputy back to the house to await the county coroner, who was an unnecessarily long time in coming.

The remaining deputy occupied the interval taking several flash photographs with an enormous camera.

The sheriff questioned both Ben and Drake, listened to the story Ben told of the water hunt, the graphic description of the speed with which the old man had darted into the brush in search of the "big spring."

"Don't take much stock in water witchin', myself," the sheriff grunted, "though I guess there's a lot of it bein' done. It's plain the old fellow had a bad heart. Too much exertion for a man his age."

The coroner finally came, fussed over the corpse. He wasn't a doctor—the coroner's post in Burton County was a political appointment—but even he could see that Ellers was dead, and he said so, with what seemed to Drake to be a great deal of unnecessary satisfaction.

"Think his heart gave out, Abe?" rumbled the sheriff.

"Ed, you know I'm not a doctor!" protested the coroner. "We'll have to send the body to the city for a post mortem. All I can say for sure is that he's dead."

The group crashed back through the brush. The two deputies carried the body. At the edge of the thicket, a pair of ambulance men with a stretcher met them. The body was put on the stretcher, carried out to the ambulance in the street. Sheriff Hamilton offered a few last words, legged into his car with his deputies, and the cortege ground away.

Drake was surprised to find Zuelda in the house when they re-entered.

"Bev called me," Zuelda explained. "I had neighbors bring me over."

Ben frowned. "You should not have come, Zuelda…"

Zuelda sparkled dangerously. "Leave Bev all alone, with you men out there crashing around in the brush?" She softened suddenly. "Poor old Tom…!"

Ben shrugged, turned to Drake.

"I guess we better be going, Jack. It's late." A cloud settled on his thin, handsome face. "There's…something frightening going on around here, Jack." He appealed to Beverly. "Aren't you afraid to stay here?"

Beverly shook her head, wondering.

Drake said, "If you're referring to those puddles, Ben, it's your turn to forget it. There's a natural explanation for everything, if you look far enough. As for being afraid of poor old Ellers' ghost...I think not!"

Zuelda spoke slowly, looking doubtfully at her husband, as if seeking support from him.

"Ben is...is psychic...Jack. You can call it that. We wouldn't blame you if you moved out right away after these things have happened."

Drake laughed harshly.

"Too big an investment to leave," he chuckled grimly. "It's over with now, so what is there to worry about? Ben...you're too sensitive. I've thought that about you all along. If I told you there were pixies in the thicket, I'm sure you would believe me!"

Ben stared at him oddly while Zuelda anxiously regarded her husband.

"Do you...do you know there is something in the thicket...?"

Drake exploded with strained mirth.

"There...what did I tell you? I didn't even say there were pixies, and you..." He exploded in another uproar.

"You listen to Ben, Jack!" Zuelda shrilled at him, shocking him out of his semi-hysteria. "Ben knows things you don't know he knows...don't dream...!"

Ben Harrian's hand came down forcibly on her arm.

"Zuelda! My dear..." He turned to Drake, smiling. "Sorry, old man. I take it, then, that you plan to stay right here?"

NOW it was Drake's turn to stare. Could there really be any other thought in the tall man's mind? Move out? Why? Ben seemed satisfied with Drake's reaction. He took his wife solicitously by the shoulder.

"Come, dear. Jack's had a bad evening."

"Sorry I'm not scared out of seven years' growth," Drake put in with a sour grin. "Like some people..."

Ben turned, flashing white teeth in a friendly smile.

"Good night, Jack...Beverly."

They heard the Harrian's car churning the furlongs to the highway.

Beverly said, "You've insulted them, John, our best friends!" She said it simply, without accusation, as if puzzled, and she awaited an explanation.

Drake passed a hand across his face. His fingers shook.

"I'm sorry, Bev. Shock, I guess. Mostly, I can't stand that guy, anyway. I'll look him up at the office tomorrow and apologize."

He wondered later about Ben's concern over their leaving this place, he and Bev, Drake laughed grimly at the thought. It wasn't in Drake's make-up to scare easily. He wasn't scared at all, he told himself. His reaction was shock...sympathy...pity for poor old Tom Ellers...tough way to end!

The apology he had contemplated making Ben for Beverly's benefit dried up like the puddles in the yard. Drake didn't apologize, and though he saw Ben frequently at the office, there was a strained atmosphere between them. And it didn't matter, Drake told himself, though Bev was worried about losing Zuelda's friendship.

FRIDAY evening, Sheriff Hamilton stopped by. Drake gave Bev that look, which both of them tacitly understood to mean vanish. Bev vanished into the kitchen and rattled crockery.

Hamilton opened the skirmish with a few questions about Tom Ellers—pointless questions. Drake shrugged.

"You'd better ask Ben Harrian about that, Sheriff. I'd never seen the man before in my life."

The sheriff grunted. "I'll get around to Harrian later. Now, about this dowsing. Tell me about that again."

Drake told him. He wanted to mention the puddles, just to spite Ben Harrian, but somehow he could make no mention of them pass his lips.

"Now, tell me again just how you found the body," the sheriff went on.

Drake said, "Aren't you making a lot of unnecessary trouble, Sheriff, over a man's dying of a heart attack?"

Sheriff Hamilton stared levelly into Drake's eyes.

"*I* didn't say Ellers died of a heart attack—leastwise, not tonight."

Drake felt a kind of sick alarm flood him.

"You mean…an accident? He could have tripped and fallen…"

"He didn't trip."

Drake felt sicker. The thought of an attacker lurking in the thicket…probably there while Bev was home alone…

"I didn't see any marks to show he might have been clubbed or stabbed, Sheriff. And we didn't hear a shot."

"Ellers wasn't knifed, clubbed or shot."

Drake wondered why the sheriff deliberately prolonged the agony of his disclosure. Did he think he and Ben Harrian had killed Ellers?

"How *did* he die—if it's any of my business?"

"It *might* be your business. It depends on whether Ellers went off into the brush under his own power, as you say, or whether he was carried in there and planted after he was drowned."

"*Drowned?*"

"The autopsy showed his lungs full of water. Ellers died by strangulation in an aqueous medium…if you prefer the language of the autopsy report."

There was a moment of leaden, swimming silence, then the sheriff's rough voice resumed the interrogation.

"Now, you're sure, are you, that Ellers went off alone into the brush…"

He does suspect us, Drake thought. A countering thought flashed through his mind. It was Hamilton's job to suspect everybody. He could have no evidence to point suspicion toward Ben or Drake.

Drake said, "I guess I've said enough, Sheriff. If I am under arrest, I'll go peacefully…"

The sheriff sighed and got to his feet.

"Sit down. You're not under arrest. I believe your story, and that's the tough part of it. It would be easier if I didn't. If you find out how a man can drown himself in the middle of a thicket without getting his clothes wet, and without a drop of water anywhere around, let me know huh?"

JOHN DRAKE awoke in the middle of the night with a feeling of palpating urgency. His ears strained against the unusual quiet of the night, as if seeking again the source of some sound that might have awakened him. Silver moonlight gushed through the bedroom windows from a nearly full moon riding high in the star-powdered sky.

The night was breathlessly still and hot. There was no murmur of insects, no raucous screams of the cicada, a blasting trumpet of sound synonymous with hot weather. He heard only the light breathing of Beverly as she slept quietly beside him, bathed in the light of the moon.

Then, faintly, he heard the sound again, the sound that had brought him awake—a low, throbbing ululation of musical quality that rose and fell on the moon-drenched night, crescendoed to a wail, and fell again to a haunting murmur that was like the whisper of dark waters caressing the smooth stones of an ancient stream bed. With the sound, there came an intensification of the urgent feeling that gripped him. He had to get up and go—someplace, he knew not where. Drake sat up in bed, head cocked for better listening, restraining the mad impulse to jump and run.

It was the sound of a voice—or of many voices, so beautifully blended as to seem one. It was a voice such as Drake had never heard before, its unhuman quality poignant with desire and the promise of sweetness ineffable. As the voice crescendoed, his ear detected the separation of syllables, but the song remained lost to his understanding, the words blurred and indistinct, yet pregnant with a lure that was more than he could resist.

Suddenly the singing was quite loud, as if swelled by an unimaginable chorus, until the room throbbed with its rhythm. Surely, Drake thought, the swelling harmonies must awaken Beverly. But she slept gently on. Drake covered his ears with his hands, but the wild song diminished not a decibel in volume.

It came to him then that the voices he heard lifted in song were not in the air at all, but in his own mind, ringing sweet and clear from some mystic, hidden well-spring of his own being. The pathos of it, the lure of it, the liquid, murmuring richness of its rhythmic fabric consumed him, dulled his senses, his power of thought, made of his mind a bright chamber where Nothingness floated in Void and he was robbed of his will.

Like a man in a dream, Drake dressed, stole to the door and out. Moments later, he picked his way through the thicket world of scrubby elms and willows, blundering through an endless, chaotic world of molten-bright moon silver and ebony shadow.

The voices still rang in his mind, neither closer nor farther away, with quickened tempo, with breathless beat, urging him frantically onward, calling, luring, promising, lulling. Drake came out in a clearing in the heart of the thicket. He might have recognized it as the place where they had found Tom Ellers' body, but his external senses were dulled to his surroundings, only the inner ones were afire with the rhythm of that delectable melody.

In the clearing he saw them…that angelic chorus…that heavenly minstrelsy…and the moon bathed with its glare their glowing bodies, effulgent silver against the shadowed backdrop of the thicket. With intricate step and flowing motion they danced…naked in the moonlight they danced…the grass blades scarcely bending under the flitting lightness of their dainty feet. Scores of female figures dancing, each perfect as cast in the mold of perfection, and from the throat of each seemed to pour that unearthly melody which held him spellbound.

The night became a blur in Drake's mind. By and by, he was vaguely aware that time had passed, that the moon had lowered itself and now poured a colder light athwart the thickety ridge. He stumbled, leaving the thicket behind him to re-cross his own back yard. He did not perceive the shape that huddled in the shadow of the garage and looked after him with complete satisfaction as he groped his way to the kitchen door and into the house. He was not truly conscious of anything until he suddenly awoke to full command of his own senses in his own bed.

Beverly slept quietly yet. She might not have stirred a muscle the whole night through. Drake's mind was a kaleidoscope of moonlight shards and shadows, and twisting, writhing, leaping shapes that glistened silver...of soft breasts and yielding torsos, clinging arms and flashing thighs...

The whole vision seemed to contract in his mind, shriveling into a core of hard brilliance, an unremembered spectacle of grandeur and passion. Drake whimpered, his face in his hands, as the last shred of delightful memory drifted beyond his ken, became a throbbing ache that answered nothing of the questioning pain in his being...and demanded much. He slept.

DRAKE could not explain, even to himself, the feeling that gripped him next day. What mystified him was something beyond his unexplainable feeling of physical exhaustion. He spent the morning out of doors, hovering at the fringe of the thicketed slope. Once he cut a forked stick as he had seen Tom Ellers do. He held it in his hands in as nearly the same peculiar manner as he could remember. But it was only a stick—a scrawny, bifurcated wooden thing, dead as a stick of wood in his grasp...a stick of wood...it was nothing more.

He drove by the Harrian's, but the shades were drawn at all the windows, and nobody answered his knock on the door.

Drake drove into the city, parked by the public library and went in. It was late afternoon when he came out, and he was ravenously hungry. He found a small restaurant, ate, and drove home. It was after sunset when Beverly met him at the door. She looked worried, wifely intuition sensing the disquiet that gnawed at him.

She said, "Your supper is waiting, dear."

Drake roused from his abstraction sufficiently to kiss her lightly.

"Thanks. I ate downtown." At her look of disappointment, he added quickly, "I'll have a cup of coffee with you while you eat.

The table was set in the kitchen. While Drake gloomed over his coffee, Beverly pecked disinterestedly at her food.

"Have you seen the Harrians today?" he asked.

She raised her brows. "No. Should I have?"

"No. I just thought—" he paused. "I stopped by their place this morning. Nobody was home, and I thought maybe they might have come here. I didn't go directly there...I drove around a bit first."

"They weren't here." She paused, wanting to ask the question. She blurted, "Where did you go today, dear?"

"No place." At her continued questioning look, he amplified, "In town to the library."

Beverly seemed suddenly more cheerful. She relaxed, smiled.

"Get any good books?"

"Huh? Get any...? No...I didn't take any out. Just looked through a couple."

"What kind of books?"

He acted as if he didn't want to talk about it, but was impelled to speak.

"Skipped through some books on dowsing...you know..."

Beverly perked up with a look of interest.

"Are there books about it?"

He chuckled hollowly. "Plenty of books, but none of them say much. There's a history to dowsing, of course, and they all treat that. The authors are either totally for dowsing as a fact, or totally against it. None of the authors, it seems, are dowsers. They're just investigators...and writers. It was a foolish notion I had, anyway."

She sensed that the subject oppressed him and wisely refrained from pursuing it further.

"Well, we don't seem to have any more springs in our yard, so I guess it doesn't matter. There's a good play on TV tonight, and I want you just to relax and forget all about..."

"Sure. I could stand some rest, hon. Feel beat up." He stood up, yawned, and went into the living room.

The television play was mediocre. Drake yawned all the way through it. At its close, he clumped off to bed and fell instantly into deep, dreamless sleep.

AGAIN the clarion call of the mystic saraband pulled him awake. Drake sat up in bed, panting, his brain astir with vague, delightful memories. Beverly slept peacefully, and the moon painted a broad band of silver across her face and night-clad upper body. The gold of her hair fought against the silver of the moonlight and lost. It looked like a cloud of fine-spun platinum against her pillow.

There was something in the elfin light that flooded the bed, which brought out a certain appealing quality no woman save Beverly had ever had for Drake. Briefly he yearned for her, then the throbbing ululation of devilish melody in his mind overcame the impulse and he found himself dressed, crashing through moon-drenched thicket.

The dance slowed its tempo as he approached, and as he stepped through a screen of young elms into the clearing, the swirling of naked figures became a closeknit weaving and swaying, their song a tremulous humming with vocal counterpoint. Suddenly there were words that had meaning for Drake, a contrapuntal repetition, now in low, murmuring melody, liquid as a clear, cold freshet springing down a piney mountainside.

"Hail the Bridegroom! ...Hail!"

The massed dancers converged upon him. Drake saw the gleam of moonglow on their eyeballs, the flashing refulgence of panting breasts, of sinuous torsos... He yielded to an intoxicating influx of passion, a living flame that ripped through his body, then flickered and failed, and nothing of it was left save a frigid ash. The hair prickled at the nape of his neck. The singers were silent, poised, staring at him, sensing that their hold upon him had somehow snapped.

Drake fell back a step. He yearned to move forward, to be swept up again in a maddening chorus of voices and flowing bodies, in a welter of passion and delight...but something deep as the shadow of the elms, as hard and bright as the floating moon, shut like a door between his mind and his feelings...and he turned and fled, back to the house, to Beverly, to...

What it was that impelled him so to run, Drake did not know. It was a consuming urgency that brooked no delay, a greater urgency than that imposed upon him by the massed singers in the thicket, and diametrically opposed, accompanied by such a sense of prickling dread that it left him gasping.

He heard the sound of its going as he launched himself against the kitchen door, heard the frantic, watery splashing of it as the door burst open. He flipped the light switch on...the floor was a sea of roiling water.

Poised on the threshold, Drake stared at it without comprehension, aware only that it seethed and boiled away from him, smote with a splash against the cellar door. The panel crashed open, and the water poured foaming into the basement.

Almost at once, the automatic sump pump woke to whirring life, began to pump the water into the French drain prepared for its outflow beside the house.

A step grated on the drive and Drake whirled. Ben Harrian stood limned in the light pouring out of the kitchen door. His face drawn and pallid. His mouth was half-open, as if he had been about to speak.

"What do you want?" Drake snarled at him.

The sump pump still whirred softly in the basement. Drake knew that Ben heard it too, and he suspected that Ben knew why it was whirring. What was Ben Harrian doing here at this time of night, anyway? Drake got hold of himself.

"Sorry. I didn't see it was you, Ben. What's the trouble?"

Ben smiled slightly, his thin, handsome face passively calm.

"I…I just dropped by, Jack. I couldn't sleep for…for thinking. I was afraid you would be in bed…"

"Beverly's asleep!" Drake announced crisply.

"Of course, Jack. I can speak to you out here. I've…I've been worrying. Sheriff Hamilton dropped by this morning…yesterday morning now, I guess. We went with him, Zuelda and I, to his office…"

Drake grunted. "So that's where you were. I stopped by to see you."

Ben's face lighted. He sat down on the kitchen step.

"He said he'd talked to you. I was wondering what you made of this drowning business."

Drake leaned in the doorway.

"Some fool of an intern got hold of the wrong corpse, naturally. Hamilton will probably get a corrected report next week. A man doesn't drown in thin air."

Ben got to his feet. He looked reassured.

"You don't think there was an assailant lurking in the thicket…?"

"With a bucket of water?" Drake snorted.

Ben grinned…almost, it seemed to Drake, as if with relief.

"Okay, you win! I'd better be getting back. I left my car down at the end of the street…didn't want to wake you if you were sleeping…"

He turned and walked off into the dark.

"Liar!" Drake thought. He stared into the dark, though Ben Harrian was no longer visible. "I'd give a nickel to know just why you *were* hanging around here!"

Drake locked the kitchen door and went into the living room. The mantel clock pointed to ten minutes past two.

Drake continued to muse about Ben Harrian as he undressed for bed. There was that dark, sombre air about him that he didn't understand, for one thing. Take Zuelda, now…her face was like an open book. She was everything her husband was not…so full of life and the love of living…but what was the almost passionate affection she expressed for Beverly, a faint glow of which he seemed to feel washed over upon himself? Both the Harrians seemed unusually devoted to the Drakes, though their acquaintanceship was short indeed.

A PROFOUND weariness assaulted Drake's frame. He started as he suddenly recalled the gushing flood in the kitchen. He had been so intent on concealing its presence from Ben that it had slipped his own mind until just now.

What manner of horror was it he had witnessed…what dark rite had he interrupted by his untimely return? Could that rush of…of water, wasn't it?...have any relationship to *them*...be one of them?

How could he ever sleep again with so frightful a question un-answered? He looked at Beverly, the sweet outline of her cheek cuddled against the pillow...then the segmented parts of his night's experience clashed in his brain, burst into jumbled fragments that whirled madly and exploded in ribbons of incandescence upon the darkness of his mind. Drake toppled over in inert slumber.

There were thundershowers the next day and Drake mooned around the house, hating the inclement weather. He blamed his feelings on a night of poor sleep, not realizing he had scarcely slept at all. His mind was confused with a chaotic non-remembrance of racing dreams from which he could isolate no single bizarre scene. He looked out the window at the rain puddles in the yard and street, remembering those other puddles with a vicious kind of wonder.

Drake had little enough to say to Beverly, and she seemed to respect his reticence, though with a puzzled crease between her eyes.

"You've not been feeling well lately, John. I think you ought to stay home from the office tomorrow...take another day of rest..."

He shrugged, switched on the TV and settled himself for a dull afternoon. By and by, the sun came out, the landscape steamed itself dry, and Drake went out for a walk.

He felt impelled, somehow, to stroll up toward the thickety ridge, in the direction Tom Ellers had taken. There was nothing in the wood but damp humus and puddles that glistened among the scrub. The earth was unaccountably dry in a clearing among the brush. It looked somehow familiar, then Drake remembered that here was where they had found Ellers' body.

He threw himself on the ground to rest, turned his eyes up to the sky and balefully studied the few woolly clouds that still lingered after the rain. He was troubled in mind and spirit, possessed of a wonder that went deeply and acutely into his perceptions. He wondered what this impelling wonder was...nothing had been the same since Tom Ellers had come up here on the hill and died...had drowned in a sea of dry grass, brush and trees...

Somehow, Drake felt no sense of personal danger from his sur-roundings. He was completely detached from the physical world as he wrestled with a thing that was in his mind alone. He let his thoughts drift over the events of the night of Ellers' death, tried to correlate them into something that resembled coherence.

The clouds drifted by as the sun declined. Slowly, Drake drifted away and away, until finally he slept in complete exhaustion of brain and body.

DRAKE felt as if he were floating. A strange, bluish luminescence engulfed him, a sparkling blueness, alive with a strange, vital sort of sentience. The sparkles waxed and waned in the blueness, and he was conscious of dim, blue shapes that swam around him. He saw their glistening eyes as they peered at him, felt the presence of naked bodies close to his own, stirring the sluggish medium in which he seemed to float.

Somehow, Drake did not care. He contemplated his surroundings with a mindless apathy. "I'm dreaming, of course," he thought, as one thinks in dreams. "I should wake up and get back to the house. Beverly will be wondering where I am."

But he made no effort to extricate himself from the dream. He allowed himself to drift, blissfully at peace, fully relaxed, a floating mote, an atom, a wretched shell of nothing among the glimmering shapes of the blue void.

Drake's perceptions seemed to sharpen after a time. The limits of the void extended themselves to floor, walls, ceiling. He was in an eerie, blue-lit cavern…the light, which lit it he knew had no physical existence, but was merely an impression of his mind, reaching out with some other-sense to palp the eternal gloom of this rift in the limestone womb of the earth. He smiled to himself for dreaming such a bizarre thing as this, knowing that he dreamed, but accepting the dream for fact, nonetheless.

He seemed to float midway between the floor of the cavern and its stalactite encrusted ceiling. The female shapes, with here and there among them the arrowing form of a male figure, swarmed around him, above, below and on both sides. He became aware then of a thrumming and humming that existed in his mind alone, as the images of the cavern-creatures existed, a wavering, chorus of melody which he identified as coming from the throng about him.

The dream-people were singing to him—a song that welcomed him to the blue-lit cavern under the earth. There was a pathos in their welcome, and a sweetness, and a lulling lure that made his presence there a thing of desire to him.

All at once, a single figure swam out of the crowding myriad, a dainty figure, her hair a cloud of shadow that caressed her shoulders, floated on the too-heavy medium of the cavern atmosphere. Her arms moved slowly, with sinuous grace, as if she actually swam in something that was as if it were water…though even Drake's sleeping mind rejected the thought, for he breathed, and the air of Earth was his medium.

There was something vaguely familiar about the elfin features that closely and more closely approached his own, but his mind was dulled, and he could not place the familiarity of her. She hovered above him—he could have touched her simply by lifting his hand, but he lacked the will to do so. Her hair floated around small, piquant features, blue-gleaming, shapely shoulders. The points of her tiny breasts pressed almost against him.

Her lips smiled, and her eyes caressed him voluptuously. He heard the murmur of her voice deep in his mind, and his perceptions fled before the ecstasy of promise in her words.

"Tonight, while the undines dance, my love...I'll wed you and you'll wed me, as it was done when the world was young..."

Drake threshed, aflame with desire, as her lips met his and clung. He flung his arms up to embrace her, but he embraced nothing, and awoke in the still darkness of the thicket.

He rolled over and sat up, head swimming, eyes still blinded by the blue glare of the dream-cavern. The world was a silent, breathless place, peopled with moveless shadows among the scrub, gashed by the glare of the rising moon...a full moon tonight...a glowing orb that spectacularly lightened the sky to dusty blue and paled the stars.

Drake made to stand, but for some odd reason, his legs refused to support him. He sat panting, his mind's eye still aglow with that world of dream, his inner ear vibrating yet to the luring promise of the witch with the floating hair...the strangely familiar witch who promised herself to him body and...

The moon rose higher and higher on his dazed musing...and the dance of the undines began.

He noticed suddenly how the moonlight sparkled on pools of water that nestled among the scrub. All at once, ripples beset the surfaces of them, though there was no breeze, so that they shimmered and winked like glowing eyes in the darkness...like giant jewels flung strew by some sublime hand.

The pools stirred...and moved. They shifted position with wills of their own, rose in mounds, then in dripping columns and bulging shapes that spun and glistened in the moonlight. Then began a slow, erratic motion, from moon-bright night to densest shadow, back and forth, gliding, slithering, bending, twisting...and slowly the undine shapes took form, became as lovely women, bending and swaying in rhythmic dance. He was swept away by the sight of them in their nakedness, by the song to which they danced, and he became as elemental as these creatures from the blue-lit limestone cavern under the earth...which he knew now had been no dream.

The woman-shapes trouped around him, unearthly in their beauty, breathing the breath of ecstasy into their song. They bent above him, caressing...

A SINGLE light glowed in the living-room window of the Drake house, where Beverly, worried and alone, tried to read a magazine. John had been gone all afternoon and evening...it was nearly midnight.

She fought against the clammy fingers of cold fear that persisted in gripping her. John had gone off today into the thicket...as Tom Ellers had gone...she cast the thought out of her mind. John would have had no reason to stay this long in such a wild place, she told herself. He could have come out of the thicket at anyone of a hundred different places. Perhaps he had taken a notion to stroll over to the Harrian's...the silent telephone mocked her. She could comfort herself, at least, with the thought that perhaps he had. If she called and found that he had not...her heart stilled...then raced at the sound of a step on the porch.

The door rattled in its frame, and a feeling of glad relief thrust through her. Then a natural caution asserted itself. John would be proud of her for her discretion if she called out first...

"Who's there?"

Totally unexpected, Zuelda's voice answered her, muffled by the heavy panel of the door.

"It's Ben and Zuelda, Bev. Let us in, please...quickly!"

Zuelda's voice was not loud, but distraught. Beverly opened up. Zuelda hurled herself into the room, followed closely by her tall, handsome husband.

"When I first heard your knock, I thought..." Beverly began.

"You thought it was Jack!" Zuelda cried. "We know he's gone. Bev...something terrible is happening..."

Beverly felt her throat contract.

"Has something...happened to John...?"

She felt faint. She groped behind her for the davenport and collapsed, stricken, horror staring out of her eyes.

Ben was briskly reassuring.

"Not at all! Beverly! Jack's all right, do you hear me?"

The meaning of his words slowly sank in and color returned to Beverly's cheeks. She gulped. Ben's voice was soothing, gentle, curiously lulling.

Ben turned to Zuelda. "Don't excite her, dear. Would you like a drink?" he asked Bev.

Beverly shook her head wordlessly, wide-eyed. She sat up straight.

"What about...John? Tell me!"

Ben looked at slim, well-kept hands. Zuelda fluttered like a small, frightened bird. She flew to Beverly's side, twittering almost, comforting with her arms.

"What I have to say is going to be difficult for you to understand, Bev. You must forget everything you have been taught as truth and fact...and remember that the scientists do not yet have the universe trapped in a test tube and wrapped up in a coil of wire.

"A long, long time ago, Bev, the world was much different from the world you know. I don't mean it was less civilized, or anything like that, which you know well enough. Perhaps I can make it plain this way— from childhood, you have been familiar with so-called fables and myths of the ancient world...of gods and goddesses, pixies, fairies, fauns, and so on. You must believe me when I say that the fables are founded on solid fact."

Beverly looked puzzled. "What has this to do with John?"

"I am getting to that. You must understand this part first. In the very long ago of which I was speaking, men knew the truth of these things I am telling you, because they actually associated with the beings who later became known as gods, goddesses, and so on.

"In those years, the streams, ponds, rivers and underground watercourses of the Earth were populated by a race of elemental beings called undines...popularly represented as being entirely female, but there were males among them too, naturally."

"You say these things are fact," Beverly put in. "How do you know?"

Ben smiled slightly. "My dear, I am a student of the...occult...a vastly misunderstood word, by the way. It simply means hidden. All my life, I have studied the hidden things...the things that are true but not evident, simply because people refuse to believe in them. The undines may be included in this classification, and they still exist in spite of man's stupid ignorance of them."

His mouth set in a thin, hard line. He mused on his next words.

"We have been watching your house every night, Zuelda and I, since the night Tom Ellers was drowned by the undines."

Beverly straightened with a gasp.

"It wasn't...his heart?"

"I assume John did not tell you. But you must know now. It is important. The undines drowned Ellers because it is their simplest and most effective means of attack against human beings. The fact that Ellers was drowned in a perfectly dry area gave me my first clue that it was the work of undines.

"You see," Ben went on, "the undines have for many centuries been forced to live away from the habitat of man. Man's attitude toward them...his vain pretense of enlightenment...made further contact between the two races impossible. In places far from men, some undines still people the surface waters of Earth, but there are many of them, and not enough isolated waters. So many, indeed, have taken to the streams and pockets of water under the earth. Occasionally, some of them come to the surface, take on human form and mingle a while with men, but they cannot stay too long away from their natural medium...a few months at most. In order to stay longer requires the peculiar spiritual nature possessed by man alone."

"I don't understand," Beverly interrupted quietly.

"You have heard a great deal of talk," Ben shrugged, "about something called the human soul. It is not exactly what you and the greater part of mankind think it is...there are not even words in the language to describe its exact nature. Anyway, no undine possesses this something called a soul."

A light of dawning comprehension gleamed in Beverly's blue eyes.

"I know! They can get a soul by marrying a human being!"

BEN smiled again, slowly. "That is how the fables phrase it. It is true in a sense, but only in the manner of speaking. We are speaking of perfectly natural powers now, and not of mythical beings and mythical souls. The human soul, as we must call it, is as real as the electricity that lights that lamp. It is a force or power that can be used, transferred, and otherwise treated like any other source of energy.

"The undines have a ritual of marriage with human beings, by which the mind-force of the group acts upon the individual human being to absorb him or her into the race of undines. In doing so, the human being is forced to give up that focus of living energy he calls his soul, which may then be trapped into the service of a waiting undine. Have I made myself clear?"

Beverly stared. Her mouth worked. "This...this marriage ceremony is some kind of witchcraft that will change a man into an undine...and the undine he 'marries' into a human being with a soul?"

"Precisely! Tonight, the undines celebrate the marriage of their queen with your husband."

Beverly's eyes blazed. Her lips tightened, white-edged.

"She can't do that! John is married to *me!*"

"The marriage of the undines is only a travesty on human marriage. The two have nothing in common. Unless we act to prevent it, the queen of the undines tonight will gain a soul…and Jack will become an immortal, soulless undine."

He held up a warning hand as Beverly attempted to speak.

"We've been watching, as I said before, and twice already—last night and the night before—Jack has kept a secret rendezvous with the undines in the thicket, where they have made an entrance to their watery world under the surface. Tonight is the last night…your husband is with them now. We need your help, Zuelda and I…we need your human soul as a catalyst in what we have to do. Will you come with us into the thicket…now?"

There was a long silence. Beverly said, hollowly, "I…I can't believe a word you've said! I…"

"Don't try. Just come with us and do as I tell you."

"Now…?"

"Now!… You want to save Jack's life, don't you?"

The bluntness of his statement shattered her reserve, penetrated where his other arguments had not. She acquiesced with vehemence. A minute later, the three picked their way cautiously through the moonlight and shadow of the dreaming thicket.

At first, Beverly could see nothing but a moonlit glade among the scrub, grass blades turned to the moon, glowing as if powdered with diamond dust. Beyond the glade, the shadows were deep and dark, and there was an uncanny stillness on the warm night air.

Ben halted her with a light touch, whispered to her to sit. Beverly obeyed, puzzled, frightened, as she peered out on the empty glade. Then Ben Harrian leaned over her and murmured something softly, a few syllables she did not quite catch. Before Beverly could ask him to repeat, she drew her breath in sharply at sight of the dancing figures, afire with moonglow, with which the glade seemed to be filled.

"These are the undines," Ben hissed. "Watch them well! Remain here…don't move or make a sound, no matter what you may see or hear. Remember…your husband's life is at stake out there…"

Then she heard the brush rustle softly as Ben departed in one direction and Zuelda in another, circling the glade as if to surround it with the three of them.

Moment by moment her eyes accustomed themselves to the treacherous light. Now she made out more plainly the dancing troupe, saw their nakedness, the lasciviousness of their gestures and dance. She could not guess how many there were…perhaps a couple of dozen…perhaps as many as fifty or more. That they were lovely she could see at a glance…lovely, graceful, and possessed of an appeal that made even her pulses quicken.

WITH joyous abandon, the undines danced in the moonlight, and, as if from far away, the sound of their singing penetrated to the ear of her mind, wailing and wonderful, utterly sweet beyond measure, throbbing with undertones of passion and grief.

It seemed to Beverly that the words of the song were half understood by her, and the undines were wailing their farewell to the queen they loved, promising a welcome to the one who was to take her place among them.

The dancing group swirled apart for a moment, and Beverly saw her husband, seated on the floor of the glade. His face was toward her, but lifted, so that the moon caught his expression in full brilliance, and she saw his lips parted in a grimace of ecstasy, his hands clutching the turf with agonized fervor.

Beverly's breath came in short gasps. She felt sticky and wet with a perspiration of anxiety. She leaned forward, peering through the shadows of the scrub, into that moonlit glade in the heart of the thicket.

Around and around the undines danced, their song growing louder, trilling more sweetly as it filled with the ecstasy of the marriage bed. The bride was coming, the song related, to meet her groom.

The bride—it must be she, Beverly thought with a jealous pang—drifted from the press of dancers, alone into the center of the circle they made. Which it was, Beverly could not tell, for the creature had her back turned, her dark hair a floating cloud about her naked shoulders. Her body swayed voluptuously to the tempo of the dance; her arms and legs writhed to the pulse of melody. The queen of the undines approached Drake, who awaited her in eager expectation.

Beverly's breath caught in her throat. It was all she could do to keep from crying out and rushing into the glade. She restrained herself with an effort, trembling, panting, her eyes straining to realize the tableau.

Any woman would know what the dancer's gestures meant...and Beverly shuddered with revulsion as she saw her husband responding. Slowly the undine bride with averted face circled her waiting groom; then she seemed to melt downward as she flung herself writhing at Drake's feet. Her body twisted—white arms reached out to embrace him as he hurled himself upon her.

Harsh upon the sudden stillness that followed cessation of the undine song, a man's voice boomed across the clearing. Beverly started with wonder and relief. It was Ben's voice, and he was chanting something not understandable, a semi-song of rolling syllables that had the sound of some ancient tongue long dead upon the face of the Earth.

What she expected, Beverly did not know, but she was not prepared for the sudden vanishment that occurred. One moment, the undines circled in a refulgent splendor of silvery flesh, in their midst an obscene spectacle of lewdness against which Beverly shut her eyes in horror and disgust. When she looked again, impelled by the silence, the glade was empty, a slice of moonlight carved out of the shadow.

Beverly fainted then, and was only dimly conscious of Ben's arms supporting her as he carried her back through the thicket to the house. She was also vaguely aware of softly thudding footsteps that followed, Zuelda's footsteps, light and indistinct on the deadening humus.

"Put her in the bedroom," Zuelda directed crisply, turning on the lights as they went through the house.

Ben deposited his burden on the bed and turned to leave the room.

"Undress her. She will be all right. She is sleeping naturally."

He went out and waited in the living room, turning off the overhead light, leaving the room dimly lit by a small television lamp on the console. Zuelda joined him softly.

He whirled, seized her arms in a fierce paroxysm of passion. His eyes gleamed fervidly in the half-light. Zuelda did not draw away. She collapsed against him, turned her face up to his with a smile of luxurious triumph. Her eyes were half-veiled, somnolent, flickering with nameless fires.

"How does it feel?" he cried hoarsely, devouring her with his eyes. *"How does it feel?"*

She laughed throatily, did a dancing pirouette out of his grasp, and threw herself breathless on the davenport.

"Not like going through the sump pump last night. That *tickled!*"

"You tried to rush things last night," he accused her. "You put us off a whole day."

"What is a day...in eternity?"

He regarded her somberly, half across the space of the living room.

"You *can* feel it?"

"Of course I can! You will know what it feels like...by and by..."

He lunged at her, seized her shoulders, shook her.

"Tell me!"

She arched her back, like a cat stretching. Her mouth was red and wide with soundless laughter, eyes closed to gleaming slits.

"Wonderful, darling! Oh...wonderful...to have a soul!"

He retreated, an enigmatic smile twisting his handsome, unhuman face. He cocked his head listening.

"It is worth the trouble then...and now, the undines sing..."

The undines were outside the house and in it, below it and on all sides, dancing their endless dance, trilling the bridal song of the blue-lit caverns of limestone far down in the earth.

Ben squared his shoulders, murmured to his wife.

"Now that *you* have a soul, you will be the catalyst for me..."

His eyes held hers and she laughed without sound again, red lips parted, pointed white teeth gleaming in the lamplight.

"Hurry..." she whispered, "...and come back to me!"

The somberly handsome undine turned, stepped toward the bedroom...

JOHN DRAKE opened his eyes in the cavern of blue spangles and encrusted limestone walls. Full memory was his now. The charm that had held him powerless had acted upon that other side of him...that part of him which was his no longer. He was an undine...as soulless as these others who swam around him, peering curiously, pathetically half-afraid, wishing to make him welcome, yet not daring the possibility of his wrath.

It was peculiar, Drake thought, that he did not feel angry. He fully understood how he had been duped, and by whom, but his mind viewed the situation with a logical philosophy. He was without emotion...and it occurred to him that perhaps that had been taken from him, along with that other...his soul. The word echoed flatly in the corridors of his thinking.

The tragic enormity of his transgression in the ethereal glade he reviewed with a calm deliberation. He remembered well the dancing undines, the poignant sweetness of their song, remembered again the ecstasy of that joyous embrace of the queen of the water-world...then he felt again in memory the sharp pangs of dissolution, felt himself flowing away into the dark earth, a watery substance that fled through minute interstices of the clay, into the phosphorescent blue sanctuary of the limestone underworld.

Remorse and disgust bit him, these being not emotions but states of mind. He knew that the life force...the soul...erstwhile his, now caressed the body and spirit of Zuelda Harrian, while her husband...he knew that, too.

The undines flashed away from him as he moved suddenly...and then he heard them singing again, their unheard voices lifted in the pagan lilt of their betrothal song.

He knew he must go...or spend eternity in this blue-lit water-world with Beverly...and the undines.

The throng was streaming away from him now, arrowing upward in full song, and Drake hurtled in the midst of them, came out with them in the moonlit glade, and flowed down the thicketed slope toward the lighted house.

Drake cast his other-sense ahead of him, palping the night for the last act of this unhuman drama.

While the undines danced, he glided and ran. He was half a man-shape when he reached the house, a water blob of a man that shone in the unwavering moonlight. He found the door and hurled it open, flung himself into the living room.

Zuelda sat with eyes closed upon the davenport, attuned to the rapture of the undine song. Drake's uncouth entry startled her into outcry. She flung herself erect.

"Jack!"

Drake halted. "So you were my bride tonight." He chuckled obscenely. "I rather think you left me at the altar, my dear!"

"No!" she gasped. "*No!*"

She voiced not a denial of his statement, but a frantic rejection of the intent she read in his mind.

"You wouldn't *dare!*"

"But I would dare," Drake mimicked her tone softly. "You forgot a few things, my pretty bride. You forgot that when you took the vital essence of my life, you took also the means by which you could control me!"

Her eyes were big and dark, pits of smoldering despair. She backed in a half-circle around him. The blood had drained from her face, taking with it her sparkling vivacity, the color of her beauty, leaving her cheeks sallow, sagging, quivering with alarm.

"I'm going to do to you," he said deliberately, "what you did to Tom Ellers out there in the thicket. Because he had a soul...and was human...he could die. You killed him then, because he came upon you taking form in the glade, and he knew you for what you are..." He chuckled with a tinge of bitterness. "Poor old devil...you were using him just for show to work me into the proper psychological mood, but you forgot to control him. Maybe if it hadn't been for him, I wouldn't have had enough on my mind to come back here from your blue cavern..." He paused.

"Jack!" Zuelda whispered desperately. "Ben is in the bedroom with..."

He laughed savagely.

"Another thing you forget, Zuelda...that I am an undine now. I can

109

see where poor humans can not. He is standing on the other side of the door, in quite as much of a funk as you are. But *you* have the soul, see? *My* soul...and I want it back. You can die now, remember, like Tom Ellers died..."

"If you kill me," she whispered in ghastly panic, "you will lose your soul forever!"

"You won't die, my dear. I won't let you...not for a long time. Drowning is not a pleasant death...but you wouldn't know anything about dying. You will learn, though...or go back to your hole in the ground!"

She moved swiftly to dart past him, into the kitchen. Drake elongated his body into a shining ribbon of water. A watery pseudopod burst from his side and plunged against her face, choking the scream that welled into her throat. His other hand, semisolid, held her fast.

"I wish the sheriff could see this," he murmured into her threshing hair. "He'd see how a man can drown without getting his clothes wet!"

Zuelda struggled piteously, floundering in his aqueous grip.

The bedroom door burst open. Ben Harrian was wild-eyed, ferocious of countenance.

"Will she let me kill her, Ben?" Drake taunted.

Alarm flooded Ben's unhumanly handsome features.

"Don't do it, Jack!"

"She can give it up...if she wants to. She is drowning now, Ben."

Ben didn't move. He called out, "Zuelda!"

The sound of water gargling in Zuelda's lungs was horrid answer to his call.

"Zuelda! Don't let him do it, darling! Give it up...hear? Let him have the damned thing back...it's probably bound for Hell, anyway!" He glared fiercely at Drake's shining form. "Give it back to him, and we'll go back to our world and our people together..."

Zuelda relaxed in Drake's grip. Her body began to lose form and substance. He knew that she had assented to her husband's plea with the last gasp of life in her tissues. Drake held his grip. He must not let go too soon.

The undine was a column of madly churning water between his hands. The base of it spread; the water-column collapsed...and *something* came out of it, like the song comes out of a bird, boisterous, vital, filled with a splendor of being.

Drake caught it, enfolded it with himself, made himself whole once more.

He stood erect, his hands empty. He was solid flesh and blood, sturdy boned...and only now did he know in full how much he had lost...and how much regained...

He swayed, naked in his own living room. There were no dancing undines anywhere. Zuelda was gone. Ben was gone. There was only a lilting splash of water flowing down the kitchen steps, and then that was gone.

Drake found that he was shaking. He went into the bedroom, looked down at Beverly sleeping, touched the soft, pale curve of her cheek. The westering moon shone full upon her. Her lips tilted in a tender smile, as if in her dreams she responded to a suggestive, unheard song...

"She knows," Drake thought, "but she won't remember...I can thank them for that, at least. I won't have to tell her, either...and I won't..."

He half-turned, cocked an ear toward the thickety ridge, seeing again the passionate surge of the undines' dance, hearing the elfin lure of their song. But it was only in fancy that he saw and heard. All was silent...no, not silent...there was sound that came to his earthly ears...the shrill music of tree frogs, the trilling of crickets, and booming above them all, the rasping scream of a cicada as it yielded its life to the predacious assault of some horny-limbed horror in the moonlight.

THE INSISTENT GHOST

By
EMIL PETAJA

A ghostly figure rippled like so many phosphorescent sea worms on a glassy night ocean...

SEAGULLS, their bellies filled with herring spawn, halted their greedy peregrinations long enough to perch on Tessa Alder's faded sign, and not infrequently to add a brief comment to Tessa's corny but commercially sound device for luring tourists and townspeople into her little gift and book shop. Her beloved landlord would do nothing at all to relieve the peeled, dilapidated condition of the double-flat's facade (or indeed any other part of the house) so Tessa, with her usual delicate counterbalance of shrewd realism and affection for whimsy, painted the legend "YE OLDE GHOSTE SHOPPE" on an old piece of driftwood, and set it to swinging on the low brick wall in front of her window. Occasionally, when some young couple breathlessly asked her who haunted the shop and why, she would blandly improvise something appropriate.

Today, the sky having produced rain several times already, remained bleak and gusty and portentous. Inside the shop Tessa was giving her friend Verbena Smith tea.

"Artists sometimes take poison. Don't they, Verbena?" Tessa was asking, in her invariably mild sweet way.

As a matter of fact they had been discussing last night's movie, a lavish musical. Verbena Smith smoothed down her lavender ruffles and smiled uncertainly. She wished Tessa would not ramble so. People frequently asked her if Tessa Alder wasn't just a little off her head and Verbena's no was not always as convincing as it might be. But she did enjoy taking tea with Tessa, and going to the movies with her. Then, too, Tessa was *old*—Tessa was sixty-seven, while she was only sixty-one.

"More tea, darling?" Tessa asked, when Verbena, in her old maid's brown study, neglected to answer her.

Verbena shook her head and sipped from her eggshell cup significantly. Tessa hummed as she reached behind the little coal stove for her own special earthen pot and poured herself a third cup. Verbena coughed to conceal her smile. Tessa was so odd. She would serve herself from that ugly earthen pot behind the stove, whereas guests were served from the pretty China pot with the cosy on it, the jaunty red and yellow cosy Verbena herself had knitted Tessa for Christmas. Well, it was likely her way of indicating that her guests were better than she was. Verbena was willing to accept this judgment.

The pursed grimace she put forth to camouflage all this mental activity was intended to be a gracious smile. She would string along with Tessa's odd fancies, humor the poor thing.

"Sometimes they hang themselves," she tittered.

"Who—ah—oh, yes! What I meant, Verbena, is that artists are peculiar. They get so intense about their work, and then when their paintings don't sell and nobody even wants to look at them—" She tilted her dark eyebrows significantly.

Verbena smiled.

"I know who you're thinking about. You're thinking about the young man in the flat upstairs."

"Mr. Teufel. Perhaps. He *is* an artist—and come to think, I don't imagine he sells many paintings."

"He doesn't sell any," Verbena corrected. "We were discussing him only yesterday at the Ladies' Sewing and Bridge Club."

"Oh?"

"Mrs. Abernathy's husband knows all about him. He can't pay his rent. He can't pay for anything. He tried to get a loan from the bank, but Mr. Abernathy wouldn't give him one because of course he has no security. Imagine him trying to put up some of his outlandish pictures as security! Mr. Abernathy said if Mr. Heckle, the grocer, wants to be silly and exchange food for those ridiculous daubs of his, let him. As for Mrs. Abernathy's husband's *bank*—"

"Poor Mr. Teufel."

Tessa wagged her head and poured herself more tea.

"What I say is why doesn't he go to work? Oh, Tessa, there's another seagull on your sign."

"Let him," Tessa said recklessly. "What else are the dear ladies doing these days, Verbena?"

"Oh, they're doing some marvelous things for the community, Tessa. Our bazaar alone made enough to plant flowers all along the boardwalk over the city dump and keep the Bird Fanciers going for another year at least."

"Poor Mr. Teufel." Evidently Tessa's thoughts were jammed on an earlier track.

"Why do you keep saying that, Tessa?" Verbena found Tessa's vagueness' very irritating. What she had really hoped from this tea was to acquire some new tidbit to dispense at the card party tonight. "Surely you must know something about Mr. Teufel by this time, something the rest of us don't. Something *definite.*"

"I never eavesdrop," Tessa said.

"Of course not, but—" Verbena wiggled her cup impatiently.

"But I don't have to with Mr. Teufel. He has a phonograph and he plays it very loudly at all hours. And you can hear every footstep up there, the ceiling is so thin."

VERBENA set her cup down and cocked an ear upwards. "I don't hear a thing."

"Mr. Teufel is sleeping."

"At three o'clock!"

"Mr. Teufel always sleeps 'til four. I imagine he paints better at night, although I always thought artists preferred sunlight to artificial light."

Verbena sniffed. "With the junk he paints I don't know what difference it makes. All great gobs of nasty colors with no pictures to them, at *all.*"

"Anyway I wish he'd paint in the daytime," Tessa sighed. "I have to put a pillow over my head to get to sleep, with all that clumping around and that wild music."

"Any visitors?" Verbena leaned forward. "Any *girl* visitors?"

"Not that I know of. I doubt if poor Mr. Teufel has any visitors at all."

"Oh." Verbena lost her gleam. She stood up briskly. "Well, dear, I must run along home and feed Poo."

"Your cat," Tessa said, without relish. There was more chitchat at the door, and out along the rococo veranda. Tessa watched her gossip-loving guest mince around the pools of water remaining in the sunken portions of the brick patio and destined for early refills. All at once came a great clatter of army surplus shoes over Tessa's head, down the open stairs leading to the upper flat. Lean Mr. Teufel swooped past Verbena so rapidly that Verbena's umbrella lost its moorings and went skittering and bobbing down the walk.

The artist's gaunt face lifted in the semblance of a smile when he retrieved and handed it back to her. Verbena emitted an explosive little shriek and drew back, as if Mr. Teufel had been a springing cobra.

Mr. Teufel scowled and said, "Boo!"

Verbena fled.

Mr. Teufel looked at Tessa and grinned. Tessa smiled politely, then went in the shop and poured herself another drink from the earthen pot.

After a while, sitting there and watching the day gradually droop and vanish, Tessa became quite tiddly. The sun made a last lavish gesture just before it dipped behind the Farallons. Its burst of brilliance highlighted Alcatraz and the populous hills of San Francisco, and put color to the muddy masses of clouds that hemmed in the East Bay horizon. While this was everyday stuff to Tessa, she was not entirely oblivious to its spectacle, and now, when the brilliance was blotted out and the Bay presented the appearance of something shrouded and good as dead, she shivered. There were seagulls, many seagulls, wheeling ambiguously across the heavy sky. But they were like vultures, and the sound they made, like that last fling of sunlight, only intensified the melancholy assurance of death...

TESSA started thinking about Herb. It was time to start thinking about him.

She poured herself another cup of sherry from the earthen pot and let him take over her thoughts. He would anyway.

Thinking about her dead husband had its amusing aspects, when you came right down to it. Maybe that was why she allowed him to keep possession of her emotions and her thoughts now, even as he had while he was alive. Oh yes. Herb had been a greedy man that way. He had expected Tessa to give him first consideration in every instance, even in her most secret thoughts. In a way she had, too. And there was no reason to assume that Herb's character had undergone any change now that he was dead, even if his physical self had. No, Herb could never change. He would remain as cantankerous, as selfish, as vindictive as ever, until there was no more anything at all.

Of course she had loved him.

He was handsome, bold, amusing. He captured her fancy completely. It was later, years later, when these traits blossomed forth and enveloped her with what was apparently a studied desire to strangle her and crush her.

But Tessa didn't crush easily. For all her flights of whimsy, Tessa was an intensely practical woman. So practical as to drive Herb insane with rage at times. She refused to accept surface excuses and reasons, dissecting each one to its very core. She saw into Herb as if he were made of plastic, and after a while that made him hate her. He couldn't lie to her and foist off cheap excuses or third-class reasoning on her. She always saw what was underneath and indicated she did, in her calm sweet voice.

When his heart went bad—mainly from self-indulgence in spite of his doctor's stern periodic admonishments—he blamed Tessa. She should have stopped him. How she could have done this, particularly with a self-willed individual like himself, was something Herb never bothered to consider. He had to blame somebody, besides himself, so he blamed Tessa. He took it out on her both in petty vindictiveness, and by a constant stream of ill-temper that would surely have crushed and destroyed a less valiant creature than wiry little Tessa.

He lost his handsomeness. The lines in his face, which had formerly suggested swaggering boldness, turned to visual evidences of mean suspicion and lurking sadism. He couldn't work, so Tessa invested the little money he hadn't squandered or needed for doctors in "YE OLDE GHOSTE SHOPPE." She made it pay, too. Not much, to be sure, but enough to keep them independent, if she were very careful.

One thing association with Herb had done for Tessa—good or bad—it had given her a taste for sherry, even mediocre sherry. There were so many remembered times when it had proved a great solace. But after Herb became really ill, so ill that he could do nothing but sit in his chair and let Tessa wait on him hand and foot while he raged and bellowed about the condition of the world and about Tessa's inadequacies, there was no more sherry. None for Herb. It would have killed him. None for her because Herb couldn't have any. They couldn't afford luxuries, to be sure, but a thimbleful of sherry now and then wouldn't have made much difference. But Herb said no, and it was folly to cross him.

Herb was a dog in the manger other ways, too. He didn't want Tessa to take a stroll down the breakwater, or go to the movies, or have any friends. Every facet of her existence must belong to him.

Tessa wanted an occasional glass of sherry, she wanted to see Gregory Peck's latest, she wanted to hear Verbena's newest gossip. She wanted to very much. But Herb always provided logical (to him) reasons why she shouldn't have these things. And it was so much easier to let him have his way. It was easier to stay home and wait on him and listen to his invalid grumblings, because if she didn't Herb would surely make her pay for it—some way.

THIS insistence on revenge for disobedience was carried to fantastic lengths. Herb was very near-sighted, so near-sighted that he couldn't even read any longer. But he seemed to develop an uncanny second-sight about everything Tessa did. He had to know everything that went on, every tiny little thing. He distrusted all her actions. He would accuse Tessa of stinting him on cream for his gruel. She was saving it for herself—or for somebody who would slip in later. Then he would proceed to take it out on her. Always he must have his revenge, even when the reason for it existed only in his imagination.

Little things, surely. And yet little horrors, piled one on top of the other, *ad infinitum*, can lead to desperation...

Tessa began to dream, and in all her dreams there was no Herb. He just wasn't there. And being essentially a practical person her dreams began to lean toward reality. Herb was near-sighted. For this reason and for selfish reasons he insisted on having a hodge-podge collection of items on a large round table near his chair. Besides his heart medicine, there was salt and catsup and mustard and picture books and a kaleidoscope—and any number of other things.

One day when Herb picked up a vinegar bottle and started spooning vinegar into the water glass Tessa had brought for his medicine, Tessa's dreams began to take definite shape. She knew about the other medicine bottle in the bathroom, the medicine that was not poison but would surely kill a person with a serious heart condition. And she knew just how to provoke Herb into waiting on himself when it came time for his medicine.

Tessa wouldn't kill Herb. Oh, no. But she would make it convenient for him to kill himself.

The dangerous medicine bottle found its way onto Herb's cluttered table. It became an interesting gamble to see just how long it would be before Herb drank some of that, believing it to be his own medicine. Tessa invented excuses for being out of the room at medicine time, then peeked between the dining room drapes behind Herb to see what happened. It was always a breathless moment. Then she would breathe a sigh of relief when Herb picked the good bottle. After several months the strained sigh of relief became just a sigh.

A year or so went by. It seemed longer. Tessa dreamed harder than ever. Not only would she be able to have her sherry again when Herb was gone, but there would be more money to afford it. During this long period of waiting and dreaming Tessa determined that *if* anything happened she would never stint herself. She would go to bed tiddly from sherry every night. She would!

It happened finally and she did.

TESSA put her cup down, regretfully, and prepared to shut up shop for the night. Humming snatches of old songs all mixed together; she took the "Open" sign out of the window, locked the shop door, and snapped off the light.

Outside the seagulls made patterns on the wind. The tide rushed in on the breakwater. Tessa's driftwood sign creaked gently. Tiny drops of vagrant rain smeared the darkness.

Tessa found her way to bed by feeling the walls, the drapes, the familiar jumble of too much furniture. She went to sleep like a baby. There was nothing to prevent. No Herb, with his querulous rasp. No Mr. Teufel, with his wild phonograph music and his clumping. Mr. Teufel was out. And the contents of the earthen pot had made her all warm and cosy inside.

But that warmth wore off—and then something cold, something ice cold, entered the dark room. It was the room Tessa and Herb had shared for so many years. And now the coldness made her shiver and waken. She yawned and half-sat up.

"Herb?" she called, after a long moment. "Is that you?"

There was no other sign—only the cold wind. But somehow she *knew*. All those years with him had given her a sixth sense where Herb was concerned. She could feel those muddy gray half-blind eyes watching her as they had when he was alive. Crafty, suspicious, vindictive.

"Herb!" She was not afraid, no. But she was startled and uneasy. It wasn't nice of Herb to come back like this. Her voice cut the darkness sharply. "I know you're there, sitting in that same chair, just as you always did. Well? Why don't you answer me?"

Still no answer.

All the same she knew he was there in that big ugly chair of his. She had meant to get rid of that chair right after the funeral, but somehow she hadn't got to it.

"Herb Alder! I know you're in this room! You might as well let me see you."

Her neck muscles twitched. She knew something strange was about to happen. It did happen. Even though this middle room was closed in so that there was no stray light from the outside at all she knew just where to look, and she was looking there. The chair began to glow. It was an untidy unrelated mass of phosphorescence, first, then it took shape and became Herb. She could still see the chair behind him; it was as if he were etched on plastic.

"Took you long enough," Tessa greeted him. "What are you up to? Oh, I see. You are back to spy on me, again. To keep track of everything I do, as you did before. Well, let me tell you, Herb. Last night I went to the movies. With Verbena. Yes, and I've seen her nearly every day since you died. And I've been drinking sherry, too. Lots of sherry, Herb. Like you couldn't have and wouldn't let me have. How do you like that, Herb?"

The figure in the chair didn't like it. It clouded up redly and elongated, as if to reach out for her.

Tessa began to laugh.

"Trying to frighten me, are you? Let me tell you this, Herb. You never did scare me, with all your yelling and snarling. You didn't then and you don't now."

She paid no attention to the ghost's feral gyrations. She had always wanted to tell Herb off. Now that he was dead she could. She flared up in a flame of righteous triumph.

"I put up with you a long time, Herb. With your childish tantrums and your petty suspicions. And your little revenge when you thought I was neglecting you or slighting you. Well, I got my share of revenge too! Do you know how, Herb? Haven't they told you where you are?"

The ghostly figure rippled like so many phosphorescent sea-worms on a glassy night ocean.

"Surprise, surprise, Herb!" Tess chortled, nearly hysterical by now with this supreme adventure of telling Herb off. "It was I who killed you, Herb! It was *I* who put that bad medicine on your cluttered table. I had to wait a long time for you to pick that bottle. But the gamble kept me amused while I waited. What do you say to all that, Herb?"

Herb expressed himself by elongating almost to the ceiling. He made himself into a luminescent tower of rage. His lips moved and although no spoken words came out he seemed to be saying: *I suspected as much. That's why I came back. Now I know for certain and now…*

"What can you do about it now, Herb?"

Tessa taunted him. "What can you do?"

She fell back, rocking with laughter.

A faint wisp of light entered the room, a tenuous harbinger of daylight. A blast of freezing cold swept the room and just before Herb vanished, Tessa was sure she heard him rasp:

"I always have my revenge, Tessa. Make the most of your freedom, because you have only until tomorrow night…"

TESSA lagged about her duties the next day. Try as she might she could never quite erase those words from her mind. Her head was fuzzy, too, from over-indulgence in the tea department the day before. She had been a fool to *tell* Herb she killed him! What a stupid thing to do! And now, typically, he wanted his revenge. That ugly rasped threat! *Tomorrow night…*

He wasn't giving her much time, was he?

The more she thought about it the uneasier she became. She hadn't a very dear idea just what Herb could do to her, dead and all. But he would do something. Trust Herb. And it wouldn't be at all nice.

Her frugal lunch of cottage cheese and canned peaches was interrupted by the strident tinkle of the cat-bell over the shop door. She hurried out in front.

"Can I help you?"

It was a young couple, happy honeymooners, trying to match their delirious mood in her quaint little shop, inasmuch as the lowering skies outside did not.

"Tell me, is the shop really haunted?" the girl twittered.

"Yes." Tessa frowned. It used to be rather fun, building up sham gothic romances for tourists. Not now.

"Really?" The new bride bubbled over. Her husband winked at her fondly.

"Who haunts it?" he asked Tessa.

"My husband."

"No!" The bride, fondling her new husband's lapel, assumed interest in the shelf nearest her to hide her smile. "Look, dear. Isn't this just the darlingest little Chinese elephant?"

"If you think so, sweet. Why does he haunt it?" The young man's lips twitched suspiciously.

"He wants revenge," Tessa found herself blurting. "He was murdered, and he's come back to—"

"Who murdered him?" The young man peeled off a dollar for the elephant.

Tessa took it, staring at him. "Nobody!" she snapped. "It's just a story!"

They left, the bride cooing about the quaintness of the shop and the darlingness of the driftwood sign and wasn't Tessa the cutest thing. Tessa picked up the nearest object to hand with the idea of hurling it after them. It turned out to be the earthen pot, and it wasn't quite empty. So she sank back in the chair by the window and had a slug.

Two more and she began to relax.

She must think, think, *think*. What did Herb have up his ghostly sleeve, and how was she going to circumvent him? It was past one already. Not much time…

Think fast, Tessa!

Something sifted into her thoughts, interrupting them. Music. Dirge-like music from upstairs. At this hour! Mr. Teufel was actually up at one-thirty, playing his blankety-blank phonograph. The dirge ended and was followed by some wild modern dissonances. Tessa couldn't help listening. After a while it struck her that there was some insidious pattern to Mr. Teufel's selection of music. It all suggested a particular train of emotion. And when a scratchy, banal interpretation of *Good-bye* began to smite her eardrums Tessa leaped to her feet.

By the time it repeated for the third time Tessa was upstairs peeking through the bamboo slats into Mr. Teufel's studio.

"Mr. Teufel, no!" she exclaimed. "You mustn't do that!"

The young artist was inside, busily engaged in hanging himself from the middle rafter.

TESSA banged on the door without result, so she whipped out her own door keys and tried them. One of them, with the added impetus of a severe inward push, sent her plunging through.

The studio was sizable but dreary. The bare floor made it ice cold, and the artist's furnishings consisted mainly of nail kegs and orange crates. Somehow the gay bohemian dash was utterly lacking. True, there was half-completed oil on his easel, but the canvas had been slashed across as if in a spasm of despondent rage.

"You stop that right now," she told the emaciated young man on the nail keg. Mr. Teufel was endeavoring to thrust his head into an ill-made noose of clothesline rope.

"Why should I?" he demanded, scowling down at her.

"For one thing you're not doing it right," Tessa told him. "Always put the noose around your neck first then wrap the rope twice around the rafter, overloop, and—never mind!" she finished off tartly.

"What are we waiting for, oh, my heart?" queried the tenor dismally. *"...the leaves must fall, and the lambs must die..."*

Tessa snapped him off. His voice deepened and mushed out and vanished. The artist stared at her sullenly, then collapsed his lanky frame to a sitting position on the keg. Tessa marched about the room briskly. Mr. Teufel's studio was an exact replica of her own bedroom, except for the lack of furniture and the rafters. Paint it up a little, apply a few rugs and pictures, and it would be livable.

Tessa turned her attention to the artist.

"You make an awful amount of noise nights," she reprimanded him. "Don't you realize you're supposed to sleep nights and work days?"

"Then why didn't you let me go through with it?" he demanded bitterly. "Suppose you go downstairs now and forget what you saw." He brightened perceptibly.

"That wouldn't help," Tessa said. "You need furniture. The place is like a barn."

"I need a lot of things—including talent." He got up and began to pace. The clump of his army surplus shoes on the bare floor was all too familiar, although easier to take here than downstairs. Pacing up and down was, then, one of the best things Mr. Teufel did. And his self-expressed lack of talent was the bone of contention.

"Who says you have no talent?" Tessa's sharp eyes traveled to a nearby corner, to a heap of canvases carelessly tossed therein. They, like the one on the easel, had been slashed across.

"Everybody says so," the artist growled irritably. "Yesterday was my last chance to prove to myself that I might someday be an artist, even a passable good artist. A critic from Paris was visiting San Francisco. All the others said I stink, but Charles Demeaux is notoriously aloof from them. He helped a friend of mine once, a nobody like me, just on the strength of what he saw in his paintings. My friend told him about me, and yesterday a letter came saying Charles Demeaux would see me if I could get over there yesterday, as he was leaving today. I waited until twelve-thirty last night in the rain, until he came home from the ballet. Demeaux was very kind. He fed me I don't know how many crepe suzettes and how many glasses of wine. But when it came to my paintings—"

"He didn't like them?"

A spasm of utter misery crossed the artist's gaunt face. "He didn't say it like that. He was too kind, too polite. But that's what it boiled down to. No talent. No expression. No future in art. Nothing!"

Mr. Teufel was plainly a man obsessed. His world had crumbled. Tessa made a tentative effort to cheer him up.

"There must be other critics. Maybe you are ahead of your time."

"They all pretend that." Mr. Teufel's lip curled. "Not me. At least I can be honest with myself. I'm no good. I never have been and I never will be."

"Of course I don't exactly understand—" Tessa said soothingly.

"No, you don't!" Mr. Teufel raged. "You don't know a damn thing about it, so why don't you get the hell out of here and leave me alone? Nobody understands anything! The world is full of sadistic morons who pretend to mean well. Bah! Bring on your atom bombs! The sooner the better!"

Tessa's sharp eyes widened, then closed.

"Well?" Mr. Teufel glared at her scornfully. "Aren't you going to go call the police or something?"

"Nope," Tessa said. "I've got a job for you."

Mr. Teufel's expression told her what he thought of work. Tessa just waited.

"Well, if I'm forced to delay my departure I guess I'll have to eat sometime. What kind of a job?"

"I want you to help me move some furniture. Yes, I'm giving it to you, Mr. Teufel—in return for a small favor."

TESSA slept well that night. She went to sleep brimming over with great satisfaction in having done a good deed. There was nothing, she told herself before Morpheus took over, quite as edifying to a human being as having performed a kindness for another human being.

Near dawn she woke with a start. The thought that awakened her was the illusion that she had missed her cue that her alarm clock hadn't gone off, that she had left a dangerous heater burning all night. *Something...*

And yet full consciousness assured her it was actually none of those things.

The springs creaked as she hiked herself up on the pillows. She cast her eyes about the darkness but she saw no shred of light anywhere. It was as if she had just missed hearing something.

"Herb?"

Her whisper vibrated into the dark, but there was no answer.

Then it came, a far-off sound like a sigh. Or was it only a seagull calling mournfully over the dark waters? Tessa chose to think it wasn't a seagull. She folded aside the covers and slid her legs down on the shag rug. Her feet groped for her sheepskin-lined slippers and invaded them. Without snapping on a light she found her robe and wrapped it around her. A habitual toss of her long black hair to unsnarl it from the collar and she went to the outside door.

She idled a second or two, listening to the swirling sucking noises the tide made as it drained away from the rocks, then she pattered to Mr. Teufel's door and listened.

She heard nothing.

She applied her key and pushed...

There had been sounds in there, mysterious sounds, and movements. She could sense their aftermath. Now there was only darkness and the cold swirling of air, as if a grave had opened and closed.

"Mr. Teufel!" she called across the room.

She knew exactly where the bed was. She knew just where everything was, inasmuch as she had given Mr. Teufel most of this furniture and had helped him arrange it.

"Are you there, Mr. Teufel?"
Still no answer.
"Herb?"
Nothing.

TESSA took a deep breath and pulled the string that switched on the ceiling light. The room leaped harshly to life. Ah. There was Herb's big chair, which she had given Mr. Teufel. And by it was Herb's old table, the one that used to be so cluttered. All there was on it now was an empty bottle.

There was no label on the bottle, none at all, but it looked like some kind of medicine Herb had taken at one time but which a normal heart could never stand. It was rather careless of Tessa not to have thrown it out, and to have scrupulously removed the label.

She didn't touch it. There would be fingerprints.

The bed was quite a mess, as if Mr. Teufel had threshed about in the throes of great misery—or under the hypnotic influence of some demanding spectre. But now that he was dead Mr. Teufel looked so calm, so peaceful, so happy with the world—or to be leaving it.

Tessa smiled there a moment, as at some teasing memory. Then she stepped softly out on the veranda and locked the door behind her. The sky was brighter now. There would be sun today, bright sun.

Tessa leaned on a rococo pillar and sighed. If Herb hadn't been quite so insistent on his revenge— Anyway, now he could rest in peace. And so could dear Mr. Teufel. He had been so definite about destroying himself, and who can stop a man from doing that if he has, firmly made up his mind? And it was so much nicer than hanging himself, so neat. No bother for anybody.

Herb had followed his cue to perfection. His ironic revenge had consisted of forcing Tessa to drink medicine that would kill her, too. Only Herb couldn't know that Tessa had got Mr. Teufel to exchange flats with her this afternoon, and poor Herb was so nearsighted—

Whisper Water

By
LEAH BODINE DRAKE

...a kind of wispy idea that something heathen and powerful from old days lived along our branch.

I ALWAYS said there was something different about Dan Redwine.

The Redwines had the big farm down the pike a piece from us and Dan was the only boy. He was a little, wispy fellow, with big gray eyes that always seemed to see a sight more than anybody else and he never was a talker. But he was happy-hearted and a right clever lad, and just about the best friend I ever had. Dan was a hard worker, too, for all his puny frame. Old Mr. Redwine was poorly, and Miz' Redwine was a slipshod, oh-let-it-rest woman, who rocked more than she worked. There were two Redwine girls, but they married early and moved into foreign parts, two—three counties away.

So it was up to Dan to bear a man's burdens, even in his youthful days. Many's the time I've wanted him to go hunting or to a play-party over in Hurdsville, and he'd say No, he had to mend a fence, or look for a cow that had strayed, or hoe the burley, or what-all. Yessir boss, Dan was a drivin' boy.

Maybe I'd better say who I am, although I have little to do with the story. I'm Jed Clay Bullion, and it was my Uncle Wade Bullion who was Sheriff of Tatum County the time we had those terrible goings-on that I will try to tell of. Uncle Wade has it all writ down and signed, what was a real, sure-enough death-bed confession, and I saw some and heard a lot of what went on, my own self.

Like I said, Dan Redwine worked hard, but he was still just a tad, time my story begins. He liked to prank around like other young ones, and he liked to fish, I mind, better than anything else. When he had the time he'd get his dad's ol' fishing pole and go down to a pretty little branch that cuts through Redwine land, named Whisper Water.

Whisper Water is well called. I don't just mean because it seems to whisper to you when you walk by its banks, 'specially at sundown

126

when the nighthawks are flying and the breeze makes spooky rustlings in the willows. I mean, there's always been whispers *about* it—mostly among the old folks—how a man might see and hear more than ripples and wind and fish jumping or a 'coon washing its dinner in those deep, brown waters. There used to be Red Indians around here, they say, in the old days—Shawnee, and Kickapoo and Cherokee. I reckon that any place where *they've* been will always have queer tales told of it. They never camped here permanent, just used to come down here for hunting and their little wars, and then go back again across the river.

But they slipped in and out of the state enough to leave shadows, so to speak, of their outlandish spooks and spirits, and there was a kind of wispy idea that something from those old times, something heathen and powerful, lived in our branch. Nobody had ever described it, and 'twasn't known if it were good or bad, but whatever lived in Whisper Water never seemed to trouble its mind over humans. That is, never till once...but I'm 'way ahead of my story.

DAN liked to hang around Whisper Water, particularly where it bulged out into a kind of little pool near an enormous old willow-tree. Many's the swim we've had together in that-there little pool. Dan liked to sit under that tree and fish, and play on a mouth-harp that he always carried in his jeans. He could play right good, too— "Sourwood Mountain" and "Hand Me Down My Walking-Cane" and "Lord Lovell He Stood By His Castle Wall." But his favorite was the one that begins, "Have you seen my true-love with the coal-black hair?" Over and over, while the willow swayed in the summer wind and the catfish nibbled his line, he'd play that sweet, sad piece.

Dan took a kind of personal pride in that branch. Whisper Pool was just below the Redwine house a ways, and Redwine property so to speak. He used to keep it cleaned out good. You know how some folks in the country are—we incline towards using a branch-bed as a kind of dumpheap. It's against the law now, I reckon, but back when Dan and I were young lads there wasn't any such law, or if there was nobody in Tatum county had heard of it. But Dan saw to it that no old blowed-out tires or tin cans were cast into his part of Whisper, and he always tidied up after any picnickers who drove in here from foreign parts. Dan was fair silly about that stream, but whatever lived in it appreciated his care, because the way the fish bit for Dan was a pure wonder!

I asked him about his amazing luck, once. Dan seemed kind of embarrassed. He muttered something about "an agreement with a brown lady."

"Brown lady?" I said scornful. I was at the scornful age then, around twelve or thirteen. "Boy, are you crazy? Don't nobody live around here except you-all and Old Man Tuttle up on the hill. *What* brown lady?"

Dan didn't answer and kept on fixing a worm on his line, pretending like he didn't hear me.

"Shoo," I went on, "she must have been one of those picnickers that worry you so. She was just a picnicker, having fun with you. Some of those foreign ladies are awful sassy."

But Dan shook his head and said No, wasn't any city-lady. That's all I could get out of him, because when it came to Whisper Water he always got mum-mouthed, for all we were friends.

Well, we got older and started going to the dances in Hurdsville and beauing the girls around and I guess Dan sort of forgot about "brown ladies," for pretty soon he was courting Honeybird Sanders.

Everyone to his own taste, is what I thought when Dan took to Honeybird. I'll admit she was a fair sight in those days—tumbled red hair, snappy blue eyes and smart and sassy. But man, was she a tartar! She could flare up over a trifle, and then her blue eyes would spark and her mouth tighten up, and she'd look like she could kill you. Besides that, she had too much of a roving eye to suit me. But Dan married up with her. Or rather, Honeybird married *him*, being a mighty purposeful woman when she wanted something. At that time she wanted Dan Redwine, and the Redwine land, maybe, it belonging to him now that his dad and ma had died.

A funny thing happened at the wedding. There was a right smart lot turned out for it, and I thought I knew most everybody present. But there seemed to be one person I couldn't quite place. It looked like a woman, but I never could see her real plain. She was always just slipping away behind somebody, or just beyond the corner of my eye, and when I'd turn to look at her she'd be a little way out of my range still. It was the aggravatingest thing! I got the idea that she was small and dark and dressed kind of odd, in what looked like old-fashioned, but handsome greeny stuff like fine, store-bought velvet, maybe. I also thought she was barefoot, and I recall saying to myself, "Well,

Missy, seems like you could have wore your shoes to a wedding!"

Nobody else seemed to notice her, and as she didn't go into the church with the rest, I forgot about her. I thought I saw Dan look around kind of sharp-like, once or twice, like you'll do when someone comes up behind and speaks suddenly to you. But—who it was, if anybody, I never did see.

The wedding party went off fine and dandy, and Dan and Honeybird settled down at his place and for a while things went along peaceable enough.

Peaceable for Honeybird, that is, but maybe not so much for Dan. Honeybird's temper didn't quiet down any, and her tongue was still razor-sharp. She had a rough hand with beasts, too. I mind one time Dan brought home a baby muskrat whose mother had died in a trap. He cared for it and petted it, just like he did all small, helpless things. Honeybird got the rifle down when he was over in Hurdsville, and killed it. But instead of being merciful and shooting it, she beat its head in with the butt! She told Dan it had bit her, but I don't think he believed her, because he never again brought any young creatures to the house.

THE worse she got, the more he took to going off by himself to Whisper Water and sitting by the willow to fish or just play his mouth-harp and brood, where it was quiet and peaceful. He had to practically sneak off, though, as Honeybird had a powerful dislike for that branch. It got to be more—it was a kind of nameless fear with her.

She showed this one day when the Redwines were walking home from church with me and my Sally. When we turned off the pike to take the short cut through the field by Whisper Water she stopped dead.

"You-all can go back along the branch," she said, "but I'm staying on the pike."

"Whatever for, Birdie?" said my Sally. "It's a slight hotter and dustier."

"Hot or dusty or not—the last time I come along Whisper that big willow hit me in the face. All right, *laugh!*" she snaps, although nobody had. "A great, long willow-wand reared back and smacked me right square across my face and left a big red welt. My laws, it felt just like some living person had slapped me!"

"Allright, Birdie girl, we'll go with you along the pike," said Dan, looking, I thought, a little worried.

We ought to have seen that—here was a token, but human beings are funny. They hate to admit that there are things in this world that are more, or less, than human, with powers for good or ill, according to whether it's good or ill that's done them by men. Honeybird never would walk by the branch again, though, and knowing what I do now, I can't blame her.

She and Dan had been married now about ten years. I reckon it got lonely for her up at the Redwine place, Dan being such a quiet man, and there never being any children. If she'd had a passel of young ones to busy her mind things might have been different. But she never did, and sometimes I wonder if Whisper Water was to blame—but maybe I'm fanciful.

ANYWAY, things perked up when some oilmen came down here and leased some of Dan's land. Pretty soon they moved in a big rig, with cable-tools, and the contractor—Mr. Bill Brady, his name was—brought in a crew and they started drilling. Two of the boys located themselves in Hurdsville and drove to work every day around noon. But Mr. Brady, who helped drill, and his tooldresser got themselves fixed at the house for room and board. They were going to run tower (as they called it) at night, and it was a sight handier to live on the place.

Mr. Brady was a youngish man, pleasant-spoken if a mite school teacherish, and no great shakes for looks. But his tooldresser, that Foley, was a humdinger!

Big, black-eyed and rowdydow, always laughing and pranking and shining up to the girls! He was the sweet-talkingest man I ever did see, poor soul! He just naturally made a set for Honeybird, and she was smitten with him from the start. After living alone with slow-spoken Dan for ten years, she was pleased and flattered to have such a big, good-looking man like Foley Mathers shine up to her. That was the toolie's name—Foley Mathers. Lard, how can I forget it?

Right away Honeybird smartened up like she hadn't since her wedding. She put herself out to cook better than since the honeymoon. Sweet potato pie and her best peach preserves on the table every day! She even took to curling her hair again and pinning on a ribbon or two, and when Honeybird set her mind to it, she was a right taking woman.

Foley just ate it up. Lots of time when I was there, around noon, when Mr. Brady and him would come off tower, Foley'd come busting in the kitchen roaring, "Where Miss Honeybird? Where's that good-looking landlady of mine?" and she'd giggle and prime herself like a girl.

Working half the night like they did, Mr. Brady and Mathers slept a good piece of the afternoon. I hate to scandalize anybody's name, especially when they're dead and gone, but seems like Foley wasn't sleeping all that time.

Mr. Brady had the spare room to himself, and he was a little hard of hearing, so what went on when Dan was down in the low ground at the corn, or hoeing the burley by the woodlot will never now be rightly known to man. But it's certain there was enough between Foley and Dan's wife to make her jealous of other women.

One noon I was over at Redwines' returning a harrow I'd borrowed. Mr. Brady was in the kitchen unlacing his field-boots, when Mathers came in the back shed. He started washing up, but pretty soon he stuck his head around the door and said, "Who's that cute little black-eyed gal around here, wears her hair in two big braids over her chest?"

"No *grown* woman'd be silly enough to wear her hair like that," snaps Honeybird, "nobody but a Red Indian, that is, and there've been none of them kind around here for many enduring years, that's certain."

"Say!" bawls Foley, "Come to think of it that's just what she looked like—a cute little Indian squaw, like I've seen out in Oklahoma, time I was working on a well near Nowata."

He stepped into the kitchen. "Mean, too, like an Indian woman can get. Man, did she give me a dirty look as she passed me! Like she's ready to scalp my hair off. Br-r-r!"

"What had you done, Mathers?" asked Mr. Brady, in a casual way. "Make a pass at her?"

"Why, Mr. Brady, you know I'm as innocent as a lamb around women!" Foley answered, big-eyed and mock solemn. "Anyway," he went on, half to himself, "I don't think she cared much for me, because she made some kind of a funny movement with her hand— like she was pushing me away, or gesturing me off or something."

"Where did all this take place, Mr. Mathers?" I asked him.

"Down by Whisper creek, Mr. Bullion," Foley answered. "It was kind of funny—I met this good-looking gal just before I come up to that big willow. You know, that real, big one by the bend, where the creek is kind of a pool. She was walking towards me, big as life and mad, like I said, when all-a sudden—whoosh! she wasn't there! Wham! Gone—just like that!" He snapped his fingers. Then he sort of studied a minute. "It looked mad, too, shaking all over," he added. "That tree, I mean."

Mr. Brady was interested by now. He leaned back in his chair and said in that school-book way of his, for all he was a young fellow, "I understand that this used to be Shawnee camping-ground once. Is that so, Mr. Redwine?"

Dan, who had kept his head turned aside during these speeches, muttered, "I reckon so," and I could tell by Honeybird's back, where she stood over the stove, that she was all ears.

Brady went on; "That's interesting what Foley said about an Indian girl, or someone who looked like one. Now if we were superstitious redmen we'd say that Foley'd met the guardian spirit or goddess of something around here, most likely something along the creek, what you folks here call the branch. Our red brothers believed that all things had their good or bad spirits, and they could take any shape or size they wanted. Indian legend is full of bear-women and tree-lovers and buffalo-girls, which sometimes fell in love with human beings. Sometimes I guess they fell into *hate*, too, if I may put it that way." He turned to Foley smiling. "Looks like the mysterious lady of the creek didn't take to Foley here."

Foley opened his mouth like he was going to say something, then shut up and sat heavily down to the table. Honeybird was setting the biscuits in front of him, and as she passed me I could tell she was shaking. I had the queerest feeling, my own self, that I'd heard something like this talk before, but I couldn't figure out why it seemed familiar.

THEN Dan spoke up all of a sudden. "If I was you, Mr. Mathers, I'd not walk that part of the branch."

"Why not?" says Foley.

"Well," says Dan, "that bank's treacherous. Even in a dry spell like we're having now it's always muddy along Whisper Water, and when we have a big rain the bank crumbles fast."

"As for that…woman you met," he went on slowly, "I reckon that was old man Tuttle's granddaughter, come from Hurdsville to visit with him. Yes, sir," he added briskly, "I'd say that-there was Willie Pearl Wakefield."

I had to smile to myself, because Willie Pearl is a tubby little towhead about eleven years old.

Honeybird wasn't smiling. All of a sudden she slapped the greens down and bust out with, "I hate that branch! I hate that Whisper Water, so dark and slimy! And I hate that big old willow most of all! Dan Redwine, I've told you and *told* you all these enduring years, to cut down that nasty old willow! It's bad—bad!"

She was just about screaming, and as we all stared at her she started to cry, ran out of the room and banged the bedroom door.

I made my fare-you-wells right soon, as I was embarrassed for Dan's sake. I went home along the branch, like I always did, anyway, but this time with all my senses alert and my ears pricked, so to speak. When I got near the big old willow something dashed out from the brush and I almost yelled my head off. It was nothing but a little old rabbit, but I was taking no chances: I called after it, "Howdy, Mister Rabbit!" the way we boys used to, for good luck. Yes, sir, boss, I was feeling very polite towards *any* creature I met down by Whisper Water right then!

Like Dan had said, it hadn't rained for weeks. August was slipping into September, and the weather held—hot, dry and terrible hard on the corn and only less so on the burley. The joe-pye weed's purple looked rusty, and the pasture grass was a sorry sight. The earth was hard as a rock. The only soft spot around was the branch-bed and banks, because even in the driest weather Whisper Water always was full. Queer, come to think of it.

I was so busy hauling water and tending to my crops that I didn't go over to Redwines' for a couple of weeks. I heard bits of news, how the oil crews were hard put to it for water; how Dan's tobacco seemed to be doing a sight better than anyone else's; and how the goings-on between Mrs. R. and Foley Mathers was getting to be a scandal and a shame. Don't ask how those things get around, but I supposed the daylight crew noticed things, coming on and off tower, and talked about it in town. It worried me, on Dan's account, but I reckon I spent more time worrying about my corn and my tobacco than I did anything else.

ONE evening, as I finished milking, Dan came slowly around the side of the barn. He looked unhappy and mad and worried, all at once. In the bitterest voice I've ever heard from him, he said, "Jed Clay, it's true. It's damn true, and I've been a tomfool not to guessed it before this."

"Boy, what you talking about?" I said, though I feared to hear— because I reckoned I knew what was coming.

"Honeybird and that Foley Mathers," said Dan. "Honeybird's been disgracing her and my name with that loud-mouthed tooldresser, that I ought to have knowed better than to take in my own house." He smashed his fist against the barn wall. "Damn these foreigners, Jed Clay! I wish I'd never leased my land to 'em. I wish they'd never come around here looking for oil."

"Hold on, Dan," I said. "What makes you so sure?" I put my arm over his shoulder. "People just naturally talk about a good-looking man or woman, and they're both that. Mathers is a big-talking fellow, but I doubt that it's any more than just sweet-talk and compliments, and such."

"It's more than that, Jed Clay," he answered. "That's all I'm going to say about it, but I'm facing them both with it tonight, and if he or she gets the least bit of a guilty expression, I'm going to light into that Foley and I don't know where I'll stop at."

"Take it easy, Dan—you're admitting right now you ain't really sure. Sleep on it tonight, boy, and don't be so hasty in your anger." I was really scared that Dan *would* jump Foley, and considering the difference in their sizes, Dan was liable to be the worst-used one in *that* ruckus.

I talked and jollied him and thought I'd quieted him down some, because he promised to think it over during the night. But when he turned away to head for home, I had the feeling that I'd never see him again. I started to call him back and ask him to stay the night with Sally and me, and I wish to glory, now, I had.

I worried so about Dan that a couple of days after that I went over to Redwines'. The house looked quiet, and I figured the night-crew were still asleep, it being around four in the evening. I knocked softly on the porch floor, and after a long while Honeybird came to the door. She looked kinda wild and sick. "Dan's not here," she said. "Dan's gone on a trip."

"Gone on a trip?" I said. "Where to?"

"Down to Memphis," she said, in a defiant, you'd-better-believe-me way.

"Memphis?" I guess I yelled it. "*Memphis?* Whatever for? What's Dan doing in Memphis?"

"He's a-visiting some of his kinfolk," she answered. "He's been away couple of days now, visiting his kin down in Memphis."

I was stumped. "I never knew Dan had any kinfolk in Tennessee. He never mentioned any to me, that I recollect."

"Well, he has, and that's where he's went," she snaps back and starts to close the door.

"He's picked a fine time to take a trip," I said. "Right when the burley needs cutting, he goes to *Memphis*—to visit his *kin!*"

"Don't you yell at me, Jed Clay Bullion!" Honeybird's temper was rising. "Can I help it if Dan Redwine's a fool? Always *was* a fool, to my mind."

"That's enough, Miss Honeybird," I said, very mannerly, because I was getting mad myself. "Dan's my friend, and if he wants to take a trip to Memphis, I reckon he knows what he's doing. Funny, though—nobody in town said anything about it when I went in yesterday. Seems like somebody would have seen him take the train, or something." Then just to end the conversation on a pleasanter note, I asked, "How's the oil-well coming? Struck oil yet?"

That did it. She just blew up. "That Foley! That big, drunken ox of a man!"

"Why, what's Foley done?" I asked. "I thought he was your star boarder, Birdie."

"You shut up!" she began, when we heard a sound which most of us had been honing to hear for weeks—a crack of thunder. Whilst we were talking the sky had begun to clabber up with big purplish clouds, and as we stood there a wind sprang up that smelled of rain not far distant. Lightning split the purple masses, thunder banged away, and the first warm drops fell. Then more of them, and faster, and cooler.

I felt like dancing. "Fare-thee-well, Miz Redwine my bonny-o!" I sang out. "I'm fixing to get home before she busts open and Whisper starts to spill over. Don't want to be caught in the low ground when Whisper starts to flood."

At that I thought she'd gone crazy. She staggered back against the screen door and put her hand to her mouth. "The branch!" she said, like to herself. "O my Lord, the branch!" and slammed both doors shut and I heard her lock the inner one.

Well, I'll swanny, I thought to myself, what a woman! No more manners than backwoods trash. But I forgot about Honeybird, because it was now raining buckets, and our Tatum county clay was already turning slippery under my boots and I had to set my mind on getting home in a hurry. The sky was now one big bruise with white forks of lightning playing over it every few minutes and the rain seemed to come down harder every step. When I passed the rig I saw the daylight crew, Collins and Mack, huddled up in their "dog-house" away from the storm. That made me think of the other crew at the house, and I thought, they won't get much sleep with all this racket. Then another thought struck me—something Honeybird had said. How she'd called Foley a drunken ox..."*drunken?*" Mathers was kind of a blow and sweet on the ladies, but he never drank anything stronger than buttermilk!

What had made him a "drunken ox" all of a sudden?

THAT night's storm was the worst I ever did see. Sally and I and the young-ones bunched up together in the kitchen, and Sally prayed a little, and I thought about Dan and Honeybird and Foley, and how troublous life can be. I said to Sally, "I'd sure hate to have to go out in *this* tonight! Don't reckon the boys will do any more drilling till it's over. It's not a fit night for a hound dog to be out in," little knowing it wouldn't be many hours before I'd be clumping around in the wind and rain and thunder, looking for a murderer!

NOW comes that part which even now seems mighty hard to credit, even though I saw some things with my own two eyes that no man could rightly disbelieve. But what with the confused and wild way in which Foley told his part of the doings, and the noise and fury of the storm that kept up while he was telling it, together with the downright unnaturalness of the whole business—well, that last part is none too clear after all these years.

Needless to say, Dan hadn't gone to Memphis. Seems that when he left me that evening and went home, he found Honeybird and Mathers talking in the kitchen. Dan walked up to him and asked him what Foley later said was "a very personal question," and one word led to another, and they started belting each other.

I'd always been afraid to see Dan get into a fight with big Foley

Mathers, but it seems like he made a fair showing. He was mad and he was hurt, and righteous wrath hath its own strength. Anyway, Honeybird thought her sweetheart was getting the worst of it. Foley said all of a sudden he heard a funny, dull sound, like a squash had been cracked open, and Dan slumped down on the floor, with his head busted wide open and Honeybird standing over him with a bloody poker in her hands.

She was like a woman made of stone. She told Foley to get Dan out of sight before Mr. Brady got back, and forbade him to go get a doctor, as Foley swears he wanted to do. She said Dan was dead, and she wasn't going to hang for it, and if Foley had any sense he'd help her bury him and pretend he'd gone out of town. They could think up what to do later, she said, and Foley was so dazed with fighting and fear of that awful woman he'd been fool enough to admire, that he followed her like a whipped dog. He slung poor Dan's corpse over his shoulder, and Honeybird got a shovel from the toolshed and they stole out of the house in the dusk.

Hard and dry as the ground was, Honeybird had presence of mind enough to know there wasn't much use digging anywhere but the one spot where the earth was always soft—by Whisper Water. Much as she hated and feared that branch-side, she realized that there was the only place to hide away her husband's poor, broken body. The two of them stole around by way of the woodlot; and down by the branch, where he used to fish and play his mouth-harp, they buried what was left of Dan Redwine. A makeshift grave it was, too, but they were in a mighty hurry and dizzy with fear and, I hope, remorse.

Those next few days must have been plain hell for her and Foley—him having to dress tools and her cooking for him and Mr. Brady, as though nothing had happened and her husband had sure-enough gone on a little trip and would be coming back soon! That was when Foley started drinking, and nobody—almost—knew why.

Then the worst happened. It rained. That downpour that everyone welcomed so was doom and destruction for the guilty pair. No wonder Honeybird mighty near fainted when I mentioned the branch flooding—she had a clear picture of that shallow grave and the way the banks crumbled in a storm!

She rushed into the house and woke Foley, and let him have the news. If he were drunk then, it sobered him up good. He could hear the rain swishing down, and knew that pretty soon the water would uncover what they wanted desperately to stay hidden from the sight of man. I don't reckon they knew what they'd do when they got there, but they couldn't sit around the house in a plight like that—they had to make a stab at covering Dan up better somehow. They crept out of the house, hoping against hope Mr. Brady wouldn't hear them, and through the wind and the lightning and the wild wet they made their way down to Whisper Water. With all that clay pulling at their feet Foley said they ran all the way as if the devil was after them, and maybe he was.

Now here's the part where Foley shook so with pain and fright, and where he'd stop so often to pray or to curse, that it's pretty much of a blur in all our minds, mine and Uncle Wade's and the others who stood around his bed there in the Redwine lean-to that night. He says that as they got to the branch, they could hear Whisper Water rushing away between her banks, like something strong and big and angry, and somehow alive. In the semi-darkness they saw that the willow was bending and shaking all over like a woe-be-gone woman, and the banks were flaking rapidly. The lightning flashes showed that they'd come none too soon! Two stiff, helpless boots and a stretch of blue jeans stuck out from the clay. The earth they'd heaped so hasty over poor Dan's body was washing away, and the husband Honeybird Redwine had murdered was silently condemning her.

The branch was boiling and churning and the trees were tossing in the wind, as they grabbed and dug in the mud with their bare hands, when a terrible glare of lightning lit up the whole place. By its wild light Foley saw the big willow, that had been bending and thrashing like the others, sort of straighten up and hold itself rigid.

Then, before their eyes it seemed to tower into the dark, wild sky, higher and higher like a horrible, huge green fountain, before it swooped down on them like a thing alive! Foley fell over backward before its rush, and in the darkness beside him he felt Honeybird go down, too. He heard her give a fearful scream, and then a kind of awful gurgling noise. Another lightning glare came, and Foley saw what no human being ought to ever see—instead of a willow tree, it was a huge, angry Indian woman, brown-skinned, black-braids and all, bending over them—but it wasn't a human woman.

"Then, O my God!" Foley'd cry, as he told and retold that awful scene. "She was reaching down for Honeybird, and choking the life out of her with her long, thin hands!"

BUT the worst is yet to tell. Foley's shrieks brought the crew from the well and Mr. Brady, and together they got him up to the house as best they could—what with his leg hanging broke, where it had caught in a root when he fell. Collins said afterwards that it was caught so tight they could hardly get him loose, "just like it was hands holding him down," he said.

There wasn't a sign of Honeybird. They laid Foley on his bed in the lean-to, and Collins got out the Ford and slid and slithered into town for Doc Luttrell. From what he'd seen and heard Collins figured he'd best get the Sheriff, too. Uncle Wade rounded some of us up, and in the wind and rain we went out to look for Honeybird. The storm had died down some, but we still had trouble with our lanterns, and I don't reckon we'd have come across her when we did if it hadn't been for Coleman Tate's old dog Luby. It was really Luby that found Honeybird.

Away down stream, caught among the brush that overhung the bank, was what looked like an old ragbag. Coleman's hound nosed it and let out a howl. It was Honeybird. Wrapped around her throat, coil on coil, so tight that it cut way into the skin, was what looked like a thin green rope. Luby set up another howl, and when Coleman and I picked her up, we almost did our own selves.

Not because she was dead. I guess we'd kind of expected that all along. But because that wasn't any rope that had strangled the life out of Honeybird Redwine—it was a long, green willow-wand!

Poor Foley died the next day. Doc Luttrell took off what was left of his leg, but he had a bad fever and what with the pain and the awful fright and...other things, like remorse, maybe...he just couldn't pull through. Dan was dug up and buried proper in the churchyard, with what was left of Honeybird—Lord pity her—along side him, although I recall there was some sentiment against it. Dan's widowed sister came over from Logan County to run the property. The drillers finished the hole with a new tooldresser Mr. Brady brought down, but they didn't get oil, so pretty soon they shut down and plugged the hole and went away. Things quieted down again, and after a while people sort of forgot about the Redwines, like you do forget things, even the worst.

But Foley had muttered something that night when he was raving and groaning—something that nobody else but me seemed to hear, and which never got into the statement my Uncle Wade writ out and had Foley sign. Yes, Foley seems to think he saw something else when that tree turned into that tall, goblin woman. He seems to have seen her bend down, after she'd cast away poor Honeybird, and sort of scoop up what looked like Dan's body out of his pitiful grave. Only it wasn't the blue-jeaned, dead body of Dan Redwine that Foley had helped bury. It was Dan, all right, but whole and unharmed, like he used to be, and naked as a newborn child! And in his hand he was holding on hard to something, some little object.

I could have told Foley what that was, and the tears come to my eyes to think on it. It was Dan's little old mouth-harp. Yes, sir, that little old mouth-harp that he was never without. And his ghost still held on to it!

Down by Whisper Water of a summer's evening, when the nighthawks are out and the fish are splashing, I've heard a sad, pretty little tune curling and creeping through the willow-wands: "Have you seen my truelove with the coal-black hair?" and the breeze in the big willow by the pool is sort of humming along with it, like a happy woman whose lover's come to her at last.

BLACK AS THE NIGHT

By
ALICE FARNHAM

...Jet's yellow eyes were on her, and Moira began to learn just how a dog could hate!

"BUT somehow," said the housekeeper slowly, "somehow I don't rightly feel that creature *is* a dog."

Her pleasant face was troubled. Behind the steel spectacles, her eyes wore a puzzled, thoughtful look.

"It's—it's more as if she was human, somehow, human as you or me—but *bad*. Bad all the way through!"

The grocer's man, on his weekly visit to the lonely house by the sea, looked uneasily down at the great black beast stretched out in the doorway, its unwinking amber gaze on the white lane that led into the London highroad.

"Look at her now!" said the housekeeper in a low voice. "Watching that road, like a jealous woman! Oh, it's fair give me the creeps, I tell you—knowing what I know, and staying here night after night alone with that beast!"

The grocer's man edged behind the table.

"Oh, no fear of that! I've a good stout stick—you see it there in the corner—and I made sure to keep it handy. My husband will have me bring it. But it's not the likes of you and me she'd trouble with. And it's not her teeth I'm afraid of—it's the cunning mind of her, and what may happen now that his honeymoon's over and he's bringing his new wife home!"

The grocer's man brightened.

"Coming today, ain't they?"

Utterly indifferent, the dog continued to stare at the empty road that wound among the rocks, away from the cliff and the sea.

"Ah!" said the housekeeper darkly. "And stand in her shoes I wouldn't, not for a million pounds, George Ottey!"

She dropped her voice, almost as if afraid the dog might overhear.

"I remember what happened to his first wife, poor thing, right here on this very spot!"

"Suicide, wasn't it?" faltered the grocer's man. "Suicide, they called it. Only some said, accident."

"It was murder," said the housekeeper, half beneath her breath. "Murder down among those, rocks, and no one the wiser but me! Murder—and I know the one who did it!"

The dog lifted its head then and looked at her steadily, its yellow eyes alight with perfect intelligence. The upper lip lifted just a trifle over the sharp white teeth in a silent snarl; and then the dog turned its head back and once again lay motionless, watching the lonely road.

At its other end, in London, Moira Glenn stepped laughing into her new husband's car to begin a long journey.

BY CHARLES' expression she could see that the laugh had been a mistake, but you can't just switch a laugh off in the middle—your face feels so foolish. Oh dear, that's the worst of marrying on such short acquaintance, she thought. I don't know which things I can laugh at and which I can't.

Charles' nice mouth set in rather a stubborn line. He was thin and dark and intensely serious, which was perhaps why lighthearted Moira loved him. That, and his wonderful skill as an artist, and the hint of tragedy in his past.

"I'm sorry it strikes you as ridiculous," he said stiffly. "Mrs. Bunty told me at the last minute she won't stay any longer than a week, and I can't very well let Jet starve just because—"

"Just because she has a rival," Moira finished gravely. "All right, darling. It's Ho for Road's End I can do with the sea breeze anyway!"

Ho for Road's End was all very well, but when Moira saw the place she felt a sinking of the heart. Lonely, Charles had said; but she had never pictured anything so savagely remote as this gray stone house on the cliff. Silent and dark and ugly it stood near the edge, under an overcast windbroken sky. Beyond it, a path led down through a scattering of jagged rocks to the sea. Three wind-bent fir trees at the back leaned inward, all their branches flung out toward the house, as if long ago they had frozen in that attitude of supplication.

Moira felt suddenly cold. Oh, why, why, did it look like this? Why couldn't the sun have stayed out? She shivered as the car drew closer, and slid her hand under Charles' arm.

"A bit out of the world." He gave her a half-apologetic look. "But you said you wouldn't mind, you know, darling. As long as we're together, you said."

"I know." She squeezed his arm. "Silly, of course that's all that matters!"

But the feeling of chill and apprehension persisted. This house wanted none of her.

A furious barking broke out within the house, high-pitched and almost hysterical. Charles laughed, the tension broken.

"Jet's heard the car! Now Mrs. Bunty will let her out!"

The heavy front door opened slowly, and a black form came bounding out to tear round the lawn in widening circles, still barking wildly.

"What a beautiful dog!" exclaimed Moira involuntarily.

"She's taken two prizes." Charles' manner was offhand, as he guided the car to a stop. "I've had her from a puppy, you know. That's seven years."

Jet continued to race about in circles, her fluid black body moving with effortless grace. Her pointed ears were laid close to her head, her long muscles rippled under the smooth silky coat.

"She's a beautiful thing—I'm going to love her. But what's she running for?"

"Showing off, for my benefit. Now she'll pretend I'm not here— it's a regular ritual. She hasn't noticed you yet."

Slowing to a stop, Jet abruptly sat down, a tall graceful creature with a fine economy of line that delighted Moira's artist soul. Conspicuously she did not look at the car, but at a point twenty feet to one side of it. Her yellow eyes were fixed upon that point with what appeared to be great interest; only the erect alertness of the pointed ears betrayed her.

"Born actress, isn't she?"

Charles spoke with pride.

JET'S head moved just a fraction. Her gaze wandered to the sky. A crow flapped across her range of vision, and she barked at it once rather mechanically.

Charles stepped down from the car, and on the instant she had covered the intervening distance in two bounds. In a frenzy of joy, she leapt to his face half a dozen times before he could quiet her.

Suddenly the dog stood back. Its body stiffened. Watchful, wary, hostile, the yellow eyes stared into Moira's.

"Get out and make friends with her. Don't be afraid!"

"I'm *not* afraid!" Moira was rather resentful as she scrambled out of the car. She held out a coaxing hand. "Hello, Jet! Good girl—come then!"

Jet backed away, her eyes still intent upon Moira's. Her coat bristled almost imperceptibly.

"It's no use, Charles." Something—reaction perhaps—caused an absurd prickle of tears behind Moira's eyelids. This overcast sky, this foreboding house, the unfriendly dog. "She—we'll just have to get used to each other by degrees."

Charles waved his newspaper at the stout aproned figure in the doorway.

"Back on time, Mrs. Bunty!" he called.

Smiling, Mrs. Bunty shook her head. She knew, and he knew, that she had stayed a day beyond her time, and that it was distinctly felt on both sides as a favor. Her presence was needed at home, and her bicycle stood waiting by the kitchen door.

"I'm glad to see you back, sir. Bunty's been that impatient he's been ringing me all day on the phone. I told him I'd be along just as soon as I'd finished the clearing up."

"Yes, yes," said Charles hastily. "We'll try not to keep you. Er—my wife, Mrs. Bunty."

Moira thought she saw an odd look of compassion on the housekeeper's face as she turned toward her. It lasted only a second, while Mrs. Bunty civilly acknowledged the introduction and withdrew, but still it was somehow disconcerting. My own servants to be sorry for me! She thought with a trace of anger, of which she was immediately ashamed.

Dinner was a rather silent meal, served with an expedition quite new to Moira but to which she was later to become accustomed. The dog lay in a corner by the empty stone fireplace, chin resting on her outstretched paws, watching them steadily as they ate.

"Mrs. Bunty's the salt of the earth," Charles said once. "Good yeoman farmer stock. Husband's an invalid—that's why she needs the job."

"I like her looks," Moira admitted, "but I have a feeling that she thinks employers should be kept in their places. Sh—here she comes now with dessert."

They fell silent again. The dog continued to watch them from her corner.

Strangely the constraint which Moira had mentally attributed to the intermittent presence of Mrs. Bunty still persisted after she had gone.

I've never felt like this with Charles before, she thought. I must be crazy. For a fleeting instant she saw the lighted coziness of their room at the hotel, felt again the warmth and gay intimacy that had so lately been theirs, saw Charles' face bright with eager longing, heard the rumble and the clatter of traffic in the streets below that intensified their delicious isolation. Already it seemed half a lifetime away.

It's a long way to Piccadilly, she thought ruefully. But it wasn't; the trip had taken them less than two hours. That was why Charles had bought the house, he told her: close enough to London for him to keep up the necessary contacts with agencies and advertisers, remote enough to provide the solitude that his work demanded. Moira felt a little homesick when she thought of the office; she wondered if they missed her. She might not be so gifted an artist as Charles, but she had carved a nice little niche there for herself all the same.

They'd tried to scare her out of her impulsive marriage, of course.

"My good girl, what do you know about the man?" Bill Conway had demanded waving his pipe. "He comes, he goes, he sells, he gets commissions—and dwells in some godforsaken hole in the rocks along the Cornwall coast. What do you think you'll do down there—count bats?"

Involuntarily now her gaze strayed to the dark beams. No bats.

"I'm going to inspire him to higher things," she had retorted. "And for your information I love solitude and I'm fond of rocks and I grow all pink and merry on sea air. And I'm going to—" she had hesitated, "make up to him a little, if I can."

For Caroline. But why had Caroline killed herself, she wondered now, looking across the room at Charles. Why, and how?

He was absently stroking the dog that lay at his feet. Looking up, he caught her eye and smiled.

"Lonely old place," he said apologetically. "Think you'll be happy here?"

Moira perched on the arm of his chair and ruffled his hair.

The dog gave her an inscrutable glance got slowly to its feet and walked away. Charles' eyes followed it, but he said nothing.

"Of course I will, silly! Especially if Mrs. Bunty goes with it."

LATER that night she was not so sure. When they went up to bed, the dog followed as a matter of course, and Moira lost her temper.

"Charles, really! You're not going to tell me that animal stays in our room all night!"

Charles looked gently obstinate.

"But she'll get lonely! She always *has* slept in the bedroom, Moira. Even when—"

Moira wanted to cry. "Even when Caroline was your wife?" but she couldn't say the words, even in her anger.

Charles persevered.

"You told me you liked dogs, Moira. You said you were used to them."

"So I do, and so I am," said Moira shortly. "But in our family dogs were slightly subordinate to the rest of the family. They didn't dominate the household. And I warn you, Charles Glenn, if that dog stays in here at night I don't. We'll sleep in separate rooms."

Charles gave in. In a rather sulky silence he put Jet outside in the passage, despite beseeching jabs at him with her forepaw. She refused to go voluntarily, and in the end had to be dragged across the room in a sitting position by her collar. Charles' lips tightened as he shut the door on her whines, but he still said nothing.

The whining kept up all night. Sometimes it rose to the pitch almost of a howl, and at others sank to a sort of sobbing; but it never stopped for more than a few minutes at a time. And all night long Moira lay quite stiff and still on her side of the bed, in the unhappy knowledge that Charles, too, was awake and unmoving.

Toward morning she must have fallen asleep. When she awoke the room was empty.

"Mr. Glenn had to go to Pembroke on business," Mrs. Bunty told her, serving her lonely breakfast in the deserted dining room. Sunlight peered timidly through the narrow windows and lay in thin fingers on the floor. The dog was nowhere to be seen.

"Mrs. Bunty—" Moira stopped abruptly. She amended her question. "Is—is Jet about?"

Again that curious look of pity, and then Mrs. Bunty averted her eyes as she set down the teapot.

"The dog went in the car with Mr. Glenn, madam."

"Too bad." Moira helped herself to marmalade and reflected on the stupidity of last night's jealousies and irritations when examined in the morning sunlight. "I was hoping to make friends."

"If you can, madam," said Mrs. Bunty gently. "I recall the first Mrs. Glenn feeling the same. But she found, poor thing, some dogs and some people won't be made friends with."

She stood for a moment in the doorway.

"If you'll excuse me, madam, I think—it's not my place to say it—but sometimes I think it's important to know who our enemies are, at the very beginning."

The door closed very softly behind her. Moira sat staring at it for a moment, and very slowly and thoughtfully finished a piece of toast.

Strange. Very strange indeed. Dogs weren't your enemies. They were your friends. You just had to know them.

Nothing in the world more natural than that Charles should have become attached to the dog in the three years that had passed since Caroline's death. In a sense Jet had been his only companion. Charles, with his almost morbid sensitivity, would have shrunk even more than his wont from meeting other people. The dog had become the friend of his solitude. How silly of her to have resented that friendship, even for a moment! And how silly of Mrs. Bunty, to seem to suggest—

With a little impatient movement of her shoulders, Moira went out into the kitchen. Mrs. Bunty was scouring a table, her back turned. Absently Moira fingered a cup.

"Mrs. Bunty, how long has Mr. Glenn had this dog Jet?"

Mrs. Bunty straightened up. "I couldn't say exactly, madam. I know he'd had her it might be three years before he married the first time. Then it was just two years after that—"

"I know," Moira struck in hurriedly. Only she didn't know; Charles would never speak of it. "You say—you say the first Mrs. Glenn didn't care for dogs?"

The housekeeper shook her head.

"She'd one herself when she came here, a cute little thing. Jet killed it. Oh yes!—Mr. Glenn would never believe it," she added, at Moira's startled look. "But Jim Roberts' boy, from the village—he saw them, up on the moors. The two of them went out for a run that day, but only Jet came back. All happy and frisky and wagging her tail. They found what was left of the little dog, three miles on the moors, but Mr. Glenn said it couldn't be so. He said the boy was lying."

Mrs. Bunty dipped a reflective brush in the bucket of soapy water.

"It was about then that Mrs. Glenn stopped trying to make friends with Jet."

Moira felt a little sick. On impulse she said, "You don't like Jet, do you, Mrs. Bunty? Are you afraid of her?"

The housekeeper put her brush down. She did not answer for a moment. When she did, it was to nod toward a stout ash stick leaning in a corner by the stove.

"I'm not afraid of her—no. But there are bad dogs as well as bad people. I'd not stop in this house without that stick for company."

Moira's eyes went to the stick for a second, and then she turned away. Gossiping with a servant, she thought shamefacedly. And probably nothing but village talk, all of it. Prejudice and dislike: I'll close my mind to it.

WHEN she had finished unpacking, she spent the day in not unpleasant exploration. There was a savage beauty in that barren spot that somehow explained the hold it had on Charles. She followed the little ravine leading from the house to the sea, and clambered over the rocks tumbled about the water's edge.

Charles found her standing there, gazing out to sea, her hair blown straight back by the strong salt wind. When she heard his voice she turned and held out her hands. Her face was alight.

"Oh, Charles, isn't it splendid? This is where I'm going to spend my time!"

For just that instant she noticed an odd look of strain about Charles' face, and then it was gone. He kissed her and held her to him for a moment.

"Darling, I did make an ass of myself last night! Can you forget it?"

"Darling, there were two of us!" answered Moira promptly. Standing on tiptoe, she kissed him again. "Let's forget it!"

When he released, her, she saw that he was staring at the rocks beyond her. The look of strain was intensified.

"Look!" She pointed to a pool just below them, hemmed in by rocks on the shoreward side, except for a narrow passage. "That's where I'm going bathing tomorrow!"

A muscle twitched uncontrollably in Charles' cheek. Turning, he pulled her roughly along the path away from the sea. The hand gripping her arm was shaking.

"Charles, what—"

He didn't look at her.

"Get away from there!" he said harshly. "Get away, stay away! Get away from those rocks!"

He pulled her faster up the path, so fast that she stumbled.

"Charles, stop it! Tell me why—"

But suddenly she knew why. She stared at him with horror.

"Oh Charles, did—? Is that—?"

Charles' pace slackened a little, but he still wouldn't look at her.

"She couldn't swim." His voice was harsh. "She just—walked into the water. There. There in that pool. Nobody ever knew why. Jet found her when the tide went out. She—Jet stood guard over her. I found Jet there, between the rocks, and Caroline lying on the sand. The tide—the tide went out, and left Caroline lying in the bottom of the pool."

She could see it. She saw Caroline lying quite still in a few clear inches of water, Jet silently watching. Her scalp prickled.

"Charles—"

"Here's Jet," he said, in a different voice. "Mrs. Bunty's let her out. Hi, girl! Good dog!"

Jet bounded down the ravine with her ears back, her whole face one laugh of delight.

"Good dog!" echoed Moira faintly. She held out her hand. "Come then! Come along, Jet."

With a shock of utter unbelief she saw the dog come toward her, wagging her black stub of a tail with a placating whine.

"You see?" Charles was triumphant. "I told you she'd make friends!"

Mechanically Moira patted the dog's eager head. Jet licked her hand, and then, barking excitedly, leapt up to lick her face. Involuntarily Moira shrank back, cloaking her revulsion with an unsteady laugh.

"But, Charles—Jet, what's come over you?"

Panting with eagerness, the dog continued to leap at her face.

"Oh, Charles, must she?" Moira pushed her away, with a look of apology. "I'm ever so happy that she's making friends—if only she wouldn't lick my face—"

"Down, Jet!" The dog groveled. "Stop it—you're making a

149

nuisance of yourself!"

Jet slunk along at his side. The three walked up the path in silence. Moira realized with a slight sinking of heart that though the dog cast her a reproachful glance now and then, accompanied by a pathetic licking of Charles' hand, Charles himself would not look at her. Somehow, in spite of Jet's new-found friendliness, Moira had managed to offend him. She had been put in the wrong—"by a dog," she thought wonderingly.

"I notice Jet's making up to you," said Mrs. Bunty, a day or two later. "Just when Mr. Glenn's here."

Moira stared at her book without answering. So I didn't imagine it, she thought. It *is* only when Charles is here that Jet acts so friendly.

More than friendly, really. Affectionate—almost embarrassingly so. So heartbroken at the faintest breath of coldness, so pointedly going to Charles for comfort. As if—

Moira gave herself an impatient little shake and tried again to concentrate on her book.

"She used to beg him to get rid of that beast," said Mrs. Bunty, going ponderously toward her pantry. "Half crying, she was over it—yes, many's the time."

Moira closed her book. Jet was lying on the hearthrug.

"Here, Jet," she called softly. "Come, girl—come over and let me pat you."

The dog raised her head. She stared at Moira with an unwinking yellow gaze, but did not move. In that total lack of response there was something almost of contempt.

Pressing her lips together, Moira crossed the room. She knelt down.

"Let's make friends, Jet. Shall we go for a walk?"

She put out her hand to stroke the sleek black head, but there was a barely audible growl. Almost in one movement the big dog got to her feet and sprang away, her hackles bristling.

Moira stared at her, her mind a confusion. Jet hadn't changed, then. But why the pretense?

AT A sound still inaudible to Moira, Jet pricked up her ears. Moira scrambled to her feet and heard it too—the low deepening hum of Charles' motor turning down the lane. The dog dashed to the front door and began to whine, pawing at it in her eagerness.

Moira stood beside the closed door and looked down at her. She was filled with sudden anger.

"Oh, no you don't!" she said through clenched teeth. "I'm sick of your always being first!"

Darting to the corridor door, she closed it swiftly behind her and drew a deep breath. When Charles switched off his motor and jumped out, she ran out the side entrance to meet him.

"Hello, darling!" she called gaily. "I thought you'd never get here!"

From the house there came wail after earsplitting wail. Charles' face darkened. He kissed her perfunctorily.

"What on earth's wrong with Jet? Is she locked up?"

Moira tried to laugh.

"No, darling—not really. I just forgot to let her out when we—I heard you coming."

Charles said gently, "You don't understand what a disappointment that was to her." Loosening her arms, he went toward the house, leaving Moira to follow. She dropped her eyes for a moment, to hide the sudden tingle of tears. But what utter nonsense—to be crying because Charles loved his dog!

Blinking the tears away with a little shamefaced laugh, she hurried after him.

Jet released, was ecstatic. Like an arrow from a bow she flew out, circled the house twice and then leapt to Charles' face over and over, with an hysterical abandon not to be denied.

When Charles finally pushed her away with a soft, "Down, girl!" she seemed suddenly to recollect Moira, standing rather stiffly to one side. Cringing, wagging her tail, her whole body writhing in exaggerated submission and supplication, she crawled over to Moira and began licking her hand. Without thinking Moira drew it away.

"Why do you do that, Moira?" Charles' voice held displeasure. "Don't you realize she's sensitive? Why must you show so persistently that you dislike her?"

"My God!" said Moira, and stopped herself. Never—and Mrs. Bunty still in the house. "Let's go in," she finished lamely. "You must be starving."

Jet followed them, walking close beside Charles, wagging abjectly and shrinking away whenever she caught Moira's eye, quite evidently in mortal fear.

"As she always does," Moira thought bitterly. "As if when Charles

151

is away I beat her!"

Dinner over, the washing-up concluded, she stood at the window watching Mrs. Bunty pedal away, sternly erect, into the gray dusk.

"Let's go for a walk, Charles," she said, with a touch of wistfulness. "On the rocks. Just—" No, not just the two of them. Never just the two of them. Only at night, and even then that haunting tragic presence just outside their closed door.

Charles looked up from his paper.

"I'm a bit tired, dear. Why don't you go—and take Jet?"

At the sound of her name the dog moved closer and laid her head on his knee.

"That's—not what I meant." There was a lump in Moira's throat. She sank down on the hearthrug. "I don't—think she wants to go for a walk. Do you, Jet?"

The dog's tail wagged. With an almost imperceptible glance at Charles, she groveled across the rug toward Moira.

"What an affectionate thing she is!" Charles' voice was fond.

Moira stretched out an unwilling hand. The dog cringed and drew back with a faint whimper, her body wagging apologetically as she shrank toward Charles. He put down his paper.

"Why on earth does she do that, Moira? She tries so hard to win your love—over and over I've seen her. But what have you done to frighten her?"

Moira sprang to her feet. She was shaking from head to foot.

"Charles Glenn, do you realize what you're implying? Are you really out of your mind?"

"I realize exactly what I'm implying," said Charles deliberately. "That your harshness and unkindness have hurt Jet's feelings so badly that she's afraid of you. A child could see that."

"I've never been unkind to an animal in my life!" Moira's voice rose, "You've put me in an impossible position ever since I came here—you and that dog between you! I've tried to be understanding. I've tried to—"

"Understanding!" His face was flushed with anger. "You don't know the meaning of the word! You're hard as nails where this poor dumb beast is concerned, and you know it. Jet's loving and sensitive—you've cut her to the heart. Don't you think a dog has feelings?"

"Don't you think a woman has feelings?"

Moira suddenly found herself screaming.

"Jet—Jet—Jet! Damn you, why did you get married at all? You don't need a wife—you've got Jet!"

She slammed the door behind her and ran up the stairs, weeping.

Charles slept in the guestroom that night. He was gone when she came down, listless and swollen-eyed, to breakfast. Jet lay in the corner, her black body relaxed in easy grace. At Moira's entrance she raised her head but did not move.

Moira crossed the room and stared down at her. The dog's yellow eyes met hers without wavering.

"I hate you!" she said softly, bending closer. "You understand that, don't you? I hate you!"

Not a muscle of Jet's face moved. Steadily she gazed at Moira.

In the end it was Moira who moved away, feeling shaken and slightly sick. She leaned against the open casement, staring at the heat-heavy garden without seeing it.

I must be losing my mind, she thought drearily. Talking to a dog like that—a dog!

For appearance's sake she attempted to eat the breakfast that Mrs. Bunty put before her, but it was no use. Her eyes kept straying to Jet in her corner. Always the dog's eyes were on her—watchful, steady, a depth of still dislike cloaked beneath that impassivity.

Abruptly Moira rose from the table and walked upstairs. Padding footsteps followed. Sitting down at the dressing table, she could see in the glass Jet stretched out in the doorway, watching her.

"Get out!" she screamed suddenly. "Get out, get out!"

Springing to the door, she pushed it with all her strength against Jet's weight, and when she had closed it leaned against it, panting.

I'm losing my mind, she thought again. This isn't me—I've changed, I've changed! Something ghastly is happening to me, and I don't know what it is!

The day was a still and breathless one, a weight of motionless heat oppressing the air. From her window she saw the sea, heavy and oily at the foot of the cliff. Not a bird was in the sky.

A dog, she thought wonderingly. A dog is breaking up my marriage. No, that's impossible! That's absolute nonsense! It's I, Moira Burton, I've had kittens and cats and dogs all my life, and a darling old pony named Whiffle!

She walked the floor restlessly, without realizing that she did it. I'll go for a swim—no, Charles didn't want her to go swimming, because of Caroline. Perhaps she could read. Perhaps—

If only Jet would die.

The day grew steadily hotter, till it was effort almost to breathe. In the afternoon Charles put through a trunk call from London.

"Darling, I'll be a bit late. Look here, I'm frightfully sorry about last night. Did you sleep?"

Sunshine flooded Moira. She drew a deep breath.

"Oh, *Charles!* Oh, darling, I was so horrid!"

"I was horrider," he said apologetically. "I've got a bit unreasonable, I think being alone so much. You know, I think perhaps we should stay in town. What do you think?"

"Oh, darling!" said Moira in a daze. "Just heavenly!"

"Better all around, I mean. You'd have company—and I imagine we could manage about Jet. Take her for walks and so on. Don't you?"

Jet! When Moira replaced the receiver a minute later, she felt curiously numb. Jet. Always Jet. Wherever they went, always Jet to be a third.

There was a slight movement behind her. She turned and looked at the dog, her eyes narrowing.

"Oh, no!" she whispered. "You won't be there! He'll never know what carried you off—but believe me, my dear dumb friend, you won't be there!"

She felt strangely light and elated as the afternoon wore on.

"I'll have an early dinner, Mrs. Bunty," she said gaily. "I'm feeling quite ravenous. And then you can go, since Mr. Glenn won't be home until late."

When dinner was cleared away she still felt restless and excited, almost feverish. She was filled with the continuing intoxication of a decision taken which cannot yet be confirmed by action.

As she stood smiling by the drawing-room window, looking out with bright unseeing eyes, Mrs. Bunty came in to bid her goodnight, her sensible hat set squarely atop her smooth head. She hesitated a moment in the doorway, regarding Moira with an odd concern.

"I'm not just easy leaving you here alone, madam. If you'd like me to stay—

Moira laughed. She felt gay and triumphant.

"Not a bit of it, Mrs. Bunty. Run along home to your family! I'm off for a walk along the cliff."

Mrs. Bunty took one step toward her. Her eyes held Moira's.

"Madam—don't take that dog with you! Whatever you do, promise me you'll not take that dog with you—or here I stay!"

Moira wanted to laugh. Mrs. Bunty was so terribly in earnest.

"All right, then—I promise. I'll lock the door behind me."

But when Mrs. Bunty had gone, her mood was a little deflated. The house was so very quiet. From the window she could see the lurid sunset. The water shone crimson as blood among the rocks.

I *will* go for a swim, she thought suddenly. Charles is an old granny, but he needn't know. After all, *I* can swim.

A few minutes later she was slipping down the rocky path in her swim suit, fastening her rubber cap. From the house behind her came a sharp, angry barking, and she laughed aloud. Silence followed, and then as she was almost down to the pool there was again the familiar sound of padding footsteps behind her.

"Oh, bother!" Moira said, under her breath. "Jet's jumped through the window!"

For a moment she stood undecided, while on sky and water the crimson stillness deepened. Should she go back to the house and lock Jet more securely? She seemed almost to hear the housekeeper's warning voice again, with that note of curious urgency.

Then she shrugged and laughed, turning once more to the sea, as Jet came down the rocks behind her. It was really rather funny. She looked back at the dog with amusement.

"I'm sure you're waiting, dear, for me to commit suicide too. What a hope! *I* can swim, you know!"

Silent, indifferent, the dog followed.

When Moira had squeezed through the twin rocks that held the entrance to the cove, Jet sat down between them, her body blocking the passage. The overcast sky, fiercely lit by an angry sun, was red.

MOIRA slid into the water, gasping at the coldness of it. The surf was rougher and stronger than she had expected, but she found it exhilarating and rolled over in the water, gasping with delight. The little pool was quite deep, the tide still coming in fast.

There in the narrow confines of the rocks the waves seemed to break with intensified force.

"I should have expected that," she thought, clinging for a moment to a rock while she got her breath. The red of the sky was fading, but the water was still like blood. "A fine idiot I'll look if a wave bangs me against a rock and bashes my silly head in!"

In a lull between waves, she loosed her hold on the rock and began swimming toward the passage. Jet still sat there impassively, silhouetted against the sky.

Moira cast an uneasy glance over her shoulder. That big wave was rushing in fast—best grab on to something—no, there was nothing to grasp—faster, faster! She could feel the swell of it beneath her, lifting her up like a feather—and then cried out in pain and fright as the wave hurled her against the sheer rock wall of the inner cove.

For a moment she lost consciousness. When she came to, choking and spluttering, she was clinging desperately to a tiny spar of rock near the water's edge. Her side was numb; there was a sickening pain in her head. The pool had faded to gray now, but around her the water was red. Dizzily, she tried to shake the water from her eyes. It was blood.

The passage. She must get to the passage, drag herself somehow over the rocks and home. Bracing herself with one hand against the sheer rock, she made a weak essay to swim with the other. Her arm hung limp and lifeless beside her.

For one instant, in a lull between waves, she thought dizzily, she heard someone calling.

"Charles!" she screamed, but her voice was drowned in the roar of the incoming surf.

With her one hand she clawed at the rock wall, feebly pushed against it with one foot. Inch by painful inch, gasping and sobbing, she crawled toward the break in the rocks where Jet still sat immobile, watching her. It couldn't have been Charles, she thought dully. Jet's still here. Something in the dog's implacable pose struck her then with a cold thrill of fear. Against the red afterglow, between black enormous rocks, she seemed to loom huge against the sky.

Her last reserve of strength carried Moira to the opening in the rocks, at the very second that she knew she could have kept up no longer. Crying weakly with relief, she started to pull herself out of the water.

With a savage snarl, the big dog leaped suddenly to its feet, every hair bristling. Moira made one last attempt to clutch at the ledge, and the dog sprang. Recoiling, she lost her grasp.

"Charles!" she screamed again, and knew it was no use. There was only Jet, and Jet had won again. Once more Jet would have Charles to herself.

In the sharp clarity of imminent death it all became plain to her. As she felt herself sinking, she looked again, with a detached and wondering vision, at that black featureless outline between the rocks. And looked again in anguished intensity, and clawed again at the rock. For another figure was suddenly silhouetted against the fading light—a sturdy figure, with a stout club which rose and fell as the dog whirled around just a second too late.

Mrs. Bunty dropped to her knees at the water's edge.

"Woman dear, catch hold my hand!" she gasped, forgetting decorum for the first time in her life. "God, I thought I was too late! I thought that black beast had done for you!"

For a second Moira hung helpless and limp from Mrs. Bunty's firm hold on her arms.

"I can't!" she whispered. "I can't make it!"

"You've got to!" Mrs. Bunty's voice was urgent. "Now!"

She pulled with a will, and slowly, with pain that seemed breaking her body in two, Moira crawled out of the water, averting her eyes from the thing that had been Jet, and lay utterly spent on the wet rock. Mrs. Bunty was breathing hard from her exertion, and for a moment neither of them spoke.

"Something seemed to turn me back," said Mrs. Bunty. "A—just a kind of feeling, when I was almost halfway home. I just knew, like as if a voice had spoke, I shouldn't have left you alone with that dog."

A sudden noise sounded above the fret of the waves, the hoot of an auto horn.

"Charles!" Moira gasped. She raised herself painfully from the rock. "Oh, Mrs. Bunty, what will we do?" Their eyes met.

"He'll never believe it!" Moira whispered. "Quick, Mrs. Bunty— push, Jet into the pool! We've got to tell him—what *can* we tell him?"

There was a splash, as Jet's body slid gently into the water. Mrs. Bunty knelt and washed the blood from the spot by the water's edge. Washing the club, she shoved it in a little recess in the rocks and pulled the scanty bushes across the opening.

"I found you in the pool together, madam," she said rapidly. "Jet was trying to save you—trying to save you, do you hear? The master would never believe what happened, not on our Bible oaths. He's deep, he'd cover it up—but all his life he'd hold it against you. Jet jumped in to save you, and a wave threw her against a rock and killed her, the same wave that nigh killed you."

"She died a heroine," murmured Moira, her eyes brightening. "Yes, he'll believe *that!*" Her mouth twisted with the irony of it. "I'll be hearing about it for the rest of my life!"

"I forgot something, we'll say, and come back and was a little worried to find you gone. Pulled you out just in time, and that's God's truth. When he sees the look of you, all covered with blood, and knows how close he was to losing you—trust me, madam, it's not Jet he'll be thinking of!"

"Moira!" called Charles, from the top of the path. "Moira darling, where are you? Where's Jet?"

Wildly, sobbingly, rocking back and forth, Moira began to laugh.

DEAREST

By

H. BEAM PIPER

"Get him to tell you about this invisible playmate of his."

COLONEL ASHLEY HAMPTON chewed his cigar and forced himself to relax, his glance slowly traversing the room, lingering on the mosaic of book-spines in the tall cases. The sunlight splashed on the faded pastel colors of the carpet, the soft-tinted autumn landscape outside the French windows, the trophies of Indian and Filipino and German weapons on the walls. He could easily feign relaxation here in the library of "Greyrock," as long as he looked only at these familiar inanimate things and avoided the five people gathered in the room with him, for all of them were enemies.

There was his nephew, Stephen Hampton, greying at the temples but youthfully dressed in sports-clothes, leaning with obvious if slightly premature proprietorship against the fireplace, a whiskey-and-soda in his hand. There was Myra, Stephen's smart, sophisticated-looking blonde wife, reclining in a chair beside the desk. For these two, he felt an implacable hatred. The others were no less enemies, perhaps more dangerous enemies, but they were only the tools of Stephen and Myra. For instance, T. Barnwell Powell, prim and self-satisfied, sitting on the edge of his chair and clutching the briefcase on his lap as though it were a restless pet which might attempt to escape. He was an honest man, as lawyers went; painfully ethical. No doubt he had convinced himself that his clients were acting from the noblest and most disinterested motives. And Doctor Alexis Vehrner, with his Vandyke beard and his Viennese accent as phony as a Soviet-controlled election, who had preempted the chair at Colonel Hampton's desk. That rankled the old soldier, but Doctor Vehrner would want to assume the position which would give him appearance of commanding the situation, and he probably felt that Colonel Hampton was no longer the master of "Greyrock." The fifth, a Neanderthal type in a white jacket, was Doctor Vehrner's attendant and bodyguard; he could be ignored, like an enlisted man unthinkingly obeying the orders of a superior.

159

"But you are not cooperating, Colonel Hampton," the psychiatrist complained. "How can I help you if you do not cooperate?"

Colonel Hampton took the cigar from his mouth. His white mustache tinged a faint yellow by habitual smoking, twitched angrily.

"Oh; you call it helping me, do you?" he asked acidly.

"But why else am I here?" the doctor parried.

"You're here because my loving nephew and his charming wife can't wait to see me buried in the family cemetery; they want to bury me alive in that private Bedlam of yours," Colonel Hampton replied.

"See!" Myra Hampton turned to the psychiatrist. "We are *persecuting* him! We are all *envious* of him! We are *plotting against* him!"

"Of course; this sullen and suspicious silence is a common paranoid symptom; one often finds such symptoms in cases of senile dementia," Doctor Vehrner agreed.

COLONEL HAMPTON snorted contemptuously. Senile dementia! Well, he must have been senile and demented, to bring this pair of snakes into his home, because he felt an obligation to his dead brother's memory. And he'd willed "Greyrock," and his money, and everything, to Stephen. Only Myra couldn't wait till he died; she'd Lady-Macbethed her husband into this insanity accusation.

"...however, I must fully satisfy myself, before I can sign the commitment," the psychiatrist was saying. "After all, the patient is a man of advanced age. Seventy-eight, to be exact."

Seventy-eight; almost eighty. Colonel Hampton could hardly realize that he had been around so long. He had been a little boy, playing soldiers. He had been a young man, breaking the family tradition of Harvard and wangling an appointment to West Point. He had been a new second lieutenant at a little post in Wyoming, in the last dying flicker of the Indian Wars. He had been a first lieutenant; trying to make soldiers of militiamen and hoping for orders to Cuba before the Spaniards gave up. He had been the hard-bitten captain of a hard-bitten company, fighting Moros in the jungles of Mindanao. Then, through the early years of the Twentieth Century, after his father's death, he had been that *rara avis* in the American service, a really wealthy professional officer. He had played polo, and served a turn as military attaché at the Paris embassy. He had commanded a regiment in France in 1918, and in the post-war years, had rounded out his service in command of a regiment of Negro cavalry, before retiring to "Greyrock." Too old for active service, or even a desk at the Pentagon, he had drilled a Home Guard company of 4-F's and boys and paunchy middle-agers through the Second World War. Then he had been an old man, sitting alone in the sunlight...until a wonderful thing had happened.

"Get him to tell you about this invisible playmate of his," Stephen suggested. "If that won't satisfy you, I don't know what will."

IT HAD begun a year ago last June. He had been sitting on a bench on the east lawn, watching a kitten playing with a crumpled bit of paper on the walk, circling warily around it as though it were some living prey, stalking cautiously, pouncing and striking the paper ball with a paw and then pursuing it madly. The kitten, whose name was Smokeball, was a friend of his; soon she would tire of her game and jump up beside him to be petted.

Then suddenly, he seemed to hear a girl's voice beside him:

"Oh, what a darling little cat! What's it's name?"

"Smokeball," he said, without thinking. "She's about the color of a shrapnel-burst..." Then he stopped short, looking about. There was nobody in sight, and he realized that the voice had been inside his head rather than in his ear.

"What the devil?" he asked himself. "Am I going nuts?"

There was a happy little laugh inside of him, like bubbles rising in a glass of champagne.

"Oh, no; I'm really here," the voice, inaudible but mentally present, assured him. "You can't see me, or touch me, or even really hear me, but I'm not something you just imagined. I'm just as real as...as Smokeball, there. Only I'm a different kind of reality. Watch."

The voice stopped, and something that had seemed to be close to him left him. Immediately, the kitten stopped playing with the crumpled paper and cocked her head to one side, staring fixedly as at something above her. He'd seen cats do that before—stare wide-eyed and entranced, as though at something wonderful which was hidden from human eyes. Then, still looking up and to the side, Smokeball trotted over and jumped onto his lap, but even as he stroked her, she was looking at an invisible something beside him. At the same time, he had a warm and pleasant feeling, as of a happy and affectionate presence near him.

"No," he said, slowly and judicially. "That's not just my

imagination. But who—or what—are you?"

"I'm... Oh, I don't know how to think it so that you'll understand." The voice inside his head seemed baffled, like a physicist trying to explain atomic energy to a Hottentot. "I'm not material. If you can imagine a mind that doesn't need a brain to think with... Oh, I can't explain it now! But when I'm talking to you, like this, I'm really thinking inside your brain, along with your own mind, and you hear the words without there being any sound. And you just don't know any words that would express it."

He had never thought much, one way or another, about spiritualism. There had been old people, when he had been a boy, who had told stories of ghosts and apparitions, with the firmest conviction that they were true. And there had been an Irishman, in his old company in the Philippines, who swore that the ghost of a dead comrade walked post with him when he was on guard.

"Are you a spirit?" he asked. "I mean, somebody who once lived in a body, like me?"

"N-no." The voice inside him seemed doubtful. "That is, I don't think so. I know about spirits; they're all around, everywhere. But I don't think I'm one. At least, I've always been like I am now, as long as I can remember. Most spirits don't seem to sense me. I can't reach most living people, either; their minds are closed to me, or they have such disgusting minds I can't bear to touch them. Children are open to me, but when they tell their parents about me, they are laughed at, or punished for lying, and then they close up against me. You're the first grown-up person I've been able to reach for a long time."

"Probably getting into my second childhood," Colonel Hampton grunted.

"Oh, but you mustn't be ashamed of that!" the invisible entity told him. "That's the beginning of real wisdom—becoming childlike again. One of your religious teachers said something like that, long ago, and a long time before that, there was a Chinaman whom people called Venerable Child, because his wisdom had turned back again to a child's simplicity."

"That was Lao Tze," Colonel Hampton said, a little surprised. "Don't tell me you've been around that long."

"Oh, but I have! Longer than that; oh, for very long." And yet the voice he seemed to be hearing was the voice of a young girl. "You don't mind my coming to talk to you?" it continued. "I get so lonely, so dreadfully lonely, you see."

"Urmh! So do I," Colonel Hampton admitted. "I'm probably going bats, but what the hell? It's a nice way to go bats, I'll say that... Stick around, whoever you are, and let's get acquainted. I sort of like you."

A feeling of warmth suffused him, as though he had been hugged by someone young and happy and loving.

"Oh, I'm glad. I like you, too; you're nice!"

"Yes, of course." Doctor Vehrner nodded sagely. "That is a schizoid tendency; the flight from reality into a dream-world peopled by creatures of the imagination. You understand, there is usually a mixture of psychotic conditions, in cases like this. We will say that this case begins with simple senile dementia—physical brain degeneration, a result of advanced age. Then the paranoid symptoms appear; he imagines himself surrounded by envious enemies, who are conspiring against him. The patient then withdraws into himself, and in his self-imposed isolation, he conjures up imaginary companionship. I have no doubt..."

In the beginning, he had suspected that this unseen visitor was no more than a figment of his own lonely imagination, but as the days passed, this suspicion vanished. Whatever this entity might be, an entity it was, entirely distinct from his own conscious or subconscious mind.

At first she—he had early come to think of the being as feminine—had seemed timid, fearful lest her intrusions into his mind prove a nuisance. It took some time for him to assure her that she was always welcome. With time, too, his impression of her grew stronger and more concrete. He found that he was able to visualize her, as he might visualize something remembered, or conceived of in imagination—a lovely young girl, slender and clothed in something loose and filmy, with flowers in her honey-colored hair, and clear blue eyes, a pert, cheerful face, a wide, smiling mouth and an impudently up-tilted nose. He realized that this image was merely a sort of allegorical representation, his own private object-abstraction from a reality, which his senses could never picture as it existed.

It was about this time that he had begun to call her Dearest. She had given him no name, and seemed quite satisfied with that one.

"I've been thinking," she said, "I ought to have a name for you, too. Do you mind if I call you Popsy?"

"Huh?" He had been really startled at that. If he needed any further proof of Dearest's independent existence, that was it. Never, in the uttermost depths of his subconscious, would he have been likely to label himself Popsy. "Know what they used to call me in the Army?" he asked. "Slaughterhouse Hampton. They claimed I needed a truckload of sawdust to follow me around and cover up the blood." He chuckled. "Nobody but you would think of calling me Popsy."

There was a price, he found, that he must pay for Dearest's companionship—the price of eternal vigilance. He found that he was acquiring the habit of opening doors and then needlessly standing aside to allow her to precede him. And, although she insisted that he need not speak aloud to her, that she could understand any thought, which he directed to her, he could not help actually pronouncing the words, if only in a faint whisper. He was glad that he had learned, before the end of his plebe year at West Point, to speak without moving his lips.

Besides himself and the kitten, Smokeball, there was one other at "Greyrock" who was aware, if only faintly, of Dearest's presence. That was old Sergeant Williamson, the Colonel's Negro servant, a retired first sergeant from the regiment he had last commanded. With increasing frequency, he would notice the old Negro pause in his work, as though trying to identify something too subtle for his senses and then shake his head in bewilderment.

One afternoon in early October—just about a year ago—he had been reclining in a chair on the west veranda, smoking a cigar and trying to re-create, for his companion, a mental picture of an Indian camp as he had seen it in Wyoming in the middle '90's, when Sergeant Williamson came out from the house, carrying a pair of the Colonel's field-boots and a polishing-kit. Unaware of the Colonel's presence, he set down his burden, squatted on the floor and began polishing the boots, humming softly to himself. Then he must have caught a whiff of the Colonel's cigar. Raising his head, he saw the Colonel, and made as though to pick up the boots and polishing equipment.

"Oh, that's all right, Sergeant," the Colonel told him. "Carry on with what you're doing. There's room enough for both of us here."

"Yessuh; thank yo', suh." The old ex-sergeant resumed his soft humming, keeping time with the brush in his hand.

"You know, Popsy, I think he knows I'm here," Dearest said. "Nothing definite, of course; he just feels there's something here that he can't see."

"I wonder. I've noticed something like that. Funny, he doesn't seem to mind, either. Colored people are usually scary about ghosts and spirits and the like... I'm going to ask him." He raised his voice. "Sergeant, do you seem to notice anything peculiar around here, lately?"

The repetitious little two-tone melody broke off short. The soldier-servant lifted his face and looked into the Colonel's. His brow wrinkled, as though he were trying to express a thought for which he had no words.

"Yo' notice dat, too, suh?" he asked. "Why, yessuh, Cunnel. Ah don' know 'zackly how t' say hit, but dey is som'n, at dat. Hit seems like...like a kinda...a kinda *blessedness.*" He chuckled. "Dat's hit, Cunnel; dey's a blessedness. Wondeh iffen Ah's gittin' r'ligion, now?"

"WELL, all this is very interesting, I'm sure, Doctor," T. Barnwell Powell was saying, polishing his glasses on a piece of tissue and keeping one elbow on his briefcase at the same time. "But really, it's not getting us anywhere, so to say. You know, we must have that commitment signed by you. Now, is it or is it not your opinion that this man is of unsound mind?"

"Now, have patience, Mr. Powell," the psychiatrist soothed him. "You must admit that as long as this gentleman refuses to talk, I cannot be said to have interviewed him."

"What if he won't talk?" Stephen Hampton burst out. "We've told you about his behavior; how he sits for hours mumbling to this imaginary person he thinks is with him, and how he always steps aside when he opens a door, to let somebody who isn't there go through ahead of him, and how... Oh, hell, what's the use? If he were in his right mind, he'd speak up and try to prove it, wouldn't he? What do you say, Myra?"

Myra was silent, and Colonel Hampton found himself watching her with interest. Her mouth had twisted into a wry grimace, and she was clutching the arms of her chair until her knuckles whitened. She seemed to be in some intense pain. Colonel Hampton hoped she were; preferably with something slightly fatal.

Sergeant Williamson's suspicion that he might be getting religion became a reality, for a time, that winter, after The Miracle.

It had been a blustery day in mid-January, with a high wind driving swirls of snow across the fields, and Colonel Hampton, fretting indoors for several days, decided to go out and fill his lungs with fresh air. Bundled warmly, swinging his blackthorn cane, he had set out, accompanied by Dearest, to tramp 'cross-country to the village, three miles from "Greyrock." They had enjoyed the walk through the white wind-swept desolation, the old man and his invisible companion, until the accident had happened.

A sheet of glassy ice had lain treacherously hidden under a skift of snow; when he stepped upon it, his feet shot from under him, the stick flew from his hand, and he went down. When he tried to rise, he found that he could not. Dearest had been almost frantic.

"Oh, Popsy, you must get up!" she cried. "You'll freeze if you don't. Come on, Popsy; try again!"

He tried, in vain. His old body would not obey his will.

"It's no use, Dearest; I can't. Maybe it's just as well," he said. "Freezing's an easy death, and you say people live on as spirits, after they die. Maybe we can always be together, now."

"I don't know. I don't want you to die yet, Popsy. I never was able to get through to a spirit, and I'm afraid... Wait! Can you crawl a little? Enough to get over under those young pines?"

"I think so." His left leg was numb, and he believed that it was broken. "I can try."

He managed to roll onto his back, with his head toward the clump of pine seedlings. Using both hands and his right heel, he was able to propel himself slowly through the snow until he was out of the worst of the wind.

"That's good; now try to cover yourself," Dearest advised. "Put your hands in your coat pockets. And wait here; I'll try to get help."

Then she left him. For what seemed a long time, he lay motionless in the scant protection of the young pines, suffering miserably. He began to grow drowsy. As soon as he realized what was happening, he was frightened, and the fright pulled him awake again. Soon he felt himself drowsing again. By shifting his position, he caused a jab of pain from his broken leg, which brought him back to wakefulness. Then the deadly drowsiness returned.

THIS time, he was wakened by a sharp voice, mingled with a throbbing sound that seemed part of a dream of the cannonading in the Argonne.

"Dah! Look-a dah!" It was, he realized, Sergeant Williamson's voice. "Gittin' soft in de haid, is Ah, yo' ol' wuthless no-'count?"

He turned his face, to see the battered jeep from "Greyrock," driven by Arthur, the stableman and gardener, with Sergeant Williamson beside him. The older Negro jumped to the ground and ran toward him. At the same time, he felt Dearest with him again.

"We made it, Popsy! We made it!" she was exulting. "I was afraid I'd never make him understand, but I did. And you should have seen him bully that other man into driving the jeep. Are you all right, Popsy?"

"Is yo' all right, Cunnel?" Sergeant Williamson was asking.

"My leg's broken, I think, but outside of that I'm all right," he answered both of them. "How did you happen to find me, Sergeant?"

The old Negro soldier rolled his eyes upward. "Cunnel, hit war a mi' acle of de blessed Lawd!" he replied, solemnly. "An angel of de Lawd done appeahed unto me." He shook his head slowly. "Ah's a sinful man, Cunnel; Ah couldn't see de angel face to face, but de glory of de angel was befoh me, an' guided me."

They used his cane and a broken-off bough to splint the leg; they wrapped him in a horse-blanket and hauled him back to "Greyrock" and put him to bed, with Dearest clinging solicitously to him. The fractured leg knit slowly, though the physician was amazed at the speed with which, considering his age, he made recovery, and with his unfailing cheerfulness. He did not know, of course, that he was being assisted by an invisible nurse. For all that, however, the leaves on the oaks around "Greyrock" were green again before Colonel Hampton could leave his bed and hobble about the house on a cane.

Arthur, the young Negro who had driven the jeep, had become one of the most solid pillars of the little A. M. E. church beyond the village, as a result. Sergeant Williamson had also become an attendant at church for a while, and then stopped. Without being able to define, or spell, or even pronounce the term, Sergeant Williamson was a strict pragmatist. Most Africans are, even five generations removed from the slave-ship that brought their forefathers from the Dark Continent. And Sergeant Williamson could not find the blessedness at the church. Instead, it seemed to center about the room where his employer and former regiment commander lay. That, to his mind, was quite reasonable. If an Angel of the Lord was going to tarry upon earth, the celestial being would naturally prefer the society of a retired U. S. A.

colonel to that of a passel of triflin', no-counts at an ol' clapboard church house. Be that as it may, he could always find the blessedness in Colonel Hampton's room, and sometimes, when the Colonel would be asleep, the blessedness would follow him out and linger with him for a while.

COLONEL Hampton wondered, anxiously, where Dearest was, now. He had not felt her presence since his nephew had brought his lawyer and the psychiatrist into the house. He wondered if she had voluntarily separated herself from him for fear he might give her some sign of recognition that these harpies would fasten upon as an evidence of unsound mind. He could not believe that she had deserted him entirely, now when he needed her most...

"Well, what can I do?" Doctor Vehrner was complaining. "You bring me here to interview him, and he just sits there and does nothing... Will you consent to my giving him an injection of sodium pentathol?"

"Well, I don't know, now," T. Barnwell Powell objected. "I've heard of that drug—one of the so-called 'truth-serum' drugs. I doubt if testimony taken under its influence would be inadmissible in a court..."

"This is not a court, Mr. Powell," the doctor explained patiently. "And I am not taking testimony; I am making a diagnosis. Pentathol is a recognized diagnostic agent."

"Go ahead," Stephen Hampton said. "Anything to get this over with... You agree, Myra?"

Myra said nothing. She simply sat, with staring eyes, and clutched the arms of her chair as though to keep from slipping into some dreadful abyss. Once a low moan escaped from her lips.

"My wife is naturally overwrought by this painful business," Stephen said. "I trust that you gentlemen will excuse her... Hadn't you better go and lie down somewhere, Myra?"

She shook her head violently, moaning again. Both the doctor and the attorney were looking at her curiously.

"Well, I object to being drugged," Colonel Hampton said, rising. "And what's more, I won't submit to it."

"Albert!" Doctor Vehrner said sharply, nodding toward the Colonel. The pithecanthropoid attendant in the white jacket hastened forward, pinned his arms behind him and dragged him down into the chair. For an instant, the old man tried to resist, then, realizing the futility and undignity of struggling, subsided. The psychiatrist had taken a leather case from his pocket and was selecting a hypodermic needle.

Then Myra Hampton leaped to her feet, her face working hideously.

"No! Stop! Stop!" she cried.

Everybody looked at her in surprise, Colonel Hampton no less than the others. Stephen Hampton called out her name sharply.

"No! You shan't do this to me! You shan't! You're torturing me! You are all devils!" she screamed. "Devils! *Devils!*"

"Myra!" her husband barked, stepping forward.

With a twist, she eluded him, dashing around the desk and pulling open a drawer. For an instant, she fumbled inside it, and when she brought her hand up, she had Colonel Hampton's .45 automatic in it. She drew back the slide and released it, loading the chamber.

Doctor Vehrner, the hypodermic in his hand, turned. Stephen Hampton sprang at her, dropping his drink. And Albert, the prognathous attendant, released Colonel Hampton and leaped at the woman with the pistol, with the unthinking promptness of a dog whose master is in danger.

Stephen Hampton was the closest to her; she shot him first, point-blank in the chest. The heavy bullet knocked him backward against a small table; he and it fell over together. While he was falling, the woman turned, dipped the muzzle of her pistol slightly and fired again; Doctor Vehrner's leg gave way under him and he went down, the hypodermic flying from his hand and landing at Colonel Hampton's feet. At the same time, the attendant, Albert, was almost upon her. Quickly, she reversed the heavy Colt, pressed the muzzle against her heart, and fired a third shot.

T. Barnwell Powell had let the briefcase slip to the floor; he was staring, slack-jawed, at the tableau of violence which had been enacted before him. The attendant, having reached Myra, was looking down at her stupidly. Then he stooped, and straightened.

"She's dead!" he said, unbelievingly.

Colonel Hampton rose, putting his heel on the hypodermic and crushing it.

"Of course she's dead!" he barked. "You have any first-aid training? Then look after these other people. Doctor Vehrner first;

the other man's unconscious; he'll wait."

"No; look after the other man first," Doctor Vehrner said.

Albert gaped back and forth between them.

"Goddammit, you heard me!" Colonel Hampton roared. It was Slaughterhouse Hampton, whose service-ribbons started with the Indian campaigns, speaking; an officer who never for an instant imagined that his orders would not be obeyed. "Get a tourniquet on that man's leg, you!" He moderated his voice and manner about half a degree and spoke to Vehrner. "You are not the doctor, you're the patient, now. You'll do as you're told. Don't you know that a man shot in the leg with a .45 can bleed to death without half trying?"

"Yo-all do like de Cunnel says, 'r foh Gawd, yo'-all gwine wish yo' had," Sergeant Williamson said, entering the room. "Git a move on."

HE STOOD just inside the doorway, holding a silver-banded Malacca walking stick that he had taken from the hall stand. He was grasping it in his left hand, below the band, with the crook out, holding it at his side as though it were a sword in a scabbard, which was exactly what that walking-stick was. Albert looked at him, and then back at Colonel Hampton. Then, whipping off his necktie, he went down on his knees beside Doctor Vehrner, skillfully applying the improvised tourniquet, twisting it tight with an eighteen-inch ruler the Colonel took from the desk and handed to him.

"Go get the first-aid kit, Sergeant," the Colonel said. "And hurry. Mr. Stephen's been shot, too."

"Yessuh!" Sergeant Williamson executed an automatic salute and about-face and raced from the room. The Colonel picked up the telephone on the desk.

The County Hospital was three miles from "Greyrock"; the State Police substation a good five. He dialed the State Police number first.

"Sergeant Mallard? Colonel Hampton, at 'Greyrock.' We've had a little trouble here. My nephew's wife just went *juramentado* with one of my pistols, shot and wounded her husband and another man and then shot and killed herself... Yes, indeed it is, Sergeant. I wish you'd send somebody over here, as soon as possible, to take charge... Oh, you will? That's good... No, it's all over, and nobody to arrest; just the formalities... Well, thank you, Sergeant."

The old Negro cavalryman re-entered the room, without the sword cane and carrying a heavy leather box on a strap over his shoulder. He set this on the floor and opened it, then knelt beside Stephen Hampton. The Colonel was calling the hospital.

"…gunshot wounds," he was saying. "One man in the chest and the other in the leg, both with a .45 pistol. And you'd better send a doctor who's qualified to write a death certificate; there was a woman killed, too… Yes, certainly; the State Police have been notified."

"Dis ain' so bad, Cunnel," Sergeant Williamson raised his head to say. "Ah's seen men shot wuss'n dis dat was ma'ked 'Duty' inside a month, suh."

Colonel Hampton nodded. "Well, get him fixed up as best you can, till the ambulance gets here. And there's whiskey and glasses on that table, over there. Better give Doctor Vehrner a drink." He looked at T. Barnwell Powell, still frozen to his chair, aghast at the carnage around him. "And give Mr. Powell a drink, too. He needs one."

He did, indeed. Colonel Hampton could have used a drink, too; the library looked like beef-day at an Indian agency. But he was still Slaughterhouse Hampton, and consequently could not afford to exhibit queasiness.

It was then, for the first time since the business had started that he felt the presence of Dearest.

"Oh, Popsy, are you all right?" the voice inside his head was asking. "It's all over, now; you won't have anything to worry about, any more. But, oh, I was afraid I wouldn't be able to do it!"

"My God, Dearest!" He almost spoke aloud. "Did you make her do that?"

"Popsy!" The voice in his mind was grief-stricken. "You… You're afraid of me! Never be afraid of Dearest, Popsy! And don't hate me for this. It was the only thing I could do. If he'd given you that injection, he could have made you tell him all about us, and then he'd have been sure you were crazy, and they'd have taken you away. And they treat people dreadfully at that place of his. You'd have been driven really crazy before long, and then your mind would have been closed to me, so that I wouldn't have been able to get through to you, anymore. What I did was the only thing I could do."

"I don't hate you, Dearest," he replied, mentally. "And I don't blame you. It was a little disconcerting, though, to discover the extent of your capabilities… How did you manage it?"

"YOU remember how I made the Sergeant see an angel, the time you were down in the snow?" Colonel Hampton nodded. "Well, I made her see...things that weren't angels," Dearest continued. "After I'd driven her almost to distraction, I was able to get into her mind and take control of her." Colonel Hampton felt a shudder inside of him. "That was horrible; that woman had a mind like a sewer. I still feel dirty from it! But I made her get the pistol—I knew where you kept it—and I knew how to use it, even if she didn't. Remember when we were shooting muskrats, that time, along the river?"

"Uhuh, I wondered how she knew enough to unlock the action and load the chamber." He turned and faced the others.

Doctor Vehrner was sitting on the floor, with his back to the chair Colonel Hampton had occupied, his injured leg stretched out in front of him. Albert was hovering over him with mother-hen solicitude. T. Barnwell Powell was finishing his whiskey and recovering a fraction of his normal poise.

"Well, I suppose you gentlemen see, now, who was really crazy around here?" Colonel Hampton addressed them bitingly. "That woman has been dangerously close to the borderline of sanity for as long as she's been here. I think my precious nephew trumped up this ridiculous insanity complaint against me as much to discredit any testimony I might ever give about his wife's mental condition as because he wanted to get control of my estate. I also suppose that the tension she was under here, this afternoon, was too much for her, and the scheme boomeranged on its originators. Curious case of poetic justice, but I'm sorry you had to be included in it. Doctor."

"Attaboy, Popsy!" Dearest enthused. "Now you have them on the run; don't give them a chance to re-form. You know what Patton always said—Grab 'em by the nose and kick 'em in the pants."

Colonel Hampton re-lighted his cigar. "Patton only said 'pants' when he was talking for publication," he told her, *sotto voce*. Then he noticed the unsigned commitment paper lying on the desk. He picked it up, crumpled it, and threw it into the fire.

"I don't think you'll be needing that," he said. "You know, this isn't the first time my loving nephew has expressed doubts as to my sanity." He sat down in the chair at the desk, motioning to his servant to bring him a drink. "And see to the other gentlemen's glasses, Sergeant," he directed. "Back in 1929, Stephen thought I was crazy as a bedbug to sell all my securities and take a paper loss, around the first of September. After October 24th, I bought them back at about twenty percent of what I'd sold them for, after he'd lost his shirt." That, he knew, would have an effect on T. Barnwell Powell. "And in December, 1944, I was just plain nuts, selling all my munition shares and investing in a company that manufactured babyfood. Stephen thought that Rundstedt's Ardennes counter-offensive would put off the end of the war for another year and a half."

"Baby-food, eh?" Doctor Vehrner chuckled.

Colonel Hampton sipped his whiskey slowly, then puffed on his cigar. "No, this pair were competent liars," he replied. "A good workmanlike liar never makes up a story out of the whole cloth; he always takes a fabric of truth and embroiders it to suit the situation." He smiled grimly; that was an accurate description of his own tactical procedure at the moment. "I hadn't intended this to come out, Doctor, but it happens that I am a convinced believer in spiritualism. I suppose you'll think that's a delusional belief, too?"

"Well..." Doctor Vehrner pursed his lips. "I reject the idea of survival after death, myself, but I think that people who believe in such a theory are merely misevaluating evidence. It is definitely not, in itself, a symptom of a psychotic condition."

"THANK you, Doctor." The Colonel gestured with his cigar. "Now, I'll admit their statements about my appearing to be in conversation with some invisible or imaginary being. That's all quite true. I'm convinced that I'm in direct-voice communication with the spirit of a young girl who was killed by Indians in this section about a hundred and seventy-five years ago. At first, she communicated by automatic writing; later we established direct-voice communication. Well, naturally, a man in my position would dislike the label of spirit-medium; there are too many invidious associations connected with the term. But there it is. I trust both of you gentlemen will remember the ethics of your respective professions and keep this confidential."

"Oh, brother!" Dearest was fairly hugging him with delight. "When bigger and better lies are told, we tell them, don't we, Popsy?"

"Yes, and try and prove otherwise," Colonel Hampton replied, around his cigar. Then he blew a jet of smoke and spoke to the men in front of him.

"I intend paying for my nephew's hospitalization, and for his wife's funeral," he said. "And then, I'm going to pack up all his personal belongings, and all of hers; when he's discharged from the hospital, I'll ship them wherever he wants them. But he won't be allowed to come back here. After this business, I'm through with him."

T. Barnwell Powell nodded primly. "I don't blame you, in the least, Colonel," he said. "I think you have been abominably treated, and your attitude is most generous." He was about to say something else, when the doorbell tinkled and Sergeant Williamson went out into the hall. "Oh, dear; I suppose that's the police, now," the lawyer said. He grimaced like a small boy in a dentist's chair.

Colonel Hampton felt Dearest leave him for a moment. Then she was back.

"The ambulance." Then he caught a sparkle of mischief in her mood. "Let's have some fun, Popsy! The doctor is a young man, with brown hair and a mustache, horn-rimmed glasses, a blue tie and a tan-leather bag. One of the ambulance men has red hair, and the other has a mercurochrome-stain on his left sleeve. Tell them your spirit-guide told you."

The old soldier's tobacco-yellowed mustache twitched with amusement.

"No, gentlemen, it is the ambulance," he corrected. "My spirit-control says..." He relayed Dearest's descriptions to them.

T. Barnwell Powell blinked. A speculative look came into the psychiatrist's eyes; he was probably wishing the commitment paper hadn't been destroyed.

Then the doctor came bustling in, brown-mustached, blue-tied, spectacled, carrying a tan bag, and behind him followed the two ambulance men, one with a thatch of flaming red hair and the other with a stain of mercurochrome on his jacket-sleeve.

For an instant, the lawyer and the psychiatrist gaped at them. Then T. Barnwell Powell put one hand to his mouth and made a small gibbering sound, and Doctor Vehrner gave a faint squawk, and then both men grabbed, simultaneously, for the whiskey bottle.

The laughter of Dearest tinkled inaudibly through the rumbling mirth of Colonel Hampton.

THE EBONY STICK

By
AUGUST DERLETH

...he even had to look the other way to kill a fly.

My UNCLE JACK was always a devil-may-care sort of fellow, debonair, handsome, with a marked aversion to work. All his nieces and nephews loved him. All his own generation, naturally, disapproved of him. On two counts—because he did not work but managed to live by his wits, and because they envied him his success at this, even though he lived from hand to mouth, so to speak, I always suspected that the only reason he kept his trim figure was that he never had enough money to gorge himself with the food and drink he loved. And the generation before his frowned on him heartily, with the exception of his mother, my grandmother, who was always slightly foolish about her children.

So it came as a distinct surprise to all of us when Aunt Maud died and left everything to Uncle Jack in a will discovered in a book in her library, which, by an earlier will, she had left to Uncle Jack, "to improve his mind and teach him that there is a great virtue and a lasting balm in labor."

We all guessed that Great-Aunt Maud, who had previously impressed us as formidably serious, had intended things to work out this way—if Uncle Jack had not begun to read the books he had inherited, he would never have found the last will and testament of Great-Aunt Maud. Still and all, it was a little strange that things should have happened this way; one would have thought she, more than most of us, would have wanted Uncle Jack to work a little harder for his windfall. And it was markedly unkind of Great-Aunt Maud to forget all the rest of us, especially Myra, who had been her favorite, and who was sure to grow up as helpless as she was beautiful, for having been petted so, and because her widowed mother, my Aunt Hester, never seemed to be able to hang on to any money whatsoever.

But that was the way things worked out, and that was the way we expected they would stay. But someone in the family had other ideas, as we found out soon enough. As soon, that is, as we found ourselves benefited by Uncle Jack's good fortune, for one weekend he invited us all to what had formerly been Great-Aunt Maud's large and imposing old house, which sat in the middle of a city block, protected from the curious by a wall of trees, and a stone wall all the way around it, so that going there was just like going out of the city into the woods. The only sounds you heard there were the clanging of the streetcars outside, and an occasional car whizzing past the gate.

I WAS twelve at that time. I remember that my mother and my father did not care very much to go, they had been so upset by Uncle Jack's good luck, but our disappointment was so pronounced in the face of their hesitation, that they decided to accept his invitation.

"I suppose we may as well make the best of it," said mother.

"He's got some reason for inviting us," said father.

"What about Hester and Myra?"

"Their turn will come."

But their turn had already come. They were at Uncle Jack's house when we got there, and Aunt Hester flew into my mother's arms, embraced her, kissed her, and, when no one was looking, leaned to my mother's ear and said theatrically, "Something's wrong with Jack!"

And something was. He, who had always been so debonair, was now distinctly preoccupied. He smiled for all of us, he made jokes— but it was not quite the same; the twinkle was not right in his eyes, his smile was insincere, and we all noticed it. When we children had a conference after dinner in the large playroom, which was part of the house, we examined the subject critically.

"Do you know what I think?" said Cousin Myra. "Uncle Jack's afraid of something."

"Hoh! Of what?" demanded my sister. "He's got all Aunt Maud's money. What's he got to be afraid of?"

"Perhaps he thinks we'll get some of it," said my younger brother, Harry.

"You know what I think," pursued Myra with dream abstraction. "I think he's planning to poison us all. Then his money will be safe."

"Not Uncle Jack," said my sister. "He wouldn't hurt a soul," she scoffed. "Why, he even has to look the other way when he kills a fly."

We laughed at this suggestion to scorn.

AFTERWARD, we made a tour of the house, to see whether

Uncle Jack had changed anything. If so, we could not find it. We thought certainly he would have taken down or turned to the wall that hideous portrait of Great-Aunt Maud which was in the living room. It showed her clad in her usual color, which was black, wearing a black velvet dress with white collar and cuffs, with one claw-like hand resting on her ebony stick with the ivory knob for a handle, and her dark, beady eyes looking out into space, and her face just as if set to say, the way she always did, "Never be afraid to work, Children. Work sweetens living and earns its due reward on earth and in heaven." But he had not touched it; there it still was, dark, grave, forbidding, a constant reminder that, by her whim in favor of Uncle Jack, we would have no choice but to work and work and wait for that sweetening and that reward of which she had spoken so often, and with such affirmation that we never had a doubt they were to come. Had they not, after all, come to Uncle Jack, even without work?

That evening at dinner we watched Uncle Jack closely. Every little while he was like his old self. He was a great tease.

He would kid Aunt Hester and poke jokes at my father. He seldom troubled my mother, who had as ready a tongue as he, and struck back fast. Aunt Hester was just helpless before his wit, and my father was too easily irritated. But when he was not his old self, he was a complete stranger; he seemed to forget all of us, and, if he had invited his sister and widowed sister-in-law and their families to that old house in order to impart some information to them, he gave not the slightest sign of it. He sat with a kind of strained expression on his face, as if he were listening for something none of us said.

After dinner, we children discussed him.

"You know what I think," said Cousin Myra again. "Uncle Jack's afraid of something."

"You said that before," accused my sister.

"I know, Jenny. I still think so."

"Why?"

"The way he sat at the table, listening."

"We didn't say anything."

I commanded my sister to pay attention to our cousin, since Myra was my personal favorite.

"He wasn't listening to us. He scarcely heard what mama or Uncle Herbert said," pursued Myra. "He was listening for something else."

We debated this proposition back and forth for a long time, and could not reach any agreement. In their own way, our parents were probably concerning themselves with a similar problem, because when we rejoined them, my mother was saying in a firm, if somewhat scornful voice, "It's perfectly plain that it's all your imagination, Jack. I've heard nothing at all since I set foot in this house."

"Wait," said Uncle Jack.

Aunt Hester, catching sight of us, said nervously, "Hush, the children."

"Are you telling fairy tales?" asked Harry naively.

"Ha! Fairy tales. That's a good one," said my father, laughing loudly. "Just what we were doing, too! That boy has the makings of a smart man."

AFTER midnight, my cousin Myra slipped into the room where Harry and I were sleeping. She shook me awake.

"Charles, listen," she whispered.

I sat up and listened.

"Do you hear it, Charles?" she asked.

I heard something, far away. "What is it?" I asked.

"Listen," she urged again.

It was a tapping sound. It came with marked regularity. *Tap, tap, tap...*

I woke Harry up, and when I had convinced him no goblins were about to devour him, told him to listen, too.

"Do you hear anything, Harry?" pressed Myra.

"Tap, tap, tap," said Harry earnestly, looking from one to the other of us.

We slipped out and into Myra's room, to awaken my sister.

She listened, too, for a moment. Then she said, "I know what that is. That's Aunt Maud's cane."

"Aunt Maud's dead," whispered Myra.

"Don't be silly," countered my sister in a superior voice. "Somebody's using her ebony stick, that's what."

"Who?" demanded Myra.

"We'll find out." My sister got out of bed, cautioned Harry not to let a peep out of him, and led the way into the hall.

Stealthily, we made our way along the hall in the direction of the sound. Uncle Jack's house was T-shaped. We were in the right wing of the T, and the sound seemed to be coming from the forend of the back wing. So we crept along in the dark in our nightgowns until we came to the hall that yawned blackly away from our wing. The tapping sound was plain and unmistakable. It came from up ahead in that blackness.

Harry began to whimper uneasily.

"You hush up," said our sister fiercely.

Being far more frightened of the immediate danger presented by our sister, Harry was obediently silent. Just to be on the safe side, he held on to my nightgown, even though I pushed out in front. I could hardly let my sister lead the way with Myra there.

We went on down the hall. The *tap, tap, tap* was right ahead.

At the end of the hall, now showing more clearly, was a double-window through which the moonlight shone. And, as we came closer and closer to it, we could see Great-Aunt Maud's ebony stick. It was moving up and down against the floor, making the sound we all heard. We could not see who was using it, only a dark shadow in the darkness of the hall. I would have pressed even farther forward, but at that point my brother planted his feet against the floor and pulled back on my nightgown. Both Myra and my sister had stopped, too, unwilling to go farther.

The stick danced up and down there in the moonlit darkness of the hall. It was somewhere near Uncle Jack's room, I figured out.

Myra put her mouth to my ear and whispered. "Who is it?"

"Don't know," I whispered back.

At that moment a door opened up ahead, and Uncle Jack stepped out into the hall. He was carrying a large flashlight, and by its reflected light we could see how wild Uncle Jack's face was. We could see something else, too. There was nobody holding on to that ebony stick.

Even before we could take that in, something wonderfully strange happened. Whoever was handling that ebony stick, and however it was being done, it suddenly jumped up and began to beat Uncle Jack about the head and shoulders while he tried in vain to catch hold of it, muttering and cursing under his breath. But he couldn't do it; he dropped his flashlight, covered his face with his hands, and fell back into his room, closing the door.

COUSIN MYRA and my sister backed away and ran. Harry let go of my nightgown, and fled, whimpering, after them. The last thing I saw was that ebony stick, still making its *tap, tap* in the moonlit hall. Then I ran after them.

We all gathered in the room where my sister and Myra slept.

"I told you he was afraid of something," said Myra accusingly. "So now you see what it is. It's Aunt Maud's ebony stick."

"That's silly," said my sister scornfully. "It's not the stick, it's who's holding it, that's what."

"Who?" demanded Myra.

My sister did not answer.

"Who?" demanded Myra again.

"I couldn't see," said my sister.

"Ha!" exclaimed Myra scornfully. "I ask you who, and you say..."

Harry interrupted. "Aunt Maud," he said in a small voice.

"Aunt Maud's dead," said my sister firmly.

"Aunt Maud," said Harry again. "I saw her."

"Aunt Maud's dead," repeated my sister.

"She's not."

"She is! You hush up, Harry Sanderson, or I'll paddle you."

Harry went around and stood behind me. "Aunt Maud," he said again in a whisper so low that my sister could safely pretend not to have heard it.

IN THE morning we were all going down for breakfast when we halted outside the large kitchen because we heard Uncle Jack's voice raised angrily.

"I tell you I chopped up that damned stick and burned it, do you hear? I did it myself. I didn't trust anybody else to do it. But you heard it last night, didn't you?"

"I heard a sound that might have been made by a cane," said my mother calmly. "But I don't know what it was, and I'm not guessing."

"Oh, Jack, what a story!" said Aunt Hester, and giggled.

"How did I get these, then?"

"Probably been drinking in your room and fell out of bed or ran into the door," said my father.

"Damn it, Herb..."

"All right," said my father in a grave voice. "Let's assume it's so. Then tell me why. What's on your conscience, Jack?"

Uncle Jack didn't say another word.

So we marched into the kitchen, after agreeing not to say anything to anybody. Uncle Jack's head and face showed angry blue bruises. That ebony stick had hit him hard. We knew, because we had seen it. We looked from one to another with that sly assurance children have when they know something their parents do not. But not one of us said anything because we were determined to corner Uncle Jack.

And corner him we did.

We caught up with him in the old coach house out in back. Even there he appeared to be listening, and of course, we knew he was listening for the *tap, tap, tap* of Great-Aunt Maud's ebony stick.

"Do you hear it all the way out here?" Myra asked.

He just looked at her, as if he could not believe what she had said.

"We know," I said. "It's Great-Aunt Maud's ebony stick. What have you done, Uncle Jack?"

Uncle Jack's bruised face got as white as a piece of paper. His bruises and his mustache stood out dark against that whiteness.

"You kids don't know what you're talking about," he said gruffly.

"Oh, yes, we do," said Harry. "We saw you get it last night."

"You saw the stick?" demanded Uncle Jack, turning on him.

Harry nodded. "And Aunt Maud," he added.

Uncle Jack swallowed hard. He hardly heard my sister's indignant denial of Harry's words.

"It was so dark we couldn't see anything except the cane in the moonlight."

Uncle Jack got up and walked away.

"I told you, I told you," chanted Myra. "Uncle Jack's afraid."

We children held a pow-wow and promised one another that the first one who heard the ebony stick again would immediately hunt up all the others and tell them. After that we separated and each of us went his own way.

In that manner we found out that the ebony stick seemed to follow Uncle Jack around. It was strange, but though we could hear it, none of us could catch a glimpse of it. And it could not always be heard, either. Sometimes it was plain, then again there wasn't any sound at all. Sometimes we couldn't hear it for an hour or more; then, of a sudden, it was there, and Uncle Jack would jump and turn around and not be able to see anything any more than we could.

TWO things happened that day, apart from the *tap, tap* of the ebony stick.

The first was Harry's find. Harry had gone to rummage about outside. He was a great one to get himself lost in the woods. That afternoon he found a place where a lot of rubbish had been burned. When he came back he had with him a charred white thing that couldn't have been anything but an ivory handle just like that on Great-Aunt Maud's ebony stick. It puzzled us all a lot.

The second was our parents talking.

Aunt Hester said, "I think it was a wonderfully generous gesture on Jack's part to offer to divide the estate with us in equal parts."

My father said, "There's something behind it."

My mother said, "We'll wait and see what happens."

That night it was Harry who heard the ebony stick first. He pinched me and whispered, frightened, "It's Aunt Maud. She's going up to whip Uncle Jack again."

I woke the others. We took a vote on following or not. Harry voted against it, but because he was too scared to stay alone, he went along anyway, hanging back as much as he could.

Once more we followed the sound of that cane down the hall.

That night it was different. Instead of moonlight, there was a storm outside, and every little while the lightning flashed and flared at the windows and into the hall. It was scary, but the four of us stuck together. I think each one of us, except Harry, was afraid to admit he was scared; so we all went on, following that ebony stick to Uncle Jack's room, where it stood tapping and dancing.

I tried as hard as I could to see who was doing it. Every time the lightning flared I looked close, but I couldn't make out anyone definite. Maybe there was someone leaning there over the stick, just the way Harry said.

"It's Aunt Maud," he kept whispering.

"You hush up," my sister said inevitably.

Maybe there was no one there, only that couldn't have been, because otherwise the cane couldn't have moved like that. So there was someone or something, and we weren't smart enough to figure it out.

This time the door of Uncle Jack's room stayed closed.

But that didn't seem to make any difference, for suddenly the ebony stick wasn't there at all, and at the same time we could hear Uncle Jack shouting in his room, and then the door flew open, and he came stumbling out in his pajamas, trying to protect himself, and the stick came *after him*, though none of us had seen the door open to let it in.

Then, in a flash of lightning, he looked straight at us.

I don't know who he thought we were, but just then he fell down to his knees, with his hands over his face, and he shouted out, "Let me alone! Go back where you belong! I'll do anything—I'll give it back, all of it."

We ran like everything.

"He saw us," said Myra, once we were safely together in our room.

Harry shook his head.

"I don't think he could make us out," I said.

Harry whispered hoarsely, "It was Aunt Maud. I saw her. Oh, but she was mad at Uncle Jack!"

My sister shook him. "Aunt Maud's dead, do you hear?"

"She isn't!"

"She is!" she said so fiercely that Harry was cowed.

"Let him alone," I said.

"Let's not quarrel, please," said Myra.

"What shall we do?" asked my sister.

"Nothing," I said.

"I said all along Uncle Jack was afraid of something."

"He said he'd give it back," said my sister thoughtfully. "He must have stolen something."

"Oh, no!" cried Myra. "Not Uncle Jack! He's got everything. He's got all the money he wants."

"That's true," admitted my sister.

Harry had noticed something the girls had not seen. After we were alone, he whispered it to me.

"Charles, you could see the window-sill right through that cane."

Coming to think of it, you could.

We had agreed to scout the kitchen next morning, the last day of our stay with Uncle Jack, so that we would not miss anything.

Nor did we.

As soon as Harry let us know that Uncle Jack had gone down, we slipped down and stood outside the kitchen to listen to what went on inside.

"And how are you getting on in your affair with Maud's stick?" my father greeted Uncle Jack.

"I asked you all down here for one purpose," answered Uncle Jack soberly. "I wanted to offer you a share of what Aunt Maud left."

"You did, and I think it was a wonderful thing of you, Jack," said Aunt Hester.

"Thank you. But apparently it was not enough for Aunt Maud."

"How you talk!" That was Aunt Hester again; I could see her giggling.

"I guess Aunt Maud means you to have it all," Uncle Jack continued.

"Except the library," said my mother. "I thought so."

"Oh, no, Jack!" cried Aunt Hester.

"All right, let's stop pretending," said Uncle Jack. "It's true. I forged that will. It was a masterpiece. No one ever suspected. But I haven't had a moment's rest since then. That damned cane even follows me to hotels and resorts. You might have guessed. I thought I could appease her by sharing all this with you—but no, she'll have her way."

"We must avoid scandal," said my mother immediately.

"We'll let the will stand," said my father. "But you'll just deed over the property, and we'll make the proper division. You might have known Maud would resent being foiled."

We all felt sorry for Uncle Jack, no matter what a rascal he had been.

But in the end, Great-Aunt Maud was foiled, after all. Uncle Jack took after Aunt Hester and they were married. They came at last to live in Great-Aunt Maud's house. Neither of them ever saw or heard that ebony stick again, though Cousin Myra said that Uncle Jack kept on listening for a long while after they had returned to the house. This time the ebony stick stayed burned.

THE SPANISH CAMERA

By
CARL JACOBI

Its lens was sensitive to vague horrors as well as concrete objects.

NO ONE would suspect Miss Lydia Lancaster of being a dreamer. She was conservative to primness, unemotional, and conventional. Yet for all that, it was a habit of hers to daydream, constantly during those off moments when she was quite sure of being unobserved.

Miss Lydia worked as private secretary in the firm of Childers, Dourley and Ganston, 21 Maiden Lane. Her residence was in Bloomsbury by Russell Square, near the British Museum. And her life, the full thirty-three years of it up to the present, had been quite devoid of interest.

At five o'clock on Tuesday, the 5th of October, a dreary rain-swept day, Miss Lydia put away her typewriter, dusted her desk, as usual, and prepared to leave the office. At that moment a messenger arrived and delivered to her a letter from a well-known solicitor. The letter was brief and to the point:

Dear Madam: I have to inform you that you have been named heir to certain monies and properties as stipulated in the will of the late George Faversham who died suddenly on Thursday last. Will you kindly call at this office at your earliest convenience.
    BENJAMIN HOWELL

Miss Lydia had to read that note twice before it dawned on her who George Faversham was. He was her uncle, but her uncle in name only. That is to say, she had never met or even corresponded with him. The last of her mother's four brothers, he long had been regarded as the black sheep of the family. She knew he had never married and that he had spent the greater part of his life wandering about the back ports of the world. Two years in Nepal, through the Khyber Pass, up the Mahakam River in Dutch Borneo into unexplored Apo Kayan, into the white Indian country of the Upper Orinoco, he had come and gone like a will-o'-the-wisp. But why he should have bequeathed her anything or indeed remember that she even existed was more than she could conjecture.

Early next morning Miss Lydia called at the office of Benjamin Howell in Lincoln's Inn Fields. Howell, a somewhat younger man than she had expected, waited until she had settled herself in the chair opposite his desk. Then he opened a filing folder before him,

"Miss Lancaster," he said, "your uncle left you a small house in East Darwich, and, the sum of fifty thousand pounds in cash or negotiable securities."

The significance of those words sank in slowly. Even at the end of five minutes after she had drunk the glass of water the solicitor gave her, she felt slightly dazed.

"Fifty thousand pounds!" she repeated. "Why, it's incredible! I'm—I'm rich!"

Mr. Howell nodded quietly. "The sum should take care of your needs for some time," he said dryly. "Now about the house in East Darwich. I should strongly advise disposing of it."

"Why?" asked Miss Lydia. "Is it run down?"

"Oh, it's in good enough repair. In fact, it's quite attractive. But..."

"But what...?"

"Well, your uncle was a strange person, Miss Lancaster. He visited some rather off-the-trail places. There may be some things about the house, or rather, in it, that..." His voice broke off significantly.

But Miss Lydia was adamant. Inasmuch as George Faversham had been good enough to leave her this money, the least she could do was accept the lesser part of his bequest. Besides, she was independent now, it would no longer be necessary for her to work or live in London, and a country house was the very thing she needed.

"Very well," sighed Mr. Howell, "I've done my part. Here are the keys: the brass one for the front door, the iron one for the back door and two small keys for some chests you'll find in the house. According to the will, my instructions were that these chests were not to be touched or opened by anyone but you."

IT WAS characteristic of Miss Lydia that she completed arrangements for her new life by the following Friday. Saturday she took the train to East Darwich, arriving early in the afternoon. As Mr. Howell had explained, the house was small and furnished in typical bachelor style. It was situated very close to the ocean shore and was quite alone, yet it appeared to be neither damp nor particularly isolated. The view from the parlor window was breathtaking with the craggy cliffs on one side and the foam-swept beach on the other.

Miss Lydia had all but forgotten the chests mentioned by Mr. Howell until she came upon them in the bedroom. Then curiosity seized her and she hastened to fit the keys into the locks.

The covers thrown back, she stared in disappointment. In Miss Lydia's eyes they contained nothing of interest whatever. Photographic equipment: three cameras of different styles and manufacture, an enlarging device, a developing tank and a quantity of the necessary papers, films and chemicals.

She remembered her mother mentioning that photography had been George Faversham's stock-in-trade. During his earlier years he was employed by a large newspaper service. But more recently he had preferred to freelance, taking and selling pictures of unusual events as he came upon them.

She closed the two chests, pushed them back in a corner and promptly forgot about them. In the days that followed, Miss Lydia attempted to live the life of a gentlewoman of ease. She employed several female servants as well as a gardener and she completely refurbished the house in a manner to her own taste. She called on the vicar. She took long walks through the countryside—but after years of activity and routine this state of affairs soon began to pall on her, and she cast about for some other means of capturing her interest.

It was thus that she thought again of the two chests. Why not photography as a hobby? She had all the materials she needed, and the picturesque shore and the town of East Darwich should offer many opportunities for a camera fan.

From the chests she selected the thirty-five millimeter camera, loaded it with film and strolled out along the beach.

Miss Lydia's ideas about picture taking were decidedly elementary, but she was familiar enough with cameras to know that this one was rather unusual. It was of Spanish manufacture with an F 3.5 Garcia color-corrected lens and a shutter speed up to a thousandth of a second. Just below the lens a small rectangle of silver had been fastened, the center of which was hollow and the outer surface covered and protected by a shield of glass. In this aperture could be seen a tiny black stone roughly carved in the shape of a coiled serpent.

In the sunlight this stone glittered from a hundred different facets. The viewfinder, too, was rather odd. At times when she peered through it, Miss Lydia could see her subject clearly and distinctly. Again, an inner fog seemed to cloud the glass and the scene appeared hazy and indistinct as though viewed through water.

She took eighteen pictures that first day: of the shore, the sea and the streets of East Darwich. Then she set about to do her developing and printing.

SURPRISINGLY enough, all eighteen negatives turned out well. But it was not until she had enlarged and dried her prints and spread them out on a table that she was able to take stock of her day's work. Then she leaned back with a glow of satisfaction.

The Spanish camera was a marvel. Sixteen of the pictures were sharp and clear with no undue highlights or shadows. There was the seashore with its smooth trackless stretch of sand and dashing spray. There was the distant fishing vessel outlined against the driven cloud. And there were the quaint crooked streets of East Darwich snapped in the clean freshness of early morning. She turned to the two remaining pictures and examined them carefully. One was merely fogged from pointing the lens into the sun. But the other—A queer thrill passed through her as she stared down upon it.

It was a sea view, taken from the top of one of the lesser cliffs. Miss Lydia remembered that picture very well, for it had cost her a torn dress climbing up the spume-wet rocks. It should have showed only an empty expanse of Atlantic with several sea gulls perched on a black pinnacle in the foreground. But at that point in the picture where the sky met the water—roughly in a space the size of a postage stamp—there appeared to be the miniature figure of a man—a man sitting in a chair with what looked to be a painted plate-glass window behind him. The whole thing was small with vague edges, yet the man's features—aquiline nose, bristly mustache, deep inset eyes— were sharp and clear. It gave the impression that one had pointed the lens of the camera through a curtain of gauze and caught a fleeting glimpse of a mirage in the sky.

"Double exposure," said Miss Lydia to herself; but even as the thought came, she realized that couldn't be the answer. For she had taken no inside shots and the surroundings about the man's figure were definitely those of an interior.

She examined the camera again. Next she got out a magnifying glass and studied the plate-glass window background behind the man. Minute printing was discernible across this window and under the glass she slowly made out the words:

CAFE CLENARO

Her excitement mounted. There was no Cafe Clenaro in East Darwich. Of that she was positive. There was, however, a restaurant by that name in Poland Street, Soho, in London.

Miss Lydia went thoughtfully to bed. A hundred questions surged through her mind. Why should a camera, which she herself had loaded with fresh film, take a double exposure picture of an interior scene in London, hundreds of miles away. There seemed no answer, and she passed into a restless sleep. Toward morning she began to dream—queer fantastic dreams. She saw herself perched on a high tower with an enormous camera strapped about her body, and every time she pressed the shutter release, a huge serpent emerged from the lens chamber to glide about her in an endless circle.

Morning, and she woke nervous and exhausted. A single thought was uppermost in her mind. She must go to London, to the Cafe Clenaro. She must wait for the man by the window, take his picture and compare that picture with the one on the table. For in her state of excitement, it somehow never occurred to her that the man might not come to the cafe or that he might not exist at all.

It was only when she was settled back in her seat on the train with the sunlit woods and fields gliding by that the utter absurdity of her action struck her. At King's Cross she took a cab out Euston, down Totenham Court Road and along Oxford to Poland Street and the Cafe Clenaro where she chose a table near the window and ordered lunch. Her camera in its case still hung by a strap from her shoulder, and her hands trembled slightly from a nervous expectancy.

Time passed, customers came and went, and Miss Lydia saw no sign of her man of the photograph. At length weariness stole over her; she paid her check and rose. Then suddenly she stiffened.

He was there, sitting in the chair by the window: a large, heavy-set man with a coffee-colored mustache and wearing singularly incongruous pince-nez spectacles. Sunlight streaming in the large window cast him in sharp relief. As in a dream Miss Lydia reached for

189

her camera. She unbuckled the leather flap and raised the viewfinder to her eye. An instant of focus and she clicked the shutter. And then an astounding thing happened.

The man leaped upward with a hoarse cry and tore at his throat. His eyes bulged, his face purpled, the veins of his neck stood out lividly. A moment later it was all over. While Miss Lydia stood there transfixed, the man slumped to the floor, twitched a few times and lay still.

A crowd gathered like magic, and in the ensuing confusion Miss Lydia sidled quietly to the door and made her escape. Outside, she walked the streets for half an hour before her heart quieted and she regained some of her composure. But even then with the reality of afternoon traffic about her, she felt weak and dazed, like a person who had just been rescued from an onrushing train.

SHE hailed a cab and rode to the offices of Benjamin Howell. The solicitor ushered her into his office with some concern.

"In heaven's name, what's wrong?" he demanded. "You look as if you'd seen a ghost."

"I believe I have," sighed Miss Lydia. "At least, I've seen a murder without apparent cause."

"Murder!"

In halting sentences she told him all that had happened. When she had finished Mr. Howell sat there, scowling.

"I think you're seeing too much in coincidence," he said. "A heart attack or a hundred other things might have caused the man's death, if he did die; however, let's take a look at that camera."

HE DID look, long and carefully. Finally he returned it to its case and handed it back.

"Unusual, but I see nothing wrong with it," he said. "I can assure you it's not a weapon of any kind. Now, may I suggest again that you sell or dispose of that house and all that's in it."

"But you said—"

"Miss Lancaster," said Mr. Howell, "you never knew your uncle. I did. Believe me when I say he was an extraordinary man. As you know, he spent the greater part of his life, photographing rare and unusual scenes. He—ah, have you ever heard of the *Trinidad Queen?* "

She shook her head. "I don't believe so."

The solicitor leaned back, closing his eyes.

"The *Trinidad Queen* was a blackbirder, an eighteenth century slave-trade vessel, plying between Africa's west coast and the West Indies. In 1784 she left Martinique, ran into a storm, was blown off her course and foundered near the island of French Key in the Grenadines. Now her approximate position was thought to have been known for a long time and also known was the fact that her strong box contained nearly two hundred thousand gold guineas. There have been innumerable attempts to rescue that gold, but the position was in deep water, exposed to the winds, and all such attempts failed."

Howell paused to tilt back in his chair and make steeples of his hands.

"In his travels, your uncle, George Faversham, came on a map purporting to show that the *Trinidad Queen* had actually gone down some miles to the east off Rojo Bank and was lodged on a comparatively shallow reef. He organized a party, hired a small motor cruiser and headed for the Grenadines. That was a year ago."

Howell opened the desk humidor and took out a cigar. Halfway to lighting it, he changed his mind and returned it to the box.

"Primarily, of course, your uncle's motive in the whole affair was photography. He saw in the underwater action, the movements of the divers about the old sunken vessel an opportunity to capture on film some dramatic scenes. He took three men with him: Garcia Perena, a Portuguese from Havana, Dane Kellogg, a non-practicing British physician, and Justis Hardesty, a nondescript American whom he found on the San Juan waterfront. It was agreed that your uncle should have all returns on the photography work while the treasure, if any were found, should be divided four ways—"

"But what has all this to do with—?" Miss Lydia interrupted.

"With your camera? It may have nothing to do with it," replied Howell, "and then again it may have everything. First of all, you should know that the *Trinidad Queen* sailed under a stigma that has continued down through these many years. It was said that on the West African coast her skipper went upriver to a native village and took from a crude altar a small particle of what was known as the Damballah serpent stone. All the black evil which surrounded its obeah worship there in the jungle was said to have followed the captain and his ship."

THE SPANISH CAMERA

HOWELL uncrossed his legs and shifted in his chair. "That's about all," he said, "except that your uncle eventually realized a part of his fortune from that expedition. He found the *Trinidad Queen* all right and he brought to the surface quite a large quantity of the gold. He also seems to have brought up that much discussed piece of the Damballah stone—that is my guess anyway as to the nature of that thing under the glass covering on your camera. But something happened on that expedition, something strange that drifted back to civilization only in the form of vague rumors. It was said your uncle very nearly lost his life on one of the underwater dives."

Miss Lydia failed to see any connection between Mr. Howell's story and the subject in hand, but she was too polite to say so. The solicitor urged her again to dispose of her newly acquired house, and a few minutes later, still nervous and unsatisfied, she took her departure.

Morning found her back in East Darwich, anxiously scanning the morning paper. Any doubt she might have had that the man of the restaurant was not dead was dispelled when she read the following:

DANE KELLOGG DIES UNDER MYSTERIOUS
CIRCUMSTANCES IN SOHO CAFE.

Kellogg! That was the name Mr. Howell had given as one of the three men who had accompanied her uncle on his expedition!

For a week Miss Lydia lived a life of tension and anticipation. The papers continued with a few more desultory accounts of the strange death; then the story died out. More than once during that week she half decided to return to London and tell all she knew to the police. But a moment's consideration changed her mind. After all, she had done nothing that would interest Scotland Yard.

As time passed, however, she found herself thinking less about the man and more about her future work in photography. While in London she had picked up a pamphlet announcing a new prize contest in camera craft, and with typical amateur enthusiasm she cast about for worthy subject material.

Her strange dreams during this period continued, and strangely enough it was one of these dreams that formed into an idea for a picture. She dreamed she was walking along the beach in the moonlight and all about her were middle-aged men pleading with her to take their pictures, but every time she focused her camera and clicked the shutter the surrounding moonlight gave way to blackest night. When the moonlight, returned again, the subject was writhing

192

on the ground, desperately fighting a huge serpent.

The more Miss Lydia thought about this dream, the more it seemed to her that a moonlight shot of the ocean shore might be an ideal entry for the photography contest.

She chose her setting with extreme care. A hundred yards down the shore from her house, half buried in the sand, was the rotting skeleton of an old whaleboat. In the background the wall of black cliffs formed a natural archway with the sand piled high in curious shaped dunes about it.

Loading the camera with a high speed film, Miss Lydia took along a collapsible tripod and went out on the shore one night shortly after darkness had set in. The sky lit by brilliant stars was shot here and there with flying spindrifts of cloud, but the moon had not yet arisen. Waiting for it, she sat on an outcropping rock and felt a vague uneasiness steal over her. At length the moon peered whitely over the tops of the trees and the rolling surf changed on the instant to silver.

Miss Lydia mounted the Spanish camera firmly on the tripod, focused it so the whaleboat would be in upper mid-center of the picture and opened the lens to its full F. 3.5. She clicked open the shutter and waited, watching the minute hand of her wristwatch.

She took several pictures. Back in her house, she set about developing and printing. As she worked, a queer feeling that she was being watched by unseen eyes seized her. Nervously she caught herself looking over her shoulder several times.

Only two of the negatives proved suitable for printing. One of these was fairly successful, but the effect was rather that of a dull daylight shot. It was the second picture that drew her up short.

Double exposure again! The sandy strip of beach was very clear with the mellow moonlight caught perfectly. But the old whaleboat was not there! In its place were the head and shoulders of a man—a Latin looking man this time, with dark features and a receding hairline. He was leaning against the front of a building, and Miss Lydia recognized that building as she studied it with her magnifying glass. It was the Drury Lane Theater.

Miss Lydia did not sleep well that night. She awoke at fitful intervals, the last time at three-thirty a. m. by the radium-faced clock on her dresser. The house was quite still, save for the distant swish and boom of the surf. Yet this time she was positive some unusual sound had awakened her. She got up, put on a dressing gown and slippers and made her way to the front door.

The moon had gone down, and the night was steeped in shadows, with only the glow of the stars. But as she stood there, the chill wind clutching at her gown, Miss Lydia suddenly stiffened. Ahead of her one of the shadows had detached itself from the others and was slowly advancing toward her. It was the figure of a man who seemed to glide rather than walk across the lawn. The lower part of his body was wreathed in mist, but to the woman in the doorway it seemed his face was clear and distinct, it was the face of a middle-aged man with mental strength and determination. Under one arm he carried a camera and in the other hand a book.

Coming to a halt in the open space before the door of the house, he suddenly poised the camera at some unseen object. Then he passed on to the far end of the veranda, took the book from under his arm and proceeded to wedge it between the ornamental porch rails. After which he turned and glided toward that point where the lawn merged into the sand of the beach. And there the mist seemed to gather about him in loose flowing coils until he had disappeared.

Was she dreaming? Miss Lydia rubbed her eyes and stared before her in sleepy bewilderment. She went back into her bedroom and returned with a powerful flashlight. But although she probed the white beam from the birches on one side to the azalea bed on the other, she saw nothing.

Morning, and she was half way through her solitary breakfast before she suddenly remembered the book. That at least would prove whether her experience of the night was an actuality. Hurrying out onto the veranda, she stopped stunned. A book was there, still wedged between the porch rails, still damp from morning dew.

Miss Lydia stepped forward, took the book and glanced at its title. It was a well worn copy of *West Indian Journal,* by Panson McBeal, published in London in 1897, and, after a quick glance Miss Lydia thought it queer that anyone would read such a book. It was out of date both in style and subject matter, containing only one yellowed map. But a glance at the map told her that this book was undoubtedly the source of her Uncle George Faversham's information as to the actual location of the *Trinidad Queen.* The actual site of the ship on French Key was carefully marked, together with the depth soundings.

One thing about the map puzzled her. On the margin at the bottom, in tiny hurried script was written *twenty-seven.* Why should anyone in the apparent haste that this writer was take the time to write those words instead of the numerals 27? Miss Lydia turned to page 27, but there was nothing unusual about it. Then words spoken by Solicitor Howell came back to her: "Your uncle was a strange man, Miss Lancaster. He did things in unusual ways." Was there a clue to his life, to the mystery of his camera in those two words written at the bottom of the map page?

She began looking on pages that were divisible by 27, without result. Then she looked simply at those pages in which 27 was a component part. She got no place here either.

ABRUPTLY she paused and began to count the letters in those two words. Counting the hyphen, they totaled twelve. She wrote down the numeral, 12, and looked at it abstractedly with the long habit of one whom appreciates numbers for what they are. During the summer of '43, Miss Lydia had worked in the cryptograph department of British Intelligence, and now, without thinking, she applied her training here. She added the two digits of 12, making three; she added a 4 for the division of 12 by 3 and then swiftly multiplied the 34 by 12 and to this 108 she subtracted the total of 34 plus 12 or 46, leaving 62. All the while she was quite aware that her actions would seem meaningless to the casual observer.

Turning to the book again, she looked on page 62, sixth line down, second word in. The word she found there— "they"—didn't mean much. But when she had followed it with words in the identical position on every subsequent page with a six or a two in it, she stared astounded at her written result.

As Solicitor Benjamin Howell had told her, three men had accompanied her uncle on his trip to the *Trinidad Queen*, the foundered slave-trade vessel: Dane Kellogg, Justis Hardesty and Garcia Perena. The message, which she had extracted from the West Indies travel book, was a black condemnation of those three men. Briefly it told of George Faversham's overhearing the three plot to murder him. Murder for his share of the salvaged gold!

Miss Lydia closed the book thoughtfully.

Why had George Faversham taken such pains to hide his message in the pages of that book? Simply because he was queer and eccentric? That might be one reason. But undoubtedly it was because at the time of the writing he was afraid one of the three —Hardesty,

Kellogg, or Garcia Perena—would discover that he knew the truth. But if such an attempt against his life were plotted, why had her uncle not made any attempt to prosecute the three after his return to civilization? Howell had told her the answer. The men fearing retaliation, had disappeared.

For two days Miss Lydia sought to forget these facts and lose herself in the routine duties of her house. The moonlight photograph with its fantastic inset of the man standing before Drury Theater entrance haunted her. On the third day she could stand it no longer. Salving her conscience with a list of things she needed in London, she caught the morning train. She took her camera along.

That night found her stumbling back into her house, dazed and haggard. Her eyes were bloodshot. She went directly to her bedroom and lay down in the darkness while a thousand mad thoughts swirled through her brain.

The camera had repeated itself. In London she had gone directly to Drury Lane Theater at Drury Lane and Catherine Street, and focused her gaze on that section of the theater entrance, which had found itself in her photograph. Within half an hour it had happened.

A man with Latin features and impeccably dressed had paused in her ellipse of stage to light a cigarette. An instant Miss Lydia stared at him. Then her arm shot sideward of its own accord, opened the leather case of her camera and jerked the instrument to eye focus. "No!" she told herself. "I must not! I must not!" But a will other than her own ruled her every move. Through the viewfinder she saw the man standing there. She clicked the shutter.

In her room now, Miss Lydia tried to expel the scene from her thoughts. The man had died there, died horribly, but drawn by the same inner hypnosis she had lingered while the crowd gathered and a phlegmatic bobby made his identification. The man was Garcia Perena, a citizen of Havana!

Out of her confused mind, as she lay there in the darkness, a single thought rose to repeat itself over and over again. The camera with its accursed Damballah stone must be destroyed, must be sent back to the depths from which it came.

Miss Lydia got out of bed, took up the camera and went out of the house. She went down the gravel path past the bed of azaleas and onto the moonlit beach. The booming surf seemed to resound in tune with her steps and the night wind caught her hair and skirts and whipped them out behind. She was heading for the Needle, a small promontory that stabbed out into deep water. There she could throw her camera away forever without any fear that it would be washed up on, the beach.

The moon was brilliant and she seemed able to see for miles in the cold light. Half way to the Needle she suddenly halted. A man was approaching her from far down the beach. As yet he had not seen her, for she was moving in the shadow of the flanking cliff. For some reason stealth appeared to be in his movements, and Miss Lydia darted behind a boulder to let him pass. The man passed her and went on, walking with a slight limp in his right foot. She waited, a moment, then began to follow.

He passed through her garden to the rear wall of her house and began to fumble with the fastenings of the window there. The window slid open, and the man gripped the sill preparatory to lifting himself through the opening. And as she stood there watching in the shadows, a feeling of something evil swept over Miss Lydia. Her camera was trembling like a thing alive in its case hanging from her shoulder. Abruptly it seemed to lift of its own accord into her hands. A cry of horror rose to her lips at the realization of what was happening.

With a jerk the man spun around, staring.

And calmly, and matter of factly, moved by another will, Miss Lydia lifted her camera to focus and clicked the shutter. A span of mist appeared to radiate outward from the lens. That mist seemed to open like a white envelope, from the depths of which the coils of a yellow green serpent emerged.

The serpent slid slowly forward, and the man at the window stared in fascinated horror. He threw himself sideways, attempted to leap over a collection of flower pots. He tripped and fell. And while his screams rent the night air, the serpent slid slowly over him and began to gather its coils about his throat.

MR. BENJAMIN HOWELL visited Miss Lydia the day after the inquest. He found his client in surprisingly good spirits, a little nervous from the ordeal of answering police questions but seemingly relieved that the jury had found a verdict of "death at the hands of person or persons unknown."

"But who was he?" Mr. Howell asked. "Your letter said something about a thief trying to break into your—"

"He was just that," replied Miss Lydia calmly. "But in addition his name was Justis Hardesty who you will remember was the third and last of the men who accompanied my uncle on the *Trinidad Queen*."

"But I don't understand," began Mr. Howell.

"The three of them—Hardesty, Kellogg and Garcia Perena—were fiends, cold-blooded fiends," continued Miss Lydia. "They deliberately plotted to murder my uncle, to sever his life-line and air hose while he was underwater on the deck of the sunken vessel. Now all three of them are dead, and my uncle can rest in peace."

Howell half smiled. "Oh come, Miss Lancaster, you can't really believe George Faversham had anything to do with the death of those three men. It was pure coincidence that two of them died when they did. As for Hardesty, he simply read in the paper of your inheriting your uncle's fortune and saw in your house a good place to rob. As for that camera—by the way what did you do with the camera, Miss Lancaster?"

"It's gone," she said.

"Gone?"

Miss Lydia nodded cryptically and left the matter at that.

THE END

If you've enjoyed this book, you will not want to miss these terrific titles…

ARMCHAIR SCI-FI, FANTASY, & HORROR DOUBLE NOVELS, $12.95 each

D-1   **THE GALAXY RAIDERS** by William P. McGivern
           SPACE STATION #1 by Frank Belknap Long

D-2   **THE PROGRAMMED PEOPLE** by Jack Sharkey
           SLAVES OF THE CRYSTAL BRAIN by William Carter Sawtelle

D-3   **YOU'RE ALL ALONE** by Fritz Leiber
           THE LIQUID MAN by Bernard C. Gilford

D-4   **CITADEL OF THE STAR LORDS** by Edmund Hamilton
           VOYAGE TO ETERNITY by Milton Lesser

D-5   **IRON MEN OF VENUS** by Don Wilcox
           THE MAN WITH ABSOLUTE MOTION by Noel Loomis

D-6   **WHO SOWS THE WIND…** by Rog Phillips
           THE PUZZLE PLANET by Robert A. W. Lowndes

D-7   **PLANET OF DREAD** by Murray Leinster
           TWICE UPON A TIME by Charles L. Fontenay

D-8   **THE TERROR OUT OF SPACE** by Dwight V. Swain
           QUEST OF THE GOLDEN APE by Ivar Jorgensen and Adam Chase

D-9   **SECRET OF MARRACOTT DEEP** by Henry Slesar
           PAWN OF THE BLACK FLEET by Mark Clifton.

D-10   **BEYOND THE RINGS OF SATURN** by Robert Moore Williams
           A MAN OBSESSED by Alan E. Nourse

ARMCHAIR SCIENCE FICTION CLASSICS, $12.95 each

C-1   **THE GREEN MAN**
           by Harold M. Sherman

C-2   **A TRACE OF MEMORY**
           By Keith Laumer

ARMCHAIR MASTERS OF SCIENCE FICTION SERIES, $16.95 each

M-1   **MASTERS OF SCIENCE FICTION, Vol. One**
           Bryce Walton—"Dark of the Moon" and other tales

M-2   **MASTERS OF SCIENCE FICTION, Vol. Two**
           Jerome Bixby: "One Way Street" and other tales

If you've enjoyed this book, you will not want to miss these terrific titles...

ARMCHAIR SCI-FI & HORROR DOUBLE NOVELS, $12.95 each

D-11   **PERIL OF THE STARMEN** by Kris Neville
         THE STRANGE INVASION by Murray Leinster

D-12   **THE STAR LORD** by Boyd Ellanby
         CAPTIVES OF THE FLAME by Samuel R. Delaney

D-13   **MEN OF THE MORNING STAR** by Edmund Hamilton
         PLANET FOR PLUNDER by Hal Clement and Sam Merwin, Jr.

D-14   **ICE CITY OF THE GORGON** by Chester S. Geier and Richard S. Shaver
         WHEN THE WORLD TOTTERED by Lester Del Rey

D-15   **WORLDS WITHOUT END** by Clifford D. Simak
         THE LAVENDER VINE OF DEATH by Don Wilcox

D-16   **SHADOW ON THE MOON** by Joe Gibson
         ARMAGEDDON EARTH by Geoff St. Reynard

D-17   **THE GIRL WHO LOVED DEATH** by Paul W. Fairman
         SLAVE PLANET by Laurence M. Janifer

D-18   **SECOND CHANCE** by J. F. Bone
         MISSION TO A DISTANT STAR by Frank Belknap Long

D-19   **THE SYNDIC** by C. M. Kornbluth
         FLIGHT TO FOREVER by Poul Anderson

D-20   **SOMEWHERE I'LL FIND YOU** by Milton Lesser
         THE TIME ARMADA by Fox B. Holden

ARMCHAIR SCIENCE FICTION CLASSICS, $12.95 each

C-3   **INTO PLUTONIAN DEPTHS**
        by Stanton A. Coblentz

C-4   **CORPUS EARTHLING**
        by Louis Charbonneau

C-5   **THE TIME DISSOLVER**
        by Jerry Sohl

C-6   **WEST OF THE SUN**
        by Edgar Pangborn

ARMCHAIR SCIENCE FICTION & HORROR GEMS SERIES, $12.95 each

G-1   **SCIENCE FICTION GEMS, Vol. One**
        Isaac Asimov and others

G-2   **HORROR GEMS, Vol. One**
        Carl Jacobi and others